D0268726

"You *slept* with me?
Without asking me if it was okay?"

Brenna didn't know whether to be outraged or disappointed that she didn't remember how it felt to have that hard body of his stretched out beside her.

"You woke me up whimpering in your sleep. The only way I could quiet you so I could get some sleep was to cuddle you." He said "cuddle" as if the very idea was repugnant. . . .

Before she could respond, he marched into the bathroom and slammed the door shut.

PRAISE FOR *DARK PROTECTOR*

"Stunned me with its raw emotion and the poignant love. . . . I raise my sword high in the air for a story well told!"

—*Joyfully Reviewed*

"Intriguing and unique . . . compelling characters who all deserve their own stories, so hopefully this is just the beginning."

—*Romantic Times*

Dark Defender

Alexis Morgan

POCKET STAR BOOKS
New York London Toronto Sydney

An *Original* Publication of POCKET BOOKS

 A Pocket Star Book published by
POCKET BOOKS, a division of Simon & Schuster, Inc.
1230 Avenue of the Americas, New York, NY 10020

This book is a work of fiction. Names, characters, places and incidents are products of the author's imagination or are used fictitiously. Any resemblance to actual events or locales or persons, living or dead, is entirely coincidental.

ISBN: 978-1-4767-8688-9

This Pocket Star Books paperback edition December 2006

10 9 8 7 6 5 4 3 2 1

POCKET STAR BOOKS colophon are registered trademarks of Simon & Schuster, Inc.

Cover art by Craig White

Manufactured in the United States of America

For information regarding special discounts for bulk purchases, please contact Simon & Schuster Special Sales at 1-800-456-6798 or business@simonandschuster.com

I would like to dedicate this book to my friends at work, both past and present. Think of all the children's lives you have touched with the gift of learning. What could be better than that?

Acknowledgments

To Janice Kay-Johnson—your friendship has been a true and generous gift in my life. Thank you for daring me to write in the first place and then sticking by me through the roller coaster ride of each book I've done. I would have never come this far without you.

Dark Defender

prologue

St. Louis, Missouri

$\mathcal{D}$ad?"

Where had he disappeared to? Not ten minutes ago he'd been looking through some papers, but now his desk was cleaned off and there was no sign of him.

That was odd—they'd planned to have lunch together to celebrate the release of her latest book. Although he'd been preoccupied all week, it wasn't like her father to forget something like that.

Then she heard the kitchen door slam. Brenna Nichols hurried toward the back door, and saw him heading straight for his car.

Stepping out onto the back porch, she called, "Dad, where are you going?"

Clearly distracted, he paused to look back at her.

Deep worry lines bracketed his attempt to smile. "Sorry, Brenna, I should have told you. Something's come up, so I have to run into the office for a while."

"Aren't we having lunch?"

For a second he looked truly perplexed, which was even more alarming. This definitely wasn't like him. Not at all. She walked to the edge of the porch. "It's okay, Dad. I thought we had plans for today, but maybe I had the date wrong."

Her father's shoulders slumped. "Sorry, honey, I forgot." He checked his watch. "I'll try to be gone for only an hour, two at the most. Maybe we can go when I get back."

Despite his offer, she sensed his heart wasn't really in it. "We'll just reschedule, Dad."

There was no mistaking the flash of relief in his eyes as he climbed into the car. "If you're sure you wouldn't mind, maybe it's for the best. I don't think I'd be very good company right now."

He fastened his seat belt and rolled down the window. "I'm sorry about this, Brenna. I love you, sweetheart."

He waved and turned the key in the ignition. The engine sputtered briefly before catching.

Then, with a flash of smoke and lightning, the world exploded. A searing roll of thunder flung

Brenna through the air, and terror mixed with the taste of blood in her mouth as she slammed into the side of the house. Her last conscious thought was that she forgot to tell her dad that she loved him, too.

chapter 1

Murmurs and whispers danced just out of reach. Brenna remained in the darkness, content to stay where she was. The fire of pain waited for her each time she tried to open her eyes; it was far better to huddle in the black chill than to let the monsters in.

But then a new voice entered the discussion, a masculine one that wouldn't be ignored. A woman answered his demands, sounding defensive and a little afraid.

A few seconds later, heavy footsteps approached and another man started to speak, trying to placate the newcomer. Though the stranger made the others nervous, the deep resonance of his voice comforted Brenna somehow.

She tried to concentrate, to make out what they were saying, but waves of agony immediately sent her diving back down into the darkness. It was enough to know he was there, watching over her. She floated under the edge of pain, content to let his voice soothe her.

Blake Trahern inched closer, making sure Brenna was still asleep. He'd arrived too late to do more than bury her father and say he was sorry for . . . so damn much. His presence would only upset her, and she had enough on her plate right now without him adding to the mess.

The need to touch her burned along his nerve endings, but he forced his hands to remain at his side.

He stayed outside the circle of light surrounding her bed, the dim glow coming from the instruments that monitored her heartbeat, her breathing, her very life force. Bandages covered the worst of the damage, and after three days, the bruises on her face and arms were fading to a sickly greenish color. Brenna shifted in her sleep, whimpering with pain at the small movement. He moved farther back into the shadows.

"Sons of bitches," Blake whispered. He vowed that whoever had planted the bomb would pay dearly for their crime. It was the least he could do for her father—and her. But revenge would have to wait. For now, he would stand guard.

A shrill alarm shattered the quiet of the hospital room, dragging Blake out of his memories. He scanned the room for any sign of danger, adrenaline burning through his veins, but relaxed when he realized the noise came from one of the machines surrounding Brenna's bed.

He shook his head to clear out the last of the cobwebs and cursed himself for a fool. Her room was on a private floor in the hospital, but that didn't mean the security couldn't be breached. A fat lot of good he would have been if the footsteps outside the door had belonged to a killer, rather than one of the nurses who came in and out regularly.

He eased farther into the shadows and pulled his hand away from the knife in his pocket. Luckily, the nurse paid him little heed as she silenced the machine. After a few failed attempts to engage him in conversation, the medical staff ignored Blake as they saw to Brenna's needs. He watched silently as the nurse hung new bags of life-sustaining liquids on the IV pole and checked her vitals.

The need to know how Brenna was doing forced him out of his silence. "How is she?"

The nurse jumped, as if she'd forgotten he was even there. "Are you family?"

"I'm all that she has left." And that was a sad statement if there ever was one. "What does the doctor think now?"

The woman stared at him for a few seconds. He

lacked the gene for charming people into talking, leaving him no choice but to wait her out. Finally, some of the tension in her stance drained away.

"The injuries are healing as well as can be expected. The concussion caused by the explosion put her in a coma, even though the concussion didn't appear to be that severe." She glanced at Brenna's pale face. "I'd guess the shock of seeing her father die aggravated her condition."

A fist-size lump settled in his throat, and Blake realized that the bitter taste in his mouth was fear. He'd often faced certain death without blinking. Hell, he'd died more times than he could count and had come back from it. But for Brenna, death was permanent—not just something to be endured until her heart and lungs remembered how to work.

"What else can be done?" He hated the sympathy in the nurse's eyes. Begging wasn't his style, but he couldn't rely on his usual technique of holding his opponent at sword point.

"Talk to her. Sometimes that seems to help bring them back." She tilted her head as if to listen. "I've got another patient calling for attention, so push that button on the bed if you need me."

Then she was gone, leaving him alone with the blinking lights and Brenna, still and pale and silent.

• • •

"Come on, Brenna, I need you to tell me what happened." Blake felt stupid carrying on a one-sided conversation, but he'd strip and run naked down the street if it would help her come back to the living. "I know it hurts, but you're strong."

He reached for his water bottle and took a big swig to soothe his parched throat. He was known for his silence, not for conversation. Reading her the front page of the paper obviously hadn't worked, and he tried to think of another topic of conversation.

He let his thoughts wander back to when he'd first met her, and without realizing it, he started talking.

"I'd never met anyone like you before—all eyes and innocence, but with one of the best minds I'd ever met. Even at age twelve, when you started high school, you saw and understood far more than most adults."

His lips quirked in a half smile. "I'd been living on the streets, more wild animal than human. Then your father picked me up by the scruff of my neck and dropped me right into your home. I don't know what he was thinking, but between him and Maisy, they got me straightened out in short order. Maybe it was all those cookies she baked for me. And, despite being five foot nothing, she could be a real terror."

Leaning back in the chair, he stared up at the

ceiling. "Once, just before your thirteenth birthday, I was on my way to the kitchen to see if Maisy had any snickerdoodles for me to eat when you came charging out of the kitchen, almost knocking me over. I still remember the look in your eyes when I caught you to keep both of us from hitting the floor. For that one moment, I could see past the glasses and braces to see the lovely woman you'd become." He dragged his gaze back toward Brenna's still form in the bed. "I wasn't too far off the mark." He drifted into silence, the past never a comfortable place for him to visit.

And once again he'd run out of conversation. "Brenna, you've got to wake up. It's not safe here in the hospital—even with the guards your father's buddies, the Regents, sent in. No place will be safe until we find out who was behind this."

Her eyes fluttered briefly. He'd been a day and a half without sleep, though, and didn't trust what he'd just seen. He reached over and angled a light so that it shone directly in her face. "Brenna, blink your eyes. I need to know if you're understanding me."

She moaned softly and tried to turn away from the glare, but he captured her chin gently in his hand and held her face still. He injected more authority in his voice, just as her father always had when she fought getting up in the morning. "Brenna, it's time to wake up."

Mumbling something about five more minutes,

she frowned for all she was worth and stubbornly kept her eyes closed. Despite her small rebellion, he felt better than he had since receiving word about the car bomb.

It was time to push the nurses' button and summon the troops. Within seconds he heard voices approaching in the hallway. He kept his hand resting softly on Brenna's cheek, for fear that if he broke off contact she would slip back down into the darkness.

The first person through the door was the nurse who had suggested he talk to Brenna. The doctor was hard on her heels, both of them looking more curious than worried. If something had gone seriously wrong, the battery of monitors at the nurses' station down the hall would have set off alarms.

"What's up?" The doctor's question was addressed to Trahern, but his eyes were focused solely on his patient.

"I think she's coming out of it. Her eyelids have been fluttering and she mumbled something about letting her sleep for another five minutes." He hoped they believed him because at the moment Brenna's face had reverted back to the same unhealthy stillness.

The nurse pushed past Blake to pick up Brenna's wrist and take her pulse. The doctor pried open Brenna's eyelids and shined his small flashlight into her eyes.

She tossed her head back and forth, and whimpered. Finally, her eyes opened briefly and stared up at the three people surrounding her bed. Confusion, then fear, clouded her expression.

"Who? Where?" she croaked.

"I'm Doctor Vega and this is Jan Windsor, your nurse." He patted her hand and gave her a reassuring smile.

It was too late for Blake to slide out the door, so he braced himself for her reaction.

"Brenna, it's me, Blake Trahern."

Her response wasn't long in coming. "Can't be. The Blake Trahern I knew disappeared years ago."

Dr. Vega frowned at him. "We were under the impression that you were family."

"I'm more a friend of the family."

The doctor was clearly not happy. "Wait here, Mr. Trahern. I need to make a phone call about this."

Trouble wasn't long in coming. The door to the ward banged open as a quintet of heavily armed guards entered the hall and spread out to block any avenues of escape, weapons ready. Trahern remained still, not wanting to startle anyone into acting rashly.

The leader came inside the room to talk to Dr. Vega, then said, "Mister, we're going to have to ask you to step out into the hallway."

Before he could answer, another man stepped into view, a man Blake recognized as a Paladin.

"Stand down." The man's calm demeanor spoke of years of having orders obeyed without question.

The leader of the guards sneered. "You're not in charge here, Jarvis. Ordnance sent us."

"I'm not in charge, but I'm trying to save you and your buddies there some pain and misery." Jarvis leaned against the wall with a hint of a smile.

"You come against us, Jarvis, and we'll see who walks away limping."

"Maybe on a good day, the five of you might be able to take me down." Though the guard out-weighed him by at least thirty pounds of pure muscle, Paladins were the finest warriors on the planet. It would take more than a few armed guards to handle a Paladin in prime condition; a good dust-up against superior numbers only whetted a Paladin's appetite for violence. Guards employed by the Regents sure as hell should know that. If the five of them took on Jarvis, Dr. Vega would have a whole new set of patients to patch up. Fatal shots only made Paladins meaner; they made guards dead.

Jarvis pushed away from the wall. "Maybe I should let your men go charging in there, Sergeant. It's been awhile since I've seen Blake Trahern in action, but from all reports, he's only gotten better. It's up to you, though."

He met Trahern's gaze and his smile warmed up a few degrees. Blake nodded, acknowledging his old friend. Jarvis had been one of the two men whom Brenna's father had introduced him to years ago. Together, the three of them had told him about a secret group called the Regents that they worked for. Throughout the world, the Regents deployed warriors called Paladins to hold the line against the constant threat of invasion from another world.

With Jarvis's help, he'd learned what it had meant to be a Paladin. Jarvis's lectures, delivered with a big brother's impatient good humor, had given Blake the first taste of self-worth and belonging he'd felt in his entire life. With Jarvis's support, the Paladins, who watched over and protected the barrier that ran along the unstable New Madrid Fault, had accepted him without hesitation.

But that had been many years and several deaths ago. Trahern had changed a lot during the interim, and not for the better; a wise man would assume Jarvis had taken a similar journey on the road to madness.

Blake widened his stance and waited for the scene to play out. A movement to his left told him that Dr. Vega had pushed the nurse into the corner and positioned himself between Blake and Brenna. Good man.

"Hey, Trahern, you want to come out and meet the locals?" Jarvis stepped in front of the doorway, blocking any chance of the guards storming the room.

It seemed like a reasonable suggestion. If the

situation turned ugly, at least Brenna and the others would be out of the line of fire. "Why not?"

When he reached the door, Jarvis moved aside to avoid being trapped between Trahern and the guards. By his action, Blake assumed Jarvis would back his play, but only so far. Jarvis used to be one of the few men he'd trust behind his back, but only time would tell if that had changed.

"I'm Trahern out of the Seattle office," he told the sergeant. "Judge Nichols was an old friend of mine. I'm here to protect his daughter."

"That's our job." The sergeant lowered his gun a little.

"Hell of a fine job you were doing. I've been here for the past two days, and this is the first I've seen any of you. Anybody could have waltzed in here unchallenged to finish the job on Ms. Nichols."

One of the other guards spoke up. "The police said the judge was the target. She was just collateral damage."

Fury, hot and violent, burned through Blake. In the space of two heartbeats, he slammed the young guardsman up against the wall, his hands wrapped around the fool's throat.

"She's not *just* anything. If you and your buddies had been doing their job, maybe the judge wouldn't have been blown all to hell. Where were *you* then? Out pressing your pretty uniforms and polishing your army boots?"

The other guards buzzed around him like flies, trying to pry his hands off their friend's neck, but Trahern ignored them. He wouldn't kill the fool. Not because he deserved to live, but because his death would only complicate matters. Trahern squeezed a bit tighter just to show he could, and then let his victim drop to the floor.

Three of the guards brought their guns up, aimed straight at Trahern's gut, while the fifth dragged their gasping compatriot to safety. Jarvis spoke up, cutting through the growing tension.

"If you shoot Trahern, Sergeant, you'll only piss him off even more. And you'll have every Paladin in the area riding your ass for the rest of your miserable life." He crossed his arms over his chest and waited.

Blake hoped the guards had the good sense to back down. He couldn't afford another death for a lot of reasons—but primarily because Brenna needed him alive and sane, whether she knew it or not.

His Handler back in Seattle had warned him that he was damn close to the edge of crossing over into becoming Other, the enemy he'd spent a lifetime fighting. Regulations had required that she send his records along to the St. Louis office . . . just in case. The grief in her eyes was all too clear. They both knew it wouldn't take much more violence for him to rage out of control. If that happened, not even Jarvis would be able to keep either the local Handlers or the Guard from putting him down like a rabid dog. Hell, Jarvis would probably *help* them. No one was safe when a Paladin went rogue, and they all knew it.

Blake only hoped he could hang on to his humanity long enough to find out who had betrayed Judge Nichols. One of the Paladins back in Seattle had also come under attack. They had traced the trouble to a traitorous member of the Guard, but he'd died before they could learn how far up in the organization the betrayal reached. Trahern had contacted Judge Nichols about it, since he was the only Regent he trusted completely, and the car bomb had come too close on the heels of his inquiry for it to be a coincidence.

He owed it to Nichols to bring his killer to justice—Paladin justice. Once he had Brenna stashed somewhere safe, he'd start looking, but he couldn't do anything until he got this bunch out of his face.

"What's it going to be, boys?" He glanced at the guns and then back at their owners. "Are you going to put those popguns away or use them?"

Dr. Vega interrupted their stare-down party. "Mr. Trahern, Ms. Nichols is asking for you."

Trahern followed Dr. Vega back into the room, leaving Jarvis to deal with the Guard. Bracing himself, he hoped like hell he wouldn't be the one to break the news that her father was dead.

• • •

Brenna hurt everywhere. The pain was bone deep and centered around her heart. Something was horribly wrong—something far worse than waking up in a hospital without knowing how she'd gotten here. A doctor and nurse hovered over her bed, doing their best to reassure her that everything was going to be all right. But it wasn't. She'd lost far more than a few days of her life; she just couldn't remember what.

Worst of all, there was the cold-eyed stranger who claimed to be Blake Trahern. She'd only gotten one clear look at him before he'd disappeared from her room, but there'd been nothing familiar in the hard planes of his face. Her thoughts were thick and slow moving, probably due to the pain medication. It took all her energy to dredge up an image of his face.

Her last memory of Blake was the night of his high school graduation. He'd stood out on the stage because of his height. With his dark blond hair and silver gray eyes, she'd thought him the best-looking boy in his class. When he'd first moved in with them, no one thought he'd graduate, much less do so with honors. Her father had been so proud of Blake.

A dark chill washed over her. Where *was* her father? He would never have abandoned her like this. If he'd been there and had to leave for some reason, he would have left a message for her. Surely they would have given it to her by now.

She forced out the question she had to ask, even if she didn't want to know the answer. "Where's my father?"

When Dr. Vega broke off eye contact, she knew. Memories flooded back into her mind, shattered and broken. She remembered standing on the small porch outside their back door. Her father had waved at her as he turned the key in the ignition, saying he needed to run by his office, which was strange because he rarely worked weekends. She had turned away to go back inside; there had been a flash of light and then the noise . . . so much noise . . . shattering glass and someone screaming . . . maybe her? . . . and then pain.

Oh, God! His car had blown up! Pain, fresh and horrendous, tore through her. She struggled to sit up, but the nurse and Dr. Vega held her back.

"Easy, Ms. Nichols. You don't want to tear your stitches open," Dr. Vega warned. "Do you want something more for the pain?"

Tears running down her face, she looked toward the nurse who was drawing up an injection. "No more medicine right now. Please. I need to think. Everything just hit me all at once."

Dr. Vega frowned as he considered her request.

"All right, but if it gets to be too much for you, don't hesitate to ask for something to help you sleep. You've been through a traumatic experience."

"I will, Doctor." But before she would allow them to sedate her again, she wanted some answers. Maybe the man out in the hall could tell her more. She still wasn't convinced he was Blake Trahern, because Blake would never have abandoned her father for years, even if he hadn't wanted to keep in touch with her. Still, she'd pretend to believe him, to find out what he knew and how.

She forced a control into her voice that she didn't feel. "Would one of you ask Mr. Trahern to come back in?"

"Certainly, Ms. Nichols, but only for a short visit. Right now you need rest. For the next day or so, I think it best to restrict any visitors as much as possible." Dr. Vega stepped away from her bed but paused in the doorway. "We do have to notify the police that you've regained consciousness. They'll want to talk to you about the incident."

For some reason, that frightened her even more than dealing with the man out in the hall. Were they coming to explain what had happened, and why? Or did they expect her to be able to shed some light on the situation for them? If so, they were out of luck.

She closed her eyes for a brief moment, but she felt Trahern's approach. He moved with the soft silence of a big cat, but she swore she could feel the intensity of his gaze from all the way across the room. When he reached the side of her bed, she braced herself and looked up at him. For several seconds, he said nothing as he allowed her to look her fill. The silver gray eyes were the right color, as was his hair. The hard set to his mouth was new but not unexpected. The young man who had made his home with them had not had an easy life; it was bound to take a toll.

"It's been a long time, Brenna." His voice was deeper, but there was a note of familiarity, something of the boy she used to know.

But she couldn't think about that right now— not with a wall of grief threatening to fall in on her and bury her in the rubble of pain and sorrow. Drawing a deep breath, she shoved the painful memories down to be dealt with later.

"How much do you know about what happened to my father?" She deliberately didn't use his name although she was beginning to suspect he really was exactly who he'd claimed to be.

"Enough, although I haven't gotten a copy of the police report yet. I drove by your house, but I didn't stop because I needed to get here."

"Why?" She had to ask the question, even if she already knew the answer.

"Don't play games with me, Brenna. You're not stupid. Someone planted the bomb that killed your father and damn near finished you off, too. Until we know who was behind the attack, you're not safe."

Tears stung her eyes, but his blunt words were somehow easier to deal with than the doctor's sympathy. "So you're convinced he was the target and not me."

The look he gave her was one of pure disgust. "Get real, Brenna. Even if the reviewers thought your latest book sucked big-time, their weapon of choice would have been words, not explosives."

She focused on the one piece of that speech that surprised her. "You know about my books?"

His eyes suddenly found one of the machines above her head to be absolutely fascinating. "Yes."

Despite the situation, that small admission made her smile. "You actually read some of them?"

He shoved his hands in his pockets. "I've read all of them, except the latest one on women pioneers here in Missouri."

"And what did you think?" She waited for his answer even as she wondered why his opinion mattered.

His eyebrows snapped together. "You have more important things to worry about right now than what I think about your writing."

But she'd learned stubbornness from an expert: him. "Did you like them?"

"Yes, damn it, I did. You have a real knack for bringing history down to the individual level, letting the reader see and feel what it was like to live back then. Now, can we move on to more important things?"

The little show of temper was almost the last bit of information she needed to accept that this man was the boy she'd last seen over ten years before. One last test and she'd know for certain.

"What kind of cookies did our housekeeper Maisy bake just because you liked them so much?"

He stepped closer and glared down at her. "You still don't believe it's me, do you? Well, too damn bad, Brenna, because I'm all that stands between you and —"

Another voice interrupted him. "Come now, Trahern, don't mislead Ms. Nichols like that. Who do you think watched over her until you came charging in here to stand guard?"

"Shut up, Jarvis."

"Is that any way to show your gratitude? I saved you from those guards just now. Surely that earns me an introduction."

"No."

There was no hostility in Blake's voice, but neither was there any welcome in his body language. Maybe the other man's approach merely reminded him that they weren't alone. Who was this Jarvis, that he would have stood guard over her in a hospital? With his dark hair and eyes, he looked nothing like Blake, yet there was a great deal of similarity in their stance—especially in the way their eyes kept checking out their surroundings every few seconds.

"I'm Brenna Nichols, Mr. Jarvis."

"It's nice to meet you, Ms. Nichols. Your father was a good man. We had nothing but respect for him."

Trahern elbowed his unwelcome companion in the ribs. "That's enough."

Jarvis put a little more space between them. "I heard the doctor tell the nurse that the police will be here in a few minutes."

"So?" Trahern said.

"If you don't want to be tied up here for hours answering questions we don't want to answer, I suggest we get out before they arrive. She'll be safe enough while they're here."

Brenna was getting really tired of them avoiding her questions and talking as if she weren't in the room. "Why would the police want to question Blake?"

Jarvis's smile was a little too practiced for her to trust it. "Because until they know who killed your father, everyone is a suspect. Especially strangers who can't explain what business they have for being here in the first place."

"Get out, Jarvis."

Jarvis planted his feet wide and stood his ground. "After you, Trahern."

Why couldn't Blake explain? And how had he

found out about her father's death so quickly? But he was already moving away from her bed, probably to disappear from her life just as quickly as he'd appeared.

"When will you be back?"

Jarvis stood in the doorway, watching down the hall. "The guards will let us know when the police have come and gone."

"We won't leave you alone, Brenna," Blake said. "Not until we get to the bottom of this." He was almost to the door.

"Isn't that the police's job?" She knew she was missing something here, something important. "Blake?"

"Not now, Brenna. There isn't time."

She didn't want him to leave, although he'd given her no reason to trust him. She just knew facing a bunch of policemen asking questions to which she had no answers would be easier with Blake Trahern standing at her side. She blinked back tears, not wanting to appear weak.

"Fine. Go ahead and leave. It's what you're good at." If she sounded bitchy, so be it.

His cold gray eyes stared across the room at her. "Snickerdoodles." Then he was gone.

Brenna pushed the button and raised the head of her bed to better face down the two detectives who had invaded her room. After their initial offerings of sympathy, their visit had quickly shifted to more of an inquisition.

She marshaled enough strength to let a little displeasure show in the tone of her voice. "I've already told you everything I know, Detective Montgomery. I have no idea who hated my father enough to kill him."

He hadn't believed her the first time she'd told him that, and he obviously didn't believe her now. His pencil stub stood poised over his notepad, but he hadn't written down a single word since she'd verified her address and phone number. She glanced from him to his partner, Detective Swan. Their attitudes puzzled her. Why would she lie? She was the one who most wanted her father's murderer brought to justice.

Detective Montgomery shifted his considerable weight in the molded plastic chair by her bed. "Tell me again how it happened, Ms. Nichols. Start with breakfast that morning and go from there."

How would knowing if she ate eggs or cereal help explain the explosion that had destroyed her world? "My father and I are . . ." Her throat constricted with pain, but she forced herself to continue. "That is, my father and I were both early risers. As soon as I got up, I went for a run while Dad read the paper. Afterward, I came home and showered. Then we each ate a bowl of cornflakes with skim milk." If he wanted details, she'd give him some. "The spoons had flowers on their handles. The bowls were white with blue stripes around the top. My glass held sixteen ounces of iced tea."

Her inquisitors didn't appreciate her efforts one bit, but at least Montgomery wrote something on his pad. "And then?"

"I did some routine chores—laundry, paid bills, that sort of thing."

"And your father?"

"He spent most of the morning at his desk in the library. I heard him make several phone calls. When I went in to see if we were still on for lunch, he was gone." She stared at the ceiling, letting the events of Saturday morning run through her mind like a movie, watching for details that might satisfy the police's need for information.

The younger detective moved away from the wall, closer to her bed. "Did he act worried or upset?"

She shook her head. "No, Dad always got lost in his work because he paid attention to the details. That's what made him such a good judge. When he was studying a case, sometimes you had to say his name two or three times to get his attention."

"Do you know which case he was working on?" The pencil was poised to write again.

"No, I don't. In fact, I had thought he was between major cases right now." But if that was true, what did he need at his office that was so important that he had to find it on a Saturday morning?

"And even though the two of you had plans, he suddenly decided to leave?"

She'd already told them that. "Yes. We agreed to reschedule for another day."

"Did the two of you often go out to lunch on Saturdays?"

"Sometimes, not regularly."

"Did you pick the restaurant or did he?"

The two detectives were both asking questions now, making her feel as if she were in the middle of a tennis match. "We both felt like Italian, so we chose accordingly."

"Do you know who any of the phone calls were to?"

The rapid-fire questions made her head ache. "No, I don't. Sometimes he shared his work with me; sometimes he didn't. It also wasn't unusual for him to go into the office if he needed to borrow a specific book. He has an extensive library at home, but not as comprehensive as the one at the courthouse."

"We'll want to get his phone records." Montgomery closed his notebook, stuck it back in his pocket, and stared at the floor for a moment, as if gathering up his scattered thoughts.

"Ms. Nichols, thank you for talking to us, especially when you've been through so much. If you think of anything else, please call us." He laid a business card down on her bedside table. "We'll be in touch."

"I would appreciate being kept informed on your progress, detectives."

"Yes, ma'am," Detective Swan answered without much conviction.

After they left, weariness washed over her, leaving her shaken and a little frightened. Due to her father's job, she'd spent a lot of time around the law enforcement community. She'd mostly found them to be dedicated to their profession—sympathetic to the victims of crime but hard on criminals. She just wished she knew which category these particular detectives thought she was.

chapter 2

Come on, Trahern, she's safe for the moment. Finish your beer."

Blake's first inclination was to refuse. Ordinarily, he wouldn't have hesitated to depend on the Guard to keep Brenna safe, but the recent betrayal back in Seattle had left him distrustful. He'd known Purefoy for years and never suspected the man would betray any of the Paladins, much less their Handler, Dr. Young.

So he sure as hell wasn't going to leave Brenna's welfare in the hands of strangers. Too many years had passed since he'd last served in St. Louis for him to be familiar with the local personnel.

But rather than argue with Jarvis, he picked up his drink and took a long swig. Considering how tired he was, he should have been loading up on caffeine rather than alcohol, but his friend had insisted on stopping for a sandwich and a couple of cold ones.

"Don't worry, Blake. If she's anything like her old man, she'll handle whatever the police throw at her." Jarvis leaned back in his chair and crossed his feet at the ankles, the picture of a man content with his life and relaxing after a long day.

Blake knew better. Despite Jarvis's easygoing appearance, he had a hair-trigger temper that simmered just beneath the surface. Almost all Paladins did; some were just better at hiding their true natures than others. Others, like Blake, didn't bother to try. Men usually moved out of his way without hesitation, not even aware of how they knew the danger he represented.

Women often had a different reaction. On some primitive level, they recognized him as the alpha male he was. In the dimmest memories of mankind, he would have led the men in the hunt and had his pick of the women to warm his bed at night. Modern women were smarter than that. They might like to walk on the wild side on Saturday nights, but he wasn't the kind of man they'd take home to meet the family.

That was fine with him.

He didn't deal well with crowds or clingy women at the best of times. Now, when all of his protective instincts were at full throttle, his nerves felt stretched to the breaking point. It wouldn't take much to shatter the fragile control he had over his need to strike out at a handy target—like the bastard who'd killed the judge.

Which brought him right back to the problem of Brenna Nichols. She'd grown into a lovely woman, her beauty unmistakable despite her bruises and unkempt hair. And though she was twenty-six now, those big green eyes of hers held the same innocence that had irritated the hell out of him twelve years ago.

"Hey, partner, you're thinking too hard." Jarvis straightened up. "You've got to be running on empty. Let's go check on your woman one more time and then hole up at my place for some sleep. Tomorrow we'll start turning over rocks to see what crawls out."

"She's not my woman, Jarvis," he said with cold anger. The last thing he needed was for rumors to start about his relationship with Brenna. She was the daughter of a former mentor. End of discussion.

His old friend raised his hands in mock surrender. "Fine. Let's get a move on before you crash." He stood up and tossed some bills down on the table.

Blake would rather stay in a hotel, or even the emergency barracks near the barrier that the Regents provided for visiting Paladins. But right now he needed Jarvis's goodwill more than he needed privacy. His friend's guest room would serve until Brenna was released from the hospital.

It didn't surprise him when Jarvis left the bar through the back rather than the front. They both paused as they stepped outside to let their eyes adjust to the darkness. There wasn't even a hint of a breeze in the narrow alley, and the smell of old garbage hung heavily in the night air.

"I left my car a block over that way." Jarvis nodded toward the end of the alley. "Why don't I drop you off at the hospital, and then you can head for my place when you're ready?"

"Sounds good to me."

After only a few steps his shirt was clinging to his skin. Damn, he'd forgotten how hot St. Louis was in the summer. They walked along in silence, for which Blake was grateful. He was thickheaded from too little sleep and too many questions he had no answers for. But before he allowed himself to rest, he'd make sure that Brenna was settled in for the night and that the guards understood their lives were in jeopardy if they failed to keep her safe.

When they reached the street at the far end of the alley, Jarvis headed for a bright blue 1969 Chevelle SS.

"I should have known you'd still be driving that beast."

Jarvis grinned and patted the roof of his baby.

"While you're here, we'll have to take her down some of those roller-coaster highways in the Ozarks and let her rip. They don't make them like this anymore."

"I'm surprised you can make it from one gas station to the next without it complaining." Though he wasn't above admiring the feel of a 396-cubic-inch engine as it tore down the road.

His friend looked insulted. "I just finished the restoration on her about a year ago. I did most of it myself—new paint job, new interior, all of it to factory specs. Except for the stereo, she looks just like she did when she first rolled off the lot."

"And for what you've spent on this thing, you probably could have bought two new cars. Something more practical in a nice beige."

His friend snorted. "Shut up, Trahern. You'll hurt her feelings."

When Jarvis climbed in and turned the key in the ignition, a deep-throated rumble purred through the car. Blake leaned back and fought to keep his eyes open. After a few blocks, Jarvis let loose with a string of curses. Blake immediately sat up and reached for his gun, only to remember he wasn't carrying one.

"What's wrong?"

Jarvis pointed straight ahead. "See all those flickering lights in the hospital parking lot?"

A sick feeling settled in Blake's stomach even as

adrenaline pumped through his bloodstream, ready-
ing him for battle. A bevy of cop cars and fire trucks,
all with lights ablaze, were blocking the road ahead.
He was already reaching for the door handle before
Jarvis stopped the car.

"I left all my weapons in Seattle, figuring on re-
stocking here. Have you got anything I can borrow?"

Jarvis reached under the seat and tossed him a
bean-shaped gun pouch. "I'll park the car and be
right behind you."

"Fine."

Blake ran through the shadows for a block before he slowed to a walk. He couldn't risk drawing
unwanted attention to himself by charging into the
hospital like the goddamn cavalry. He wouldn't do
Brenna any good cooling his heels in a jail cell, especially if they pulled his old police records.

The activity seemed to be centered around the
entrance to the emergency room, so he circled to
the front of the hospital. A handful of the medical
staff stood huddled together, smoking as they ignored the chaos a short distance away.

He waited until a couple of the employees
ground out their cigarettes and broke away from
the group before making his approach.

"Excuse me, but could you tell me what's going
on? I was on my way to visit a friend in the hospital
when I saw all the lights."

The two men, both orderlies judging by their uniforms, shrugged. "The fire alarm went off. Evidently some trash caught on fire, and a few patients in the far wing had to be evacuated just in case. The all clear came through a few minutes ago, and the patients have already started returning to their rooms. The police are just finishing up their paperwork."

"Thanks."

If someone wanted to get at Brenna, what better way to do it than throw the whole hospital into chaos? Even with police and firemen crawling all over the place, there would be a window of time before they arrived during which anyone could slip in and out of the hospital without a soul noticing. And in a medical center the size of this one, there would be enough personnel turnover to cover the presence of an unfamiliar face.

Maybe the fire and commotion had nothing to do with Brenna, but Blake had never liked coincidences. He headed for the staircase and took them two at a time up to Brenna's floor.

No guard was on duty at the door to the stairs. Son of a bitch! He ran down the hallway, sliding to a stop when he spotted the cluster of guards standing around Brenna's bed. He shoved his way through to the front, only to see that her bed was empty and the machines that had been monitoring her vitals were dark and silent.

He grabbed the nearest guard by the front of his uniform and shoved the barrel of Jarvis's gun against the man's throat.

"Where the hell is she?" Blake's eyes flicked down to the man's name badge. "Speak quickly, Baxter, and you'd better have a good answer—because there's nothing I'd like better right now than to squeeze this trigger."

The sound of a door opening and closing and the sound of shuffling footsteps caught Blake's attention. He froze, unwilling to release his victim, but aware that everyone's attention had shifted to the person or persons behind him.

"Blake Trahern! What are you doing?" A hand grabbed his arm and tried to tug him away. "Stop scaring him like that."

Brenna's voice, weak and hoarse, sounded like heaven to him. He slowly lowered the gun, not wanting to startle one of the other guards into a rash act, then stuck it in the back of his waistband.

When he turned to face Brenna, she was swaying slightly.

"What are you doing out of bed?" he snarled.

She managed to straighten her shoulders and stand her ground. "When the fire alarm went off, we had to evacuate. Once the all clear was sounded, we came back."

"Back where? Your bed was empty and these piss-poor excuses for guards were all clustered

around your empty bed, instead of standing watch."
He put his hands on his hips and glared down
at her.

A faint blush crept up her face. "I needed to
use the restroom, not that it's any of your business.
Now if you'll excuse me, it's been a long day and
I'm tired."

When she moved to step around him, she almost fell. Blake swept her up in his arms, muttering about stubborn fools. Despite the urge to just
dump her on the bed, he gently settled her back
on the mattress and pillows. After yanking the
blankets up around her, he gave the guards a look
that sent them scurrying for their posts.

Brenna counted to twenty before opening an
eye to see if the room had quit spinning. When her
vision cleared, she turned her head to face Blake.
"Did you have to be so rude to them?"

"I'll be nicer when they convince me that
they're taking their jobs seriously." He ran his
hands through his hair in frustration. "You should
not have been allowed out of this room until one of
them verified in person that the fire alarm was
going off for a legitimate reason. It could've been
set off just to create confusion for your father's
killer to get in here to finish the job he started.
They're supposed to be professionals and should
have known better."

"But the nurse and doctor said we had to—"

"Damn it, Brenna, I don't give a rat's ass what they said! Someone killed your father and damned near killed you in the process." Blake grabbed onto the railing along her bed, his knuckles white with the strain. "Your safety comes first. The next time those bozos out in the hallway screw up, I *will* pull the trigger and do the whole damned world a favor."

His eyes had darkened to the color of a summer storm, sending a chill through her. "You can't go around threatening to shoot the police, Blake."

"They're not the police," he sneered. "Which reminds me. What did the detectives have to say for themselves? Do they have any leads?"

The sudden change in subjects and in his mood confused her. What did he mean, the guards weren't sent by the police? Who else would post men to guard her door?

"Two detectives stopped by. It was strange. They seemed more interested in what my father had for breakfast and where we'd planned on having lunch, than who had planted the bomb. I didn't like their attitudes one bit."

She finally gave in to the need to close her eyes and had almost succeeded in drifting off to sleep when Dr. Vega came back into the room.

"Ms. Nichols, I'm sorry about all the chaos this evening. I'll have the nurse reattach only the most necessary monitors. Now that you're awake and lucid, we want to start backing off on some of this stuff. Once she has you taken care of, try to get a good night's sleep. That will go a long way toward getting you back to normal."

As if anything would ever seem *normal* again.

Tears stung Brenna's eyes and trickled down her cheeks as she finally drifted off to sleep.

Awareness returned to her slowly. The familiar beep and whir of machines kept pace with her heart and lungs, and the scent of disinfectant and other chemicals stung her nose. She was still in the hospital. She'd been hoping that it all had been a nightmare and that she'd wake up to her old life.

She heard a murmur of low voices and immediately recognized Blake Trahern's. The second one took her a bit longer. It belonged to Blake's friend . . . Jarvis? She had no idea if it was his first name or his last.

For the moment, she was content to float between the dream world of sleep and harsh reality, listening to see if she could learn something about Blake and what had brought him back to St. Louis.

"The doctor says she should be able to fly in a couple of days." That was Trahern. "I'll see about chartering a private plane to take her to Seattle."

"I see two problems with that. First of all, she isn't going to want to go, not until she finds out what happened to her father. Second, no matter how much you trust your Handler, I don't know the woman at all, and I'm not about to send the judge's daughter halfway across country alone to stay with strangers. Now, if you were to go with her . . ."

"We've already discussed that, Jarvis. I'm not going anywhere anytime soon."

"So we're back to where we started: finding a safe place for Ms. Nichols here in town. After we track down the killers, then she can decide for herself what she wants to do."

Brenna opened her eyes. "I'm not going anywhere, gentlemen, with or without one of you as an escort. As soon as the doctor releases me from this place, I'm going straight home. And why would you two be searching for the killers? Isn't that a job for the police?"

Two pairs of eyes swung toward her, one neutral, the other glaring at her with their usual intensity. She might not be up to full speed yet, but she wasn't about to have her future dictated by these two.

"Well?" She crossed her arms over her chest and prepared to wait them out.

Jarvis broke first, not a particular surprise. "Good morning, Ms. Nichols." He offered her a broad smile. "I hope you had a good night's sleep, unlike some people I could mention."

"Shut the hell up, Jarvis."

The dark gray T-shirt Blake had worn the night before looked slept in, and the shirt he wore over it had definitely seen better days. The fact that he hadn't shaved in at least twenty-four hours only added to the intense masculinity he radiated. A woman would have to be dead not to respond to him, and the ache she felt when she looked at him had nothing to do with her injuries.

She quickly steered the conversation in a safer direction than how his prickly beard would feel against her skin. "How I slept is not important. Now would one of you please answer my questions?"

The two men went back to glaring at each other, neither of them willing to be the first one to speak. Before she could muster up the energy to insist, a nurse came bustling into the room with a bright smile.

"Ms. Nichols, glad to see we're wide awake. How are we feeling this morning?" The woman headed right for the closed curtains and threw them back to let the morning sunshine flood the room.

"Shut those curtains right now!" Trahern's bellow dimmed the nurse's practiced smile.

"Now that Ms. Nichols is awake there's no reason to keep the room dark, and . . ."

He reached past her to jerk the curtains closed with so much force that he tore the fabric loose from a couple of the rings. The savagery of his action startled Brenna and made the nurse gasp.

"Trahern, stop acting like a crazy person! She didn't do anything wrong." What had set him off? She looked to Jarvis for help, but the expression on his face was every bit as harsh as Trahern's.

Blake froze, only a tight muscle in his cheek revealing how angry he was. Slowly, ever so slowly, he stepped back, then he stared a hole through the hapless nurse. "Someone has already tried to kill Ms. Nichols once. I would appreciate your keeping these closed to avoid giving a sniper a clear shot at her while she's a patient here. She survived the first attack. She might not survive the next."

Then he walked out of the room.

The nurse's face was ashen. "Ms. Nichols, I'm sorry. I didn't think."

"I'm sure Mr. Trahern is being overprotective. Please think nothing of it."

She threw back her covers to climb out of bed. While she might not like his heavy-handed tactics, she didn't want Blake to leave. Jarvis reached out to steady her as she stood up. When he was sure she wasn't going to keel over, he brought her a robe.

"Where will he have gone?" she asked as they took the first shuffling steps toward the door.

"Not far. No matter what mood he's in, he won't leave you alone. His conscience won't allow it."

Jarvis stuck his head out the door and looked both ways. "He's at the far end, away from the nurses' station, staring out the window. Make sure he hears you walk up behind him. He never did like surprises."

Jarvis's remarks raised even more questions. For now, though, she concentrated on keeping her balance as she made her way down the hall. What was she going to say to him? The situation seemed to call for an apology, but she wasn't sure what she'd said that had upset him. She'd only asked him to stop scaring the nurse. No, wait. Her exact words were for him to quit acting like a crazy person. Surely he knew that was just an expression, that she didn't really think he was mentally unstable.

She stopped a short distance away and waited for him to acknowledge her.

He glanced back over his shoulder at her, his expression shuttered and cold. "What's the matter? Afraid to get too close to a crazy person?"

Somehow she doubted a sincere apology would work with this man. Temper, though, was something he understood. "Don't be so thin-skinned, Trahern. It was just a figure of speech. You're the least crazy person I know, but you can't go around scaring innocent nurses like that. If I didn't know you so well, I might have been scared myself."

He turned back to the window. "You don't know me at all, little girl. You never did."

"I may not know what you've done or where you've been for the past twelve years, but some things never change about a person. You would never hurt me. Ever."

"What makes you think that?"

"You're trying too hard to protect me from the person who killed my father—not that I believe I'm in any real danger."

"Until we know why your father was killed, we can't assume anything." The temper was back in his voice, but not the bitterness. "I'll feel better when we get to the bottom of this."

"I'm sure the police are doing their best."

Trahern snorted in derision. "They couldn't find their backsides with two hands, especially when they have no idea what or who they are dealing with."

"And you do? If you know why my father was killed, Blake, you need to tell me and the police right now." She grabbed his arm, trying to make him look at her. It was like trying to move a granite cliff.

"No."

"You can't mean that, Blake. If you have any respect at all for my father's work, you have to trust the legal system. Let the police catch his killer and bring him to trial. My father hated vigilante justice."

"Which work are you talking about, Brenna?"

He shook his head and looked away again. "You always were a wide-eyed innocent. Obviously that hasn't changed."

"Trahern, that's enough."

Neither of them had heard Jarvis's approach.

"Stay out of this." Blake said the words at the same time Brenna did. Under other circumstances she might have found that amusing. At the moment, it only made her mad.

"No, you both stay out of it! The police are handling the investigation, not the two of you."

Both men stood well over six feet tall, at least ten inches over her own average stature. Right now they used their height advantage to communicate by eye contact alone. Craning her neck was only giving her a headache, so she gave up in disgust.

"Fine. The two of you have a fine time all by yourselves. But until you decide to let the police do their job—"

The sound of shattering glass brought her up short. Blake grabbed her by the arm and shoved her into a nearby treatment room. She started to protest, but he effectively silenced her by wrapping his arm around her and covering her mouth with his hand. The temperature seemed to plummet, but that may have been the sudden rush of fear. In the blink of an eye, both Jarvis and Blake produced handguns, looking all too comfortable with the way they fit their hands.

Blake whispered a warning close enough to her ear for her to feel the warmth of his breath. "Stay quiet, Brenna, and you might just live long enough to tear a strip off my hide."

When she nodded, he loosened his hold on her. For a few seconds, the only sound she heard was the pounding of her heart, but then she heard a couple of popping noises and shouting. Blake pushed her behind him. Both he and Jarvis looked decidedly grim.

"Stay with her." Jarvis started out the door, looking lethal with his gun gripped in two hands.

Trahern shook his head. "This isn't the time to play hero, not when we don't know how many of them there are. We've got to get her out of here. Now."

They could hear the sound of running feet from the far end of the hallway. "The cops will be crawling all over this place soon. This confusion is our best chance to get her out of here without being seen."

A female scream rang out down the hallway, and Brenna understood all too well how the woman felt.

"Is anybody looking this way?" Blake asked.

Jarvis poked his head out of the room long enough to scope out the hallway. "No, it's clear for the moment."

"I'll lead. Bring her when I give the signal." Trahern ducked out into the hall, turning away from the commotion at the other end. He kept his back to the opposite wall, looking from side to side as he made his way to the exit sign a short distance away. When he reached the door to the staircase, he opened it and disappeared for a few seconds. Then he stuck his head back out and waved them forward.

Jarvis shielded Brenna's body with his as they silently slipped across to where Trahern waited. She tried to check out what was happening down at the nurses' station, but Jarvis blocked her view. She only caught a glimpse of a guard writhing on the floor outside the door to her room, his uniform shirt soaked in blood.

"Oh, God, how bad is he hurt?"

"I don't know, but one of his buddies will get him help. Move!" Trahern's orders were abrupt, but his touch was gentle as he supported her with his free hand.

Jarvis shoved the door closed behind them. "Up or down?"

Trahern jerked his head up. "Up one floor, then across to the other wing and down. There's an exit to the parking lot from the day surgery on the second floor."

How did he know that? Brenna didn't have enough breath to ask; it was just another in a long list of questions she'd want answers to when they reached safety. If they ever did.

"Brenna, can you keep up this pace or do I need to carry you?"

"I'll make it."

Jarvis waited on the landing, his gun and eyes aimed on the steps above them. When they reached the top step he slowly opened the door and peeked out. "No one seems to be aware that there's a problem." He slipped his pistol into his waistband and pulled his shirt down over it. "I'll be back in a few."

He disappeared, leaving the two of them alone again. Brenna leaned against the wall. This was far more excitement than her battered body needed; her legs trembled with near exhaustion, and it was hard to catch her breath. Trahern looked remarkably unperturbed; he and Jarvis acted as if this was second nature to them.

"Is this how you spend your time?" she whispered.

The dim light in the staircase cast his face in harsh lines. "Not now, Brenna." The flat words didn't invite conversation. Then Jarvis was back, motioning that the hallway was safe.

She said, "All right. But you owe me answers, and I intend to have them."

Then she joined Jarvis out in the busy hallway, letting Blake follow as he would.

●　●　●

Blake wanted to throw Brenna over his shoulder and run like hell; her face was gray with exhaustion and pain. But their best disguise was to blend in with all the other patients and their families going about their business as if nothing were wrong. As long as they were inside the hospital, they were sitting ducks. Each and every person they passed could be a paid assassin on a mission to end Brenna's life—or his or even Jarvis's, for that matter. Whoever wanted the judge dead had to wonder who he'd talked to about his suspicions. He and Brenna were the obvious choices, but no one within the Regents was safe if the judge had left any records that could be traced back to them.

It was hard to keep to such a slow pace, but the three of them would draw less attention if they walked at a rate comfortable for Brenna. In a few more seconds, they'd reach the sky bridge that led to the other wing. For the length of the bridge, they'd be exposed to prying eyes from both inside the hospital and anyone keeping watch from the outside.

Stepping out onto the sky bridge, the two men sandwiched Brenna between them. Even that was a poor excuse for protection. If the sniper knew his business, he could take out all three of them with one shot, two at the most.

"See anything?"

He shook his head. "It's empty. Let's go."

He took Brenna's arm and motioned for Jarvis to do the same, then they lifted her up and ran across to the surgical center.

"Put me down before someone sees us!"

Once she was back on her own two feet, Brenna rubbed her arms. "Just what I needed—more bruises."

Blake gave her a hard look. "Better a new bruise than a bullet hole. We go to the left here, then straight out toward the door."

By the time they reached the final turn, all of Blake's fighting instincts were running at full bore. Keeping Brenna out of sight around the corner, he studied the lobby. Two women at the desk were talking on the phone and shuffling through paperwork. An elderly gentleman held a magazine but stared worriedly at a pair of double doors, no doubt concerned about someone in surgery.

Finally, there was an orderly leaning against the wall near the water fountain, wearing a crisply pressed surgical uniform and gleaming black boots as he worked a crossword puzzle. Trahern frowned. The shoes were wrong; he couldn't remember seeing anyone else wearing black boots. This guy wasn't wearing a hospital employee ID badge, either.

Trahern turned his back to the supposed orderly while he pointed him out to Jarvis. "He doesn't belong here."

Jarvis nodded. "See any others?"

They both turned slowly, as if they were unfamiliar with the lobby and trying to get their bearings. "No, looks like he's alone."

"Leave him to me." Jarvis's smile would have frightened the dead.

He split off, heading for a table that offered coffee and cookies for those waiting for patients to get out of surgery. He filled a cup, took a sip, and then started for the door. Just as he reached the orderly he deliberately stumbled, tossing the scalding hot liquid right at the man's crotch. The orderly bellowed in pain and shock as he backed away straight into the water fountain.

Jarvis did a great imitation of a man trying to make amends for his clumsiness. One of the women came out from behind the desk to help, but Jarvis waved her off, dragging his victim around the corner into the men's room. Trahern doubted the would-be orderly would be coming out anytime soon, especially under his own power.

Then he noticed that Brenna was no longer hiding behind him. She was standing off to his side, glaring at Jarvis as he disappeared from sight.

"What was that all about? That poor man was just standing there. You can't tell me that Jarvis didn't spill his coffee on purpose. There's no way he'd ever be that clumsy."

Good God. To shut her up, Blake kissed her.

His temper was running hot, but he gentled his lips over hers as he teased her lips apart with his tongue. And damn, her sweet taste had his prick sitting up and begging for attention. He'd been too long without a woman, and it didn't help that Brenna was kissing him back.

Brenna moaned as her hands fluttered up his chest to settle around his neck. She pressed against him, making him painfully aware of the soft crush of her breasts against his chest. He wanted to drag her to the floor and bury himself in her sweet heat, but the hospital lobby was hardly the place.

He ripped his mouth from hers, his breath ragged as he stared down into her bewildered eyes. Her confusion faded as she remembered where they were and what Jarvis had done, and the stubborn set to her jaw told him she wasn't going anywhere until he convinced her that Jarvis hadn't lost his mind. Keeping her inside the circle of his arms, he whispered near her ear, "That guy was watching for us."

"You couldn't possibly know that. No one could."

He saw red, tired of her arguments, tired of her doubts, and just plain tired. "Listen closely, Brenna. It's my job to know such things. Jarvis is going to come out of that bathroom alone with an extra gun tucked in his belt and a transmitter that he's taken off that guy you're feeling so sorry for—who would have started shooting as soon as he recognized us."

"But—"

"Chew my ass all you want later. Right now, either you walk out of here on your own or I'll carry you out. Your choice." He glared down at her, his teeth clenched in frustration.

She must have realized that she had pushed him as far as she could, because she backed down. "Fine. Lead on."

He released his hold on her and walked close by her side, ready to pull his gun or respond to a physical attack. Jarvis caught up with them just as the doors slid open. Judging by the extra energy in his step, Trahern knew they had been right. For Brenna's benefit, though, he asked, "What was he carrying?"

His friend grinned, even as his eyes began an automatic sweep of the hospital parking lot. "Picked up a nice little Glock. I've wanted one for my collection for some time. His transmitter was a piece of crap, so I just flushed it."

The fear in Brenna's eyes was back, but maybe now she'd follow their orders without arguing. Once she was feeling better and the memory of the past few days faded a bit, she'd be right back to standing toe to toe with him and arguing. He couldn't wait; the defeat in her slumped shoulders was painful to see.

"Let's get her to my rental car. Your car sticks out like a sore thumb, and we don't want to draw any more attention to ourselves."

Jarvis shook his head. "I don't know how many more insults I can take from you about my car, Trahern. I think you're just jealous."

"Yeah, right. Keep her here while I check things out."

Blake approached his rental slowly, watching for anyone who might be paying too much attention to their actions. He could hear sirens approaching. If they didn't hurry, they could end up trapped in the parking lot by the emergency vehicles. Dropping to the ground, he checked the undercarriage for any telltale signs that someone might have left them an unwanted present.

Nothing.

He checked all four doors, especially the driver's side, noting the small piece of grass he'd left over the bottom edge of the door was still in place. It didn't guarantee that no one had been in the car, but he had also left a hair across the edge of the hood in two places. When he spotted both of them, he felt reasonably certain that the car hadn't been tampered with.

He opened the door and turned the key in the ignition. For a brief second he held his breath, wondering if it would be his last. But the engine caught and ran smoothly. Jarvis hustled Brenna across to the car and guided her to the back door.

"Get in and lie down, Brenna. Once you're away from here, you can sit up front. But if anyone is watching the exits, they'll be looking for a woman in a hospital gown, not a man alone."

She winced in pain as she obediently stretched out across the seat.

"Where are you going to take her?" Jarvis asked Blake.

"I don't know." Even if he did, he wasn't going to tell. The fewer people who knew where Brenna was, the better.

His friend nodded. "Call me when you get settled, and we'll plan our next step. Keep your head down, Ms. Nichols, and trust Trahern to protect you. There's no one I'd rather have at my back." He took one last look around the parking lot before slapping his hand on the trunk of the car to signal all was clear.

Blake backed out of the parking spot. As he started for the nearest exit, a couple of men charged out of the hospital, their heads turning from side to side. Luckily, other vehicles driving through the lot had two people in the front seat, and by the time the searchers had checked them out, Blake was safely out of the parking lot.

"We're on the street now, Brenna, and I'm going to stick to side streets for the next mile or two to see if we've picked up a tail."

He wasn't used to explaining his every move, since he normally worked with men used to urban combat. The Paladins were natural-born killers, but fortunately for the rest of mankind, they came hardwired with a strong conscience and a need to protect. Each time they were badly wounded or killed, they healed quickly, but at the cost of becoming more like the Others—the human-like creatures that tried to invade Earth every chance they got.

He'd killed his fair share of Others while protecting the barrier that separated their world from his, but he'd died at the end of their swords way too often over the past couple of years. He and Dr. Laurel Young, the Handler who oversaw his care, knew that his test scores were rapidly reaching the point at which he could lose his humanity and become a danger to anyone around him. She was intensifying her research into what kept her Paladin lover, Devlin Bane, alive and stable for longer than any other of their kind in recent history. Blake didn't hold out much hope that she'd find answers soon enough to save him, but he wished her luck.

"Trahern, can I get up now?"

He had driven several miles without realizing it. Damn, he couldn't afford to lose his concentration now. After checking the mirrors, he glanced back over his shoulder.

"I'm going to pull into the discount store parking lot just ahead. You'll have to wait in the car while I pick up some clothes for you."

"Okay. I wear a medium in most things." She pushed herself up into a sitting position. "My shoe size is eight and a half."

"And your bra size?" The question probably embarrassed her, but he wasn't about to guess.

"I take a 32C. I prefer a front clasp, but either kind will do."

Sweet. More than a handful: just what he liked. He remembered all too clearly the feel of her breasts crushed against his chest back at the hospital—not that he should be having such thoughts about her, especially now. "Is there anything else you need, other than a few toiletries?"

"Some ibuprofen would be appreciated. Otherwise I'm fine."

He pulled into a space near the busy main door. In the unlikely event they'd been followed, it would be harder for anyone to make a play for Brenna with so many people around.

"I'll be back in about fifteen minutes." He got out, taking a casual look around the lot. "Stay in the car and lay low."

"All right. And Blake . . ."

"Yeah?"

"Please hurry."

chapter 3

I can't believe you didn't find the judge's files." He let silence express his displeasure with the bumbling fools.

Detective Swan shifted uncomfortably in his seat. "We just got back from searching Brenna Nichols's office at the university. We didn't find much because she's taking the summer off, evidently to work on her next book. We plan to return to the judge's house later today to continue our search. No one will question the detectives of record reexamining the crime scene alone, especially with Brenna Nichols's mysterious disappearance from the hospital."

He rolled his eyes, although that fiasco was his fault, not theirs. "What makes you think you'll have any better luck searching his house this time?"

Detective Montgomery shot his younger partner a look meant to shut him up. It didn't work.

"Last time we had half the department swarming around. If we'd started tearing out walls looking for a hidden safe, there would have been questions we—and you—don't want to answer. And if we'd actually found the files, we'd have had the devil's own time keeping them from being collected as evidence."

Montgomery stepped in. "He's right about that, sir. From what you've told us, the last thing you want is the judge's files coming to light. And if we go down, you'll be right there with us."

So they had teeth and weren't afraid to show them when cornered. As long as they served their purpose, he'd ignore the little display of bravado—for now. He wasn't one to leave loose ends unclipped when his mission was accomplished, and their deaths had always been a part of the plan.

A whisper here, a rumor there, and their precious reputations would be ruined. Despite their greed, their images as good cops were important to them. He'd burst that little balloon for them, right before he took them down. It would be a shame to let them keep all that lovely money he'd promised to pay them, but it might come in handy when Internal Affairs started their investigation.

Brenna Nichols was also on the short list of collateral damage. It was really too bad. By all reports, she was both lovely and brilliant. While beauty was common enough, genius wasn't. Oh, well.

"Gentlemen, I expect better results for my money." He ticked off their instructions on his fingers. "First, get back into the judge's house. Burn the damn thing down if you have to, but no one— and I mean no one—gets their hands on his files."

Both men nodded.

"Secondly, find out where Blake Trahern has stashed Ms. Nichols."

"Do you want us to take him out?"

The insolent young pup actually sounded excited by the prospect. Of course, in his world, when a man died, he stayed that way. Trahern and the others like him would be quite a shock to these cops, who probably thought that they'd seen it all. It might be amusing to let them shoot a Paladin, just to teach them a lesson. He'd love to see how these two would react when Trahern showed up, pissed off and very much alive again.

But now wasn't the time for games, no matter how amusing. "No, just locate them. It shouldn't be hard for two of St. Louis's finest."

Swan nodded happily, oblivious to the hint of sarcasm in his voice. His partner didn't miss the small jab, nor did he appreciate it.

He stood, signaling to his unworthy companions that the interview was over. He had his own agenda for the rest of the day. "Gentlemen, you have my cell number. Don't call it unless you have good news. You'll find I have little patience with failure."

"Yes, sir." Detective Montgomery heaved his considerable bulk up out of his chair. While his words were respectful, his attitude definitely was not. He might have more control over his mouth than his younger partner, but he was just as much an insolent fool.

They left the nondescript hotel room, closing the door with a little more force than was absolutely necessary. As soon as he knew they were really gone, he began packing. He'd already made reservations at another hotel for the night. The two cops were hardly his biggest fans and Trahern must hate him, even if he didn't know his identity yet. It never paid to be where your enemy expected you to be.

Once he was settled in his new room, he would study the pieces in this chess game and decide on his next move.

"How did you know about this place?" Brenna eyed their surroundings with suspicion.

Blake had rather fond memories of this isolated roadside park. Not much had changed, except the old picnic table had been replaced with a plastic one that wouldn't leave splinters in your naked ass—not that he'd been paying attention to the rough surface at the time.

Kelly's particular talents had kept him focused

on other things the night she'd introduced him to sex. He'd had a hell of a time getting those damn splinters out of his knees and backside the next day, but the pain had been worth it. His mouth tugged up in a grin at the memory.

"I'm not sure I like that smile, Blake." Brenna eyed him with dubious suspicion. "You've been gone for twelve years. You never wrote, never called, and yet you remember one out-of-the-way little park."

"I lost my virginity right there on that table. That's the sort of thing a guy never forgets." Honesty made him add, "Well, not that exact table. It was wooden and painted dark green."

"Who?" She slapped her hand over her mouth. "Never mind. I don't want to know."

"I wasn't going to tell you anyway." Even though curiosity was eating her up, judging by the way her eyes kept darting to the table and then back at his anatomy. "Why don't you change into your clothes so we can get a hotel?"

"Where should I change?" She looked around for some kind of shelter, other than the surrounding trees.

"This is no time for modesty, Brenna. If we walk into a hotel lobby with you in your hospital gown and slippers, they're going to know something is fishy. We can't use a public bathroom for the same reason. I promise I won't look." Unless he was sure he could get away with it.

To give her some semblance of privacy, he walked over to the picnic table and stretched out on top of it. He thought about closing his eyes, but as tired as he was, he couldn't risk it. Exhaustion was playing hell with his concentration already. The sooner they found sanctuary for the night, the better off they both would be.

The sound of a car door opening startled him into sitting up, then he realized that Brenna was using it as a screen to change behind. It worked pretty well; in fact, too damn well. He could see her shoulders and a tantalizing hint of her cleavage, then nothing at all until below the door, which revealed her lower calves and bare feet. Who would have thought such glimpses would be so erotic?

Despite his promise, he couldn't pull his eyes away as she slid the straps of her bra up her arms, then leaned forward to adjust the fit of the cups before fastening the front clasp. It was like a reverse striptease, but with the same effect on his body. When had putting on a T-shirt turned into a seductive dance?

First one foot and then the other disappeared into the lightweight running pants he'd bought her. When she stood to tug them up to her waist, there was a quick flash of white, no doubt the plain cotton panties he'd picked out. He didn't think she would have appreciated getting skimpy, lacy ones from him, but he'd had a hard time reining in the urge to buy them.

The car door slammed shut. "I thought you weren't going to watch."

No use in denying it. "I lied."

Looking thoroughly disgusted, she stuffed her hospital gown and robe into the shopping bags. Turning her back on him, she used the brush he'd bought to work the tangles out of her dark brown hair. If she thought she was shutting him out by facing away from him, she was sorely mistaken. She looked damned fine from any direction.

As if sensing his continued scrutiny, she glanced back at him. "Don't stare."

"Sorry." Not that he was. The genetic anomaly that made a man a Paladin had also gifted him with a very healthy sexual appetite, and he'd been on a starvation diet for far too long. Still, one look at the fading bruises on her arms had him banking the fires.

"Let's get out of here." He stood up and stretched, trying to get the kinks out of his back and neck before climbing into the car.

Brenna winced as she settled into the front seat and fastened her seat belt. He had to admire her stamina. She'd been through hell the past few days, with no end in sight, yet she didn't complain and kept going. It shouldn't surprise him. She had a lot of her father in her, including a similar, frighteningly powerful intellect.

"There's a hotel not far from here."

She opened one eye and gave him a suspicious look. "Another vivid memory from your past? If so, pick another hotel."

Her tart remark startled a laugh out of him. "Back then, the backseat of a car or a picnic table were the fanciest accommodations I could afford."

She didn't look convinced.

"I spotted this place on the way here." He held his hand up in a mock salute. "Scout's honor."

"You were never a Boy Scout."

"True, but I wouldn't lie to you about this."

"Which means there are some things you *will* lie about." She turned to stare out the window.

Just that quickly, his good mood was gone. Because she was right: he would lie if necessary. And when she found out about her father's lies, it might just destroy her.

Trahern checked them into the hotel with his usual efficiency. Brenna wasn't happy about sharing a room with him. She still felt hot, flushed, and embarrassed from his earlier kiss. But short of pitching a fit right there in the lobby, there wasn't much she could do. Once they were alone, he was going to get an earful—if she could stay awake long enough.

"Come on, honey, let's go on up to the room. I

can bring in our luggage later. Right now I've got other plans for us."

The cad actually winked at the cute little blonde behind the counter. Lord save her from women who giggled. Then he had the nerve to throw his powerful arm around her shoulder and nearly drag her toward the elevator, as if he couldn't wait to get her alone.

Once the elevator doors closed, she jerked free. Some of the makeup she'd slathered on to disguise her bruises had left a streak on his shirt, which pleased her.

"What was that all about?"

"Hotels find it odd when customers have no luggage. I don't have anything but the bare essentials with me, and you have nothing. If she thinks we're in a hurry to get to our room, she won't wonder why I've only got this one small bag."

Logical, but that didn't mean she had to like it, or him leering at some sweet young thing in front of her. A flash of what felt suspiciously like jealousy burned through her. Intellectually she knew she had no right or reason to feel that way, but Blake's reappearance in her life was too new for her to want to share.

When the elevator doors pinged, Blake pulled his gun from his waistband and checked the hallway outside before he'd let her come out. She didn't like the unspoken reminder that she needed his protection.

A few seconds later, he pushed the door to their room open and tugged her inside. She was *so* ready to shower and crawl between clean sheets and sleep for hours. Trahern stopped abruptly, blocking her view of the room. She tried to shove him out of the way.

"Brenna, I swear I didn't know."

"Know what?" She leaned over to look past him, at the bed.

THE bed. As in a single place to sleep. If he didn't look so shocked, she might have suspected this was another of those things he felt safe in lying about.

"So ask for another room."

He sighed. "She said it was the last room available. I suppose we could go someplace else, but . . ."

"Never mind. I'll sleep on the floor." If she didn't get horizontal soon, she'd probably fall asleep standing up.

"Like hell."

"Fine, I'll sleep in the chair then. Right now I don't care."

She headed for the bathroom, only to realize that she had nothing to sleep in except that hideous hospital gown. If they'd gotten separate rooms, she would have slept in her underwear, but that wasn't going to work with him in the room.

No matter how battered she was, he managed to stir up thoughts and feelings she had no business having. Like how it had felt to be held so carefully in his arms, and the spicy male taste of his kiss. Desire, hot and liquid, settled at the apex of her legs. She couldn't remember the last time, if ever, that she'd had such strong reactions to a man. She wanted him, plain and simple.

Eyeing the queen-size bed, she had a wayward thought. Sharing that mattress with Blake would be a heck of lot more comfortable than that old picnic table.

"Here. Thought you might want something clean to sleep in." Blake tossed her a white T-shirt as she went into the bathroom.

"Thank you." She blushed at the thought of wearing his clothing, but the alternative was unthinkable.

As much as she would have enjoyed a long soak in the tub to soothe her aches and pains, there wasn't time. She wasn't the only one in need of sleep. At least she'd had a decent night's rest at the hospital; Blake had spent it in a chair. Skewing the water to the hot side of comfortable, she stepped into the shower and let the spray wash away some of the day's problems.

The bandages on her arm got soaked in the process, and once she dried off, she carefully pulled them off and checked the stitches underneath. The wounds looked as if they were healing just fine, with no hint of redness.

All in all, she'd gotten off pretty lightly, considering how close she'd been to the explosion. Her poor father . . . NO! She was not going to think about him. Not yet. If she allowed even one tear to fall, she might not be able to stop.

She toweled her hair dry before pulling on Blake's T-shirt, happy that it came to midthigh on her. Thank goodness he was as tall as he was. Feeling a bit shy, she hesitated before opening the door. When he'd lived in their home, she'd thought nothing of running around in not much more than what she had on.

But that was then, when he was a teenager and she was in most ways still a little girl. He had always acted older than most of the other boys his age, probably because of the hard times he'd experienced before her father had rescued him. Neither of them had ever told her any details, but she'd done what she'd always done when she had questions—she'd gone to the library to do research. She hadn't learned much, but it had been enough to give her nightmares for a week.

But he definitely wasn't a boy anymore, not with those broad shoulders and powerful muscles. He didn't have the beefy build of a weight lifter, but more the kind of strength that one often saw in well-trained military or firemen. Somehow, she didn't think either of those were what he did for a living. He'd hated rules and regulations as a youth, and judging by his actions over the past two days, he still did.

And he hadn't wanted to be with her when the police came to interview her in the hospital. Was he afraid of them for some reason? She poked at that idea for a second or two before rejecting it. The idea of Blake being afraid of anyone was absurd. He had good reason to not care for the law in general and she'd already seen him bend more than one rule, but he'd never walk on the wrong side of the law.

A niggling little voice reminded her that Blake had left twelve years ago; how much could she really know about the man he'd become? Enough to know that he'd keep her safe for the night, and for now, that was enough.

Stepping out of the bathroom, she braced herself for a fight over which one of them got the bed and which would make do with the chair. But Trahern was already sprawled in the chair, sound asleep. If she tried to move him, it would only start another argument that she'd probably end up losing.

The cool sheets felt like heaven to her as she snuggled between them, and she turned to better see Blake. The faint light she'd left on softened his features as he slept, making it easier to see the boy she'd known in the hard-edged man he'd become. Clinging to that small familiarity, she let her eyes drift closed and slept.

• • •

Blake frowned. Normally he didn't mind a raccoon or possum invading his yard, but right now all he wanted to do was sleep. If the creature didn't quiet down soon, it would find out the hard way what a crack shot Blake was.

The whimper came again, this time loud enough for him to recognize the sounds of pain and fear. Crap, it was probably an abandoned baby looking for its mother. That was all he needed; another night spent trapping a scared animal and getting it to one of the wildlife rescue shelters.

After a bit, the noise stopped. Satisfied that mother and child had been reunited, he tried to turn over to sink back into deep sleep.

Something was wrong, though. Either his bed had shrunk or he was sleeping in a chair. His eyes reluctantly opened, first one and then the other. Son of a bitch, he *was* in a chair, not his decadently comfortable king-size bed. And the whimpers he'd been hearing weren't from some lost animal, but Brenna crying in her sleep.

He managed to stand up, every joint in his body screaming in protest, and pulled the chair closer to the head of the bed.

"It's all right, Brenna. I'm right here." He rubbed her shoulder and back slowly, hoping the dubious comfort of his touch wouldn't startle her awake. From the way she was crying, she was trapped in a dream, most likely a replay of the explosion. He hoped like hell that she wasn't one of those people who dreamed in color. She didn't need to see her father blown to bits in vivid clarity.

"Hush, Brenna. Don't cry."

Please don't cry. He could face down a dozen Others armed with razor-sharp swords and not blink an eye, but a woman with a tear-streaked face unmanned him completely. He bet Devlin Bane, back in Seattle, would be rolling on the floor watching Blake try to comfort Brenna. Then again, maybe he wouldn't be. Devlin was just about the biggest, baddest Paladin of all time, and now he was in love—with his Handler, of all people.

The two of them seemed very happy together, making all the other Paladins more than a little jealous. What Devlin and Laurel shared was much more than good sex; in all the years that he'd known him, Blake had never seen Devlin more content.

He suddenly realized that Brenna's crying had tapered off. He slowly pulled back his hand, hoping the worst was over, but she began thrashing around until he put it back again. He left his hand on her shoulder, figuring it was little enough when she was in such obvious pain. After a few minutes, though, his back was protesting loudly over the awkward position.

He couldn't stay that way for the rest of the

night; it was hours until dawn. So, he did the only thing he could think of: he joined her on the bed. As long as he stayed on top of the covers and she stayed tucked nice and safe under them, her virtue would remain intact.

Would she have found comfort in his touch if she knew the truth about him? No rational woman would. Even if she could accept that he was hard-wired to fight and kill Others, he was rapidly losing his humanity. The last time he'd been badly wounded, his Handler had bought extra strong chains just for him. That hadn't kept him from trying to break free from that cold steel table, screaming for hours and shredding the skin around his wrists and ankles until they bled.

He could remember the pain in Devlin's voice as he offered to end Trahern's life permanently to stop his misery. He'd been so tempted to accept, but that would have been the coward's way out. When his time came to be put down, he wanted it to count for something—not because he was afraid to face another day as a Paladin.

A woman like Brenna Nichols deserved a gentler man to comfort her, one who knew all the right words to brush away her nightmares. But selfish as it might be, that wasn't going to stop him. When he gathered her into his side, she came willingly, snuggling in to rest her face on his chest with his arm wrapped around her.

It felt like heaven, even if the predictable effect on his body was a living hell. How many times over the years had he dreamed of this exact moment, holding her in his arms with her warmth and scent filling his senses?

Of course, in his dreams they were both naked and sated after a night of wild monkey sex—but this version would do.

"Quit pounding so loud, damn it. I can't concentrate."

Swan glared at him and went right back to whacking his fist on the wall every few inches.

"I said stop it!" Montgomery had his own investigating to do and listening to that racket wasn't going to help.

"How am I supposed find a hidden safe if I don't check out the walls?"

"A hidden safe is going to be behind a picture on the wall or under a rug on a hardwood floor, not under sheet rock where the only way the judge could access it is with a crowbar."

Swan wasn't stupid, just too young on the job. "Okay, so I'll start looking behind things. How about all those books in his office?"

"Perfect. Take a few out at time and look behind them. Let me know if you see anything suspicious." When his partner left, he continued his methodical search of the living room. The office was the obvious place for the judge to have hidden files, but his detective's nose told him the judge wouldn't go for the obvious.

So as his friend checked behind the heavy law books in the next room, Montgomery slowly made his way around the living room. Running his fingertips over every surface, he checked each table, every picture, and every cushion for anything taped to the bottom or hidden between the cushions. It took him the better part of half an hour to do just that one room.

He was about to start in the hallway and then go on to the kitchen when his cell phone rang. Technically he and Swan were still on duty, so he couldn't ignore it. Pulling out his phone, he checked the number. It was his boss, all right, but not the one he'd been expecting. Damn. He'd *told* the man they knew as Mr. Knight that he'd call when they had news. Remembering the chill in the man's eyes, a shiver curled up his spine. It wouldn't be wise to ignore the call.

"Montgomery here."

"Well?" The arrogant bastard conveyed a wealth of disdain in just that one word.

"We got here less than an hour ago. There was a double homicide we were called in on until . . ." Mr. Knight didn't want excuses, only results. "We're looking now. I've checked the living room. Swan's in the old man's office."

"You won't find anything there."

"That's why I left that room for Swan." His partner had strong suits, but subtlety wasn't one of them. If he wanted to hide something, he'd probably put it in an envelope and write "do not open" on the front.

"Wise thinking, Detective Montgomery."

He didn't give a damn what Mr. Knight thought about him. The only thing that mattered was that the man paid well for results.

"I'll be out of touch for the next twenty-four to thirty-six hours. Leave any messages on my voice mail, but I won't be able to get back to you until tomorrow night or the next morning." The phone went dead.

Montgomery stared at his cell as he muttered every curse word he could think of. A few bucks for some inside information on their investigation hadn't seemed like such a big deal, at first. They should have known that if it seemed like easy money, it would turn around and bite them on the ass.

He just hoped their asses were still alive when the dust settled. Maybe he'd pack a suitcase when he got home. Just in case.

Trahern had never had much use for cell phones, and the tinny music chirping away before the sun was up was enough to make him homicidal. He eased his arm out from around Brenna, hoping to silence the damn thing before it woke her up.

Snatching up the phone from the bedside table, he stepped into the bathroom and shut the door. "This better be important," he growled into the receiver.

"Shut up, Trahern. I've already been up for hours and don't want to hear any complaints from you." There was a lot of static on the line, but Jarvis's bad mood came through clearly.

Rather than getting into a pissing contest over which of them was in a worse mood, Trahern started over. "What do you need, Jarvis?"

"I'm going active down near the boot heel. Seismology has been picking up reports of swarms of weak, shallow earthquakes. They're calling all the locals in. Sounds like we'll be dancing with the darkness tonight."

"How bad is it?" He knew from his days along the barrier in that area that minor earthquakes were common. The Paladins who stood guard along the New Madrid Fault saw more active duty than some of those assigned to better-known fault lines. But when the earthquakes came in swarms, there just weren't enough Paladins and guards combined to protect the whole area. If he didn't have responsibility for Brenna's welfare, he would have offered his sword. He was no longer as finely tuned to the local barrier, but could still feel it well enough to know it was under attack.

"Don't know yet. The Regents say reinforcements will be sent in from out of state if needed, but they've made that promise before. Hopefully, I'll be back in St. Louis within a couple of days. Until then, you're on your own."

No surprise in that. "Fine. Call when you get back. And Jarvis?"

"Yeah?"

He wanted to wish his friend luck in battle, but couldn't find the words. "Uh, never mind. Look, I'll talk to you when you get back."

Jarvis understood him, anyway. "You watch yourself, too, Trahern. Gotta go." The line went dead.

He and Jarvis had lived hard, fighting and drinking with equal abandon. But they had also done a lot they could be proud of, too. The average human might not be aware of the battle that raged along the fault lines and near the volcanoes to keep the Others from pouring across and into this world, but the Paladins didn't fight for glory. They fought because someone had to, and they were the best at it.

"Who was that?"

Brenna stood outside the bathroom door, looking rumpled and warm and too damn sexy.

"Jarvis."

"What did he want at this ungodly hour?" She

was rubbing the stitches in her arm, which probably meant it was healing.

"Stop picking at your arm. You'll get it all inflamed."

"Quit trying to avoid the question. What did Jarvis want? Is something wrong?" She was more awake now and the fear was back in her eyes.

"No, nothing is wrong. He got called out of town on business for a couple of days and wanted to let me know."

"What kind of work does he do?"

"Same kind I do."

She gave an exasperated sigh. "I told you yesterday that I'd only let things slide until we both got some rest. Sleepy time is over, buster, so start talking or I'm out of here."

Trahern snorted. "And where would you go, and how would you get there? You've got no money, no purse, and you didn't seem overly impressed by those two detectives you spoke to."

She threw back her shoulders, drawing herself up to her full height, almost a foot less than his. It was cute.

"I'm a big girl, Blake Trahern. I can and will take care of myself. I've been doing so for years."

She turned away, leaving him staring after her. He hadn't meant to rile her, but he wasn't free to tell her what he and Jarvis did for a living. It was unlikely she'd believe him, anyway.

The reality of the Others had been hard enough for *him* to accept, right up until they came at him with their wide-bladed swords and throwing knives. That kind of action made a believer out of a man pretty damn quick.

Brenna had turned on the television, no doubt looking for news about her father's death. He joined her sitting on the end of the bed, just as the judge's picture flashed across the screen with a voice-over promise that it was the next story after they broke for a commercial. Brenna hunched her shoulders as if her father's image caused her a great deal of pain. She had accepted Blake's comfort in her sleep. Would she do the same now that she was wide-awake?

He eased closer to her, offering his unspoken support. She didn't move in his direction, but neither did she shift away—maybe because all her attention was focused on the television. The two reporters launched right into the sordid details as soon as they were back on camera. The first day or so, all they had talked about were the judge's sterling character, his distinguished career, and how much he would be missed.

But now, there was a different feel to their report. The first words out of the woman's mouth had Blake on his feet, ready to punch his fist through the TV screen.

". . . an unnamed source at the police department has indicated that they are investigating allegations that Judge Nichols's recent death may have been due to his suspected involvement in some questionable financial activities. Examination of his personal bank records have revealed sums of money that exceed the normal salary of a judge."

"Liars! I'll sue them for every dime they've ever had!" Brenna's eyes shot sparks. "Wait until I get my hands on them—they do NOT know who they are messing with."

"Brenna, can you tone it down? There's more." Her picture appeared on the screen behind the two reporters.

"Ms. Nichols, also injured by the car bomb, has mysteriously disappeared from the hospital where she had an armed guard. However, both the police and a spokesperson for the hospital have denied knowledge of any such guards. Furthermore, a nurse was wounded when an unknown gunman shot through the window of Ms. Nichols's room. In the resulting confusion, Ms. Nichols disappeared, apparently in the company of an unidentified male companion. It is not known at this time whether she went willingly or was taken by force."

With a look of feigned concern, the reporter leaned slightly forward and spoke directly to the camera as a phone number appeared at the bottom of the screen. "Anyone who has knowledge of

Ms. Nichols's current whereabouts should call the police at the number below."

"Son of a bitch." Could it get any worse?

Blake turned to Brenna only to find her flipping through the phone book on the desk, muttering under her breath. When she picked up the receiver and started dialing, he pushed down the button to disconnect the call. She tried to bat his hand out of the way.

"Stop it, Blake. I need to set those people straight."

He didn't budge. "Yelling at them over the phone is only going to make things worse. If you stop and think, you'll know I'm right."

She was gripping the phone so hard her knuckles were white. "They're spreading lies about my father. Isn't it bad enough he was murdered, without killing his reputation, too? Being a judge was his life's work. He would not have jeopardized that for any amount of money."

As a rule, the Regents didn't involve themselves in matters outside their mission to prevent the world from being overtaken by the Others. But if they felt their secrecy was threatened, they could and would take decisive action. If Brenna began screaming loud and long that her father was being framed, she would be vulnerable to attack from the Regents, as well as the rogue members who were likely behind the car bomb that had killed her father.

Trahern had enough on his plate, tracking down the corruption within the Regents, without having to ride herd on Brenna at the same time. Damn it all, he was going to have to break his vow of silence and tell her the truth—about the Regents, about her father, and worse yet, about himself.

It was a total cluster fuck.

chapter 4

*T*rahern's eyes took on a decided chill. "Look, I need to shower. When we're both dressed, we'll check out and then get breakfast and talk."

She should have expected him to duck out of answering her questions. "What excuse are you going to use next, Blake? When the weather cools off, we'll talk? Or when the sun comes up in the west?"

"Damn it, Brenna, give it break."

They stood in awkward silence until, unable to stand his hard gaze any longer, she turned away to face the bed—the one with the covers and pillows messed up on both sides, not just the one where she'd slept.

"You *slept* with me? Without asking me if it was okay?" Brenna didn't know whether to be outraged or disappointed that she didn't remember how it felt to have that hard body of his stretched out beside her.

"You woke me up whimpering in your sleep. The only way I could quiet you so I could get some sleep was to cuddle you."

He said "cuddle" as if the very idea was repugnant. Was touching her so awful? He certainly hadn't seemed to think so yesterday when he kissed her at the hospital.

Before she could respond, he marched into the bathroom and slammed the door shut.

The shower ran for a solid twenty minutes. Blake's duffel was sitting on the desk across the room; how long before he came out for his clean clothes and shaving kit? Long enough for her to rifle through it, she decided, though she didn't know what she was looking for. Answers, sure, but he wouldn't have left anything lying around that would be of much help—he was too smart and too secretive for that.

Rather than risk his ire, she'd keep her hands to herself. Maybe she was being naïve, but she had to trust someone. The police certainly hadn't endeared themselves to her, with their prying questions and the false reports they had leaked to the press about her father.

She picked up the duffel and set it outside the

bathroom, then rapped on the door. "Blake, here's your bag. I thought you might want it."

He mumbled something that may or may not have been "thanks." She backed away, figuring he wouldn't open the door as long as she was standing there. Did he think she was trying to get a quick peek of him, naked and still damp from his shower? Whoa, she did NOT need that image in her head. Just that quickly, her breasts felt heavy and her nipples stirred and hardened, aching for a man's touch—Blake's touch. How would that stern mouth of his feel, nuzzling or suckling them? Her hand strayed toward the knob on the bathroom door and she jerked it back.

It was bad enough that every time she stared into those silver gray eyes of his, her entire body sat up and took notice. Giving into a bad case of lust was the last thing she needed right now. She'd had such an awful crush on him the whole time he'd lived with them, except when she was hating him for putting up with all those girls who hung on his every word in high school. She had known that they had been attracted to his air of danger even then. Hadn't it bothered him to know that while they were willing to sneak out to be with him, none of them wanted him knocking on their front door?

No doubt it had been one of them who had introduced him to that little roadside park. Not that she was jealous. Well, maybe a little bit, but hot sex on a picnic table was not exactly one of her fantasies.

The click of the bathroom lock snapped her back to the present as he stepped out surrounded by a cloud of steam. Blake's white T-shirt clung to his torso, clearly outlining every one of his lean muscles. His jeans looked as if they'd been bought for comfort rather than style. The soft, faded denim suited him, and the small hole at the knee made him look more approachable.

But it was his bare feet that made her annoyingly aware of him as a man. There was just something about a man walking around barefoot that she'd always found sexy.

He reached for his socks and shoes. "Let's settle up our bill and get out of here. The less time we spend in one place, the better. I also need to change cars, because rentals are too easy to trace."

"Sounds like a plan." She reached for the bags with her hospital gown and the few things he'd bought for her. "And then we'll talk."

He didn't look happy, but he didn't argue. "Yes, we'll talk."

They each did a last sweep through the room to make sure they hadn't forgotten anything. When she started to open the door, he held it shut with his hand. "But there's something you need to think about, Brenna."

"And what's that?"

"Before you starting asking questions, make sure you really want to hear the answers." Then he walked out.

The lights flickered for the third time in as many minutes. Jarvis shivered, the chill in the air not entirely due to the depth of the cavern. The night had been a long one and it wasn't over yet. For the moment the barrier was at full strength, but it wasn't likely to stay that way.

At least they'd had enough time to clear away their wounded and dead. Rumor had it that hot food was on the way, but that was probably wishful thinking. Right now, he'd settle for some of those MREs that the military used for field rations, or even a peanut butter and jelly sandwich. Water would be good; hot coffee even better.

"Sir, the last of the dead have been transferred to headquarters for treatment." The guard looked unbelievably earnest and young, until you looked into his eyes. He'd seen enough action over the past two days to ensure his eyes would never look young again.

"How many were there?" Jarvis leaned against

the wall of the cave, too tired to care if he ever moved again.

"Two of ours dead, with another half dozen seriously wounded."

Considering the number of Others who had crossed the barrier, that was miraculously low. "Tell your men to stand down for the next four hours. We'll take the first watch."

"Yes, sir."

His fellow Paladins might not appreciate his decision, but they had more stamina than the purely human guards. If the barrier resumed blinking on and off like a damned lighthouse, they would need the guards rested and ready to fight.

When the guard was out of earshot, he pulled out his radio and signaled headquarters. A blast of static had him cursing; nothing electronic worked quite right this close to the barrier.

It quit crackling long enough for him to hear a voice.

"Where the hell are the reinforcements you promised?" he demanded.

He could only understand about every other word, but they didn't add up to good news. Help was days away, not hours. He felt like hurling the radio against the cave wall.

"Yes, sir, I understand. I also understand that you and the others never take this fault line seriously. One day it's really going to flex its muscles, and we'll be lucky if we live long enough to say we told you so."

He hit the disconnect button before the Regent could offer more excuses. He'd heard it all before, and it had been decades since he'd believed anything they had to say. The New Madrid fault line might not have the glitz and glory of the Pacific Rim, but it was just as deadly. He was sick and tired of seeing his fellow Paladins die over and over again with little relief, and it had been almost five years since he'd taken a vacation longer than a three-day weekend.

He could always ask for a transfer. The local command, tired of his constant demands for more help, would probably be glad to see him go. But he was too old, too close to the end of his journey toward madness, to want to learn the resonance of a new section of the barrier or to memorize all the tunnels that provided access to it.

Pushing away from the wall, he headed down the passageway to where the next Paladin stood watch. He ignored the row of dead Others, their faces contorted in the final pain of knowing they'd failed to find sanctuary in this world. Generations of Paladins had fought off the constant threat of invasion, never knowing what drove the dark warriors to suicide rushes across the barrier.

Or caring.

He approached the Paladin with caution. Their

nerves were all stretched to the breaking point from too much fighting and so much death. A wrong move on his part and his comrade would swing his sword first and ask questions later.

He pulled a couple of breakfast bars from the pocket of his cargo pants. "Thought you might like something to hold you until the meals arrive."

"Thanks." The weary warrior took the bar without taking his eyes off the barrier.

"I let the guards grab some sleep." Jarvis ripped open his own bar and took a bite. It tasted like sawdust but it took away the coppery taste of battle. "We're on our own for another couple of days."

"I figured."

"I'll tell the others."

Jarvis continued on down the passageway, repeating the conversation at every station. By the time he'd made the complete circuit back to his own post, he had to force himself to take each step. Bone-aching weariness and frustration drained the last bit of his reserves.

The young guard was waiting for him at his post.

"I thought I told you to stand down."

"Yes, sir, you did, but I thought we'd stick around until you all had a chance to eat. I've sent hot rations around to all of the Paladins. Once they've eaten we'll retire as ordered, sir."

They both knew he should have followed orders, but they also knew Jarvis wasn't about to complain. Sometimes the relations between the Paladins and the guards were strained, but twenty-four hours of nonstop combat was a good reminder that they were on the same side of the fight.

"Thanks."

"Your food should be here in a couple of minutes."

"Great."

Jarvis sank down against the wall and stretched out his legs. It felt damn good to be off his feet, even if the rough floor of the cave wasn't comfortable. He was too tired to care. He'd eat and then make rounds again.

And once the barrier settled down, he was going to get in someone's face about the fiasco of the past two days. Paladins weren't goddamn superheroes. They hurt and bled and died, sometimes for good. It was one thing to throw them in too few numbers against the invading Others when the barrier went down unexpectedly. But to keep asking the impossible from those still left standing was both unfair and unwise.

"Here's your food, sir."

Jarvis accepted the tray and took a grateful sniff of the rich aroma. At least someone upstairs had done one thing right. He dug into the meal as if it were his last. Time spent here on the front line of the secret war between this world and the darkness on the other side of the barrier had taught him to eat fast, because a hot meal was a rarity not to be wasted.

He was about to eat his dessert when one of the other Paladins called his name. "Hey, Jarvis, look at this. I found it by one of the dead Others."

A small rock about the size of a marble came flying through the air. He snagged it with a flick of his wrist and held it up between his forefinger and thumb. The many-faceted blue stone caught the light and fractured it into all the colors of the rainbow. He'd never seen anything like it. He'd have to show it to Trahern; there'd been some pretty strange rumors coming out of the Seattle sector.

Just that quickly, his apple pie lost its appeal. Although he ate it anyway, he didn't enjoy it, knowing the trail of death Trahern had been following now led right into Jarvis's neck of the woods.

"I want to go home. I *need* to go home."

Trahern prayed for patience. He'd already told Brenna twice that stopping by the house wasn't a smart move, but she wasn't listening. Whoever wanted her dead probably had the place under surveillance. That's what he would do under the circumstances.

Breakfast had consisted of a drive-through at a

fast food restaurant. They still hadn't had their little talk, so that was hanging over his head. Enough was enough. It was time for Brenna to face some cold, hard facts. Without signaling, he cut across traffic to make a left turn, causing several cars to hit their brakes. The sudden maneuver made Brenna squeal in fright, but he didn't care. He was pretty sure they hadn't picked up a tail, but if someone was following them, they'd likely reveal themselves now.

Other than a few nasty looks, no one seemed overly interested in them. Good.

"What was that all about?" Brenna had moved on to temper. "Are you crazy? You could have gotten us killed!"

He shot her a nasty look. "You're getting your wish, Brenna. I'm taking you home."

She narrowed her eyes, trying to guess his real intent. "But you said it was too dangerous."

It seemed that she didn't trust him. Smart woman. "It is, but you don't believe me. Besides, you want the truth. I'm going to give it to you."

They rode in angry silence as he took an indirect route to the judge's house, finally turning down the street a block over from her father's home to park the car.

"Why are we stopping here?"

"Because if we walk up to the front door, we might as well stop at the sporting goods store and buy a couple of targets for our backs. Coming in from the alley gives us a fighting chance of making it inside."

Her eyebrows drew together as she weighed his words and decided how much to believe him. "Won't they be watching the alley, too?"

"Good question. And that's why you're going to wait here until I see what we're walking into. Once I'm sure the approach is clear, I'll return for you."

He handed her his cell phone along with the car keys. "If I'm not back in twenty minutes, get the hell out of here and then call Jarvis. His number is on speed dial. He might not be able to come get you right away, but he'll know what to do to keep you safe."

"Watch your back."

"I will. Stay in the car and be ready to make a run for it."

"But—"

He surprised them both by planting a quick kiss on her lips. He could tell himself that it was the fastest way to quiet her, but he knew better. Before he could pull back to get out of the car, she latched on to his shoulders and dragged him closer to her. The green of her eyes darkened and the tip of her tongue darted out to moisten her lips.

"What?" He could hear the same heat in his voice.

"I've waited a lot of years for you to kiss me right. Even allowing for yesterday's attempt, I suspect you can do better."

With a groan, he settled his lips over hers. Her arms went around his neck as she tilted her head to one side to allow them a better fit. He nipped at her lower lip and his tongue met hers.

Brenna surprised him with her boldness. Her fingers tangled in his hair as she murmured her approval when he tried to pull her across the console into his lap. He banged his elbow on the steering wheel in the process, reminding him where they were and what was at stake.

As much as he wanted to finish what they had started, Brenna deserved better than being groped in the front seat of a car. When—and if—he ever bedded her, it wouldn't be a quickie where anybody walking by could see.

He broke off the kiss and reached for the door handle. "I'll be back."

Ignoring her look of frustration, he stepped out of the car into the bright summer sun. He wished he'd thought to grab his sunglasses, but he wasn't about to set foot in the car until he got his testosterone back down to a manageable level.

The neighborhood was a quiet one, the kind where little old ladies spent their days sitting by the windows, making note of who mowed their lawns on Sunday and of anyone who didn't belong.

If he spent too much time looking around, someone would likely report him to the police. But that
meant it was just as difficult for the enemy to do
much prowling around.

He cut through a narrow side street to the alley
bordering the judge's backyard. The high hedges
that offered him protection would do the same for
anyone waiting to catch Brenna returning to her
home. He checked his gun, making sure he could
reach it in a hurry.

The old gate had been replaced but there was
no lock on it. A chain with a lock wouldn't keep out
determined intruders, but it would have slowed
them down. Even a dog would have provided some
protection, raising hell when someone tried messing with the car.

But that was all water under the bridge. When
the house was once again safe, he'd make sure
Brenna had a top of the line security system installed.

The latch on the gate screeched softly as he
eased it open. He left the gate propped open in
case he had to leave fast and loped across the grass,
up the charred porch to the back door.

After a careful look around the perimeter of the
yard, he used the key he'd lifted from Brenna's
purse. Had it even crossed her mind to wonder
how he was going to get into the house? Probably
not—another sign of her innocence. Well, that was

about to go the way of the dodo. She'd never be safe unless she learned and accepted that there was more to her father than sitting on the bench and pronouncing judgment.

Inside, the whisper of the air conditioner filled the silence. The house had the empty feel of abandonment about it. Cereal bowls sat on the kitchen counter where Brenna and her father had left them. The small pool of milk at the bottom smelled sour and the few flakes of cereal had hardened along the edges.

The police had left chaos in their wake. Brenna would hate knowing that someone had gone through every drawer and cabinet, perhaps even her dresser upstairs. Just the thought of some ham-handed cop groping through her underwear made Blake want to punch someone.

Flexing his hands and wishing he had a handy throat to choke, he took a quick walk through the house, noting the disorder in each room. What had they been looking for? And who were they? The police would have looked through the house, checking for clues to the bomber's identity, but it was doubtful they would have been quite this thorough since the attack had taken place outside.

No, someone was searching for the judge's files—but not the court cases he'd handled. A chill ran down his spine. He hoped that Nichols had managed to stash the papers or disk where no one else would think to look.

Trahern left the house. The longer he was away, the more likely Brenna would decide to come check on him, despite his orders. He rounded the corner just in time to see her climbing out of the car. Muttering, he jogged the last distance, ready to tear into her.

Before he could launch into his tirade, she held out his cell phone. "Jarvis wants you to call him ASAP. He said it was important."

He growled and punched in Jarvis's number. It rang half a dozen times and then cut over to voice mail. If Jarvis was in such an all-fired hurry to talk, why wasn't he answering? He must be underground, which played hell with reception. He snarled "Call me" into the receiver and then disconnected.

"Let's go." Grabbing Brenna by the arm, he set off toward the house.

Brenna jerked her arm free from his grasp and stopped. "What's the matter with you?"

"Nothing, unless you count trying to keep you out of the line of fire while you fight me every inch of the way." If he was being unreasonable, too bad. No one had ever offered him any prizes for charm.

"If you'd give me explanations rather than orders, maybe I'd cooperate a bit more."

Her chin came up. Cute, but not particularly intimidating. On the other hand, it did take some of the heat out of his anger even as it tempted him to kiss her again.

"Look, let's just get inside. Standing out here leaves us too exposed." He took a couple of steps and was relieved she did the same.

When they reached the backyard, he quickly hustled her past the damaged porch and scorched bushes. She was all but running for the door and, unless he was mistaken, crying, as well. Inside the house she froze, her gaze riveted on the two bowls sitting by the sink. He wished he'd thought to stick them in the dishwasher, but it was too late for that.

"I wouldn't cook eggs for him because his doctor wanted him to watch his cholesterol. Instead, he ate cold cereal for his last meal." A lone tear streaked down her face and fell onto her shirt.

His hand settled on her shoulder in awkward comfort. "You fussed at your father because you loved him. He knew that."

She sniffed and used the hem of her shirt to wipe her face.

"Come on, Brenna. I'll look around down here while you pack a few things." He gently shoved her toward the door into the dining room. From there, she could head upstairs while he stood watch.

"Why can't I stay here?" There was no real energy in her question, as if she had already accepted the need to keep moving.

"We'll get you back here as soon as it's safe." Which might be never, but he wasn't going to say that. Not yet, anyway.

She trudged up the stairs. As soon as she was out of sight, he started through the lower floor to see how thorough the police's search had been. It didn't take long for him to realize they had checked every crack and crevice in the house. What did they know or suspect that had them digging so deep?

He decided to wait until Brenna came downstairs before checking her father's secret hiding places. When she learned that her father had led a double life, she was going to feel betrayed on so many levels. The only way she was going to believe him was if she saw the evidence herself.

He could hear her footsteps echoing overhead in the silent house. He'd always thought of this house as warm and inviting. Generations of people had lived and died within its solid brick walls, leaving their mark on the worn woodwork and the hodgepodge of remodeling jobs done over the years.

Now the stain of violence had changed that, making the house feel old and sad. He ran his hand over the marble fireplace, liking the feel of the smooth, cool tile. There was a row of family photos in a variety of sizes scattered along the mantel, and it shocked him to realize that he was in one of the pictures.

He couldn't resist picking it up. The judge stood smiling with one arm around Brenna's shoulders and his other hand on Blake's shoulder. Brenna had grinned at something her father had said just as Maisy snapped the picture. At that age Brenna had usually tried to keep her lips together when she smiled, but this time she'd grinned with her braces glinting in the afternoon sun.

Had he ever been that innocent? Not that he could remember, and certainly not past age five or six. Life had a way of stripping away the rose-colored glasses early for a boy living with a mother who was little better than a whore, and who had no idea which of her customers had knocked her up. He'd been accused of being a cold-hearted bastard; it was the truth.

He closed his eyes and thought back to the night when Brenna's father had welcomed him into their home to live. To this day, he had no idea how the judge had seen past the bitter anger of a sullen, abused teenager and seen someone worth redeeming. In those days he'd had been more of a feral animal than a human, barely surviving life on the streets. But between the judge's stern but fair discipline and his housekeeper, Maisy, spoiling Blake with cookies, they'd gradually tamed his need to strike out at anyone who came too close. He ran his fingers over the picture, missing both the judge and Maisy.

"My father loved that picture. He always meant for you to have it."

Brenna's quiet words almost startled him into dropping the picture. He carefully set it back on the mantel. How had she managed to walk up behind him without him hearing her?

"When you disappeared I was so angry, but my father never was. He was proud of how much you changed while you lived with us." She touched her father's face in the picture. "He was a great believer in second chances."

"And third and fourth." There'd been more than one night that her father had talked him into giving school another chance. If he'd learned one thing from the judge, it was that a man couldn't change his past, but he could choose his future.

And now he was going to have to change Brenna's view of her father. She was going to hate knowing that he'd had secrets he hadn't shared with her. Even more, she'd hate finding out that he'd shared that secret life with Blake. Unfortunately, he couldn't explain the reality of her father's death in such a way that she could understand and even forgive. But this wasn't the time for pussyfooting around the truth, anyway.

He took a deep breath and looked her straight in the eyes. "Brenna, you're not going to like this—but the police are right. Your father wasn't killed because he was a judge. He died because of me."

She backed away as if he'd slapped her, and all the color drained from her face.

chapter 5

*B*renna sank down on a chair. What was he trying to tell her? Her father was killed just because he knew Trahern? What had Blake gotten her father involved in?

She clenched her fists as white-hot anger burned through her.

"Explain yourself. And if you implicated my father in something illegal, I'll turn you into the police myself, Trahern."

He shook his head in disgust. "That's it, Brenna, think the worst of me on every occasion."

His reaction to her threat was infuriating. "What am I supposed to think, considering that little bomb you just dropped?"

He squatted down to eye level. She didn't want him to be considerate, only truthful.

"Start at the beginning." She crossed her arms over her chest.

"All right, but promise me you'll listen to everything I tell you before you start asking questions, or we'll never get through this."

"Fine."

"I met your father when I was accused of attacking a police officer. I was living on the streets back then, and the cop hassled me every chance he got. When he got rough with me I fought back, but I wasn't the one who damn near killed him. Unfortunately, his friends in the department didn't care that the bastard made a habit of picking on anyone weaker than him. When I was arrested, a few of them got carried away with their interrogation techniques."

"I saw the bruises," she whispered.

"Yeah, well, I heal fast so don't sweat it. And your father sure gave them hell for it."

"And that's when he invited you to live with us."

Trahern's stern mouth softened and his icy gray eyes warmed up a few degrees. "No, that's when he ordered me to either move in with him, or let the juvenile authorities take control of my life until I turned eighteen. The wily bastard gave me no choice at all."

It sounded like something her father would do. On the other hand, he'd faced hundreds of juvenile offenders over the years without bringing them home. What had made Blake Trahern different?

"It took your father some time to convince me that I could trust him enough to feel comfortable living in a place like this." He looked around the room, his gaze so serious, making her wonder how it looked through his eyes. "Getting enough to eat every day played a big part in making me stick around."

"Maisy's snickerdoodles."

He nodded. "He kept me on a short leash until he was reasonably sure I wasn't going to bolt. I don't know which of us was more surprised when I brought home good grades. I made up for all the time I'd been out of school in less than a year."

The story was going to take longer than she expected. She gave Blake a soft shove, causing him to lose his balance. "Sit down, Blake—you're making my legs hurt, seeing you stay in that position so long. It can't be comfortable."

Her action clearly surprised him, but he obligingly leaned back against a handy chair before resuming his narrative. "One night he called me to the library to meet a couple of men." He stared into her eyes as if daring her to doubt what came next. "That was the night I found out what I really am."

"And that would be?" she prompted.

"A Paladin, just like the two men he introduced me to. Jarvis was one of them."

A Paladin? Wasn't that some kind of knight? "Jarvis would have been little more than a boy, twelve years ago."

Blake's eyes narrowed. "How old do you think he is?"

"Late twenties, maybe thirty."

"He turned forty-five on his last birthday."

"That's not possible. Not unless he's had a lot of plastic surgery or something," she said.

"It's the 'or something' that accounts for his youthful appearance. Most of us mature to the physical appearance of an adult human male in his prime—roughly the early thirties. After that, the physical aging process slows to a crawl. It's only each time we die that we change at all, and that's only for the worse."

Blake was talking as if he and Jarvis were some other kind of species and that death meant something different for them. If he weren't so completely serious, she would laugh.

"Blake, you're not making any sense." Maybe she could steer him back to the matter at hand. "You were saying something about my father introducing you to Jarvis."

He nodded. "I told you this was going to be hard to believe, Brenna, but I'm telling you the truth: a truth that I've taken an oath to keep secret, just as your father did."

Now *that* was too much. "My father was not a

Paladin, or whatever you're calling yourself. He was a judge—and that's all."

"I didn't say he was a Paladin. I said we had sworn the same oath of silence. He was a Regent." He held his hand parallel to the floor. "On top, you have the Regents. They're the administrators and watchdogs who control the whole organization."

He dropped his hand slightly. "Then there's Research and Ordnance. Think of Research as a high-tech medical facility. The top dogs there are called Handlers, doctors who take care of the Paladins who are wounded or killed in battle. Ordnance is more like the military branch. They dispatch the human guards for security and back up and send Paladins where they are needed."

Then he dropped his hand again. "Then there are the Paladins themselves. We're more like commandos than soldiers—or maybe warrior is a better description. Your father was a Regent. Through him, I joined the other Paladins."

His pride in that was unmistakable. Too bad she didn't believe a word he said. She couldn't get her mind around such a far-fetched idea. "Tell me more."

He obliged her. "Paladins are born with a unusual set of genes that enable us to fight a battle that's been going on as far back as we can remember. There's an energy barrier that runs between our world and another one, a sort of shared border along two dimensions. Most of the time it keeps the two worlds separate, nice and neat. But there are weaknesses, especially along the fault lines like the New Madrid line here and the San Andreas, and the volcanoes along the Pacific Rim. Anytime there's a small earthquake or a volcano starts throwing its weight around, that barrier can be damaged."

"Really, Blake, you should have told me that you wrote science fiction for a living."

His eyebrows snapped together. "You wanted the truth, Brenna. I'm giving it to you."

"No, you're telling me wild tales and expecting me to believe them. There's no way anyone could have kept a group like you're talking about secret all this time. Besides, none of these crazy claims have anything to do with why my father died." She started to get up.

Faster than she thought a man could move, Blake rose from the floor and blocked her way, putting one hand on each arm of her chair and forcing her to sit back and listen. "When those barriers go down, Brenna, the people from that world spill over into ours. They come armed with swords and knives and fight to the death. It's our job to send them back or kill the ones who won't return home."

"That sounds like one of the fantasy games that have been all the rage the past few years." She didn't try to keep her angry disbelief from showing.

"Believe me, Brenna, it's no fantasy when one of those bastards shoves a sword in your gut and twists." He yanked up his shirt, revealing several scars. "It hurts like hell each and every time. But because that's what I was born to do, I pick up my sword again and head right back down to protect the barrier. Without men like me and Jarvis, this world you live in would be choking with the evil filth those crazy Others bring with them."

He remained silent, no doubt waiting for her to cave in and accept his bizarre story. Well, he was in for a long wait.

After a prolonged silence, he started in again. "I serve in the Pacific Northwest, in the Seattle area. Recently, a friend of mine there was killed once and almost a second time before we caught the guy who was after him. The traitor was a local guard, but he died before we could find out who was paying him. It was obvious he had help from someone higher up in the organization."

She rolled her eyes. "So why didn't you wait for him to revive and ask him then?"

"Because the guard was human, not a Paladin. Our genetic makeup allows us to return from what would be permanent death for humans. Once he was dead, he stayed that way."

"But you wouldn't have. How nice for you and your friend." She pushed at his arm, trying to get up. This time he let her.

"Nice doesn't enter into it, Brenna." He crossed the room to stare out the window toward the street. Though he looked calm, she could feel the frustration coming off of him in waves. "It's up to you whether to believe me or not, but you asked for the truth. I called your father with our suspicions that someone was making illegal deals with the enemy, because he's the only Regent I trusted completely and without question. Within days, he was dead."

There was no mistaking the very real grief in his words.

"Your father would have hidden any notes or files he had, in a place where he knew one of us would find them. Once we do, we can stash you someplace safe while I hunt down the bastards responsible for his death."

She wasn't about to let him shuffle her off to the side while he carried on some bizarre vendetta. Even though she'd like to lash out at her father's killers, she trusted the legal system to work.

"Any evidence we find will be turned over to the detectives to process, Blake. My father would have wanted it that way."

"Your father wasn't murdered by common criminals, Brenna. If he had been, I'd have come to make sure you were okay and then disappeared again. But too many things point at this being a major conspiracy arising from within the Regents."

"So you're telling me that my father has known

all along where you were, and didn't tell me?"

Blake nodded.

"And that he lived a double life that he kept hidden from me?"

His hard gaze softened. "For your protection, Brenna. He loved you too much to want you to get caught up in the world he and I lived in."

She hated what he was telling her, every single word. Even more, she was afraid he was speaking the truth, at least as he knew it. Her father was an honorable man who had believed in old-fashioned values like honor, truth, and protecting the weak and innocent. He would be just the man to join a secret organization to save the world if he believed the threat was real.

Her heart hurt. Because she'd lost her mother at such an early age, her father had worked hard to be both parents to her. They'd been as close as any father and child could be, able to talk about anything and everything. The man she had known would not have hidden secrets from her.

Not unless he'd taken an oath, one he held as dear as the one that had changed him from a prosecuting attorney into a judge. As much as she wanted to deny it, that small voice in her head was insisting she trust Trahern, despite his saying that she'd never really known her own father.

Ignoring the stab of pain, she made her decision. "What are we looking for?"

"Something small—a computer disk, maybe. Or notes." He glanced back over his shoulder toward her. "I assume he still trusted pencil and paper over a PDA or computers."

The reminder of her father's small foible brought a fleeting smile to her face. "He did switch to mechanical pencils. We both thought that was real progress."

Trahern's slight smile lightened the tension. "If he was worried or felt threatened, he would have put the information in a place that one of us might know about but that the police would most likely overlook."

Brenna gave the matter some thought. "That would eliminate his home office. I'd have to say no to his bedroom, too. We both considered our bedrooms to be private."

He nodded. "That makes sense. So do you want the kitchen or this room?"

"I'll take the kitchen. I think I'd recognize something that didn't belong in there more easily than you would."

"We can only stay an hour, two at the most. When the daylight starts fading, we need to be gone. Turning lights on could attract unwanted attention."

"Fine." She hated—HATED—feeling like an intruder in her own home. "Yell if you need me."

Once out of sight of those gray eyes that saw

too much, she allowed herself to sag. She wanted more than anything to press the rewind button on her life and make this all go away, but that wasn't going to happen. It was time to get busy.

She started in the nearest corner of the kitchen and slowly made her way through every cabinet and drawer, checking under every dish in the stacks. She could tell that someone, most likely the police, had already been through the room. Damn them! How dare they act as if her father had had something to hide!

But then . . . according to Trahern, he did.

She checked the refrigerator, throwing out any food that had outlived its usefulness. After bagging it up, she headed out to the trash can. Before she'd gone two steps out the door, Trahern was right there dragging her back into the house.

"Damn it, Brenna! Haven't you been listening to me? You just made a hell of a target for anyone watching the house." He jerked the bag of trash from her hand. "And if that weren't bad enough, cleaning out the fridge ices the cake. Why not just take out an ad in the paper announcing where you are?"

She didn't like being bossed around, but he was right. Mumbling an apology, she returned to the kitchen, leaving him to deal with the trash.

He joined her a minute later. "Any luck?"

"No." She made herself keep rooting through

the drawer of cooking implements. Maisy would have hated the disorganized mess. Lord, she missed that woman with her fussy ways and warm heart.

"Me, either. If he left anything in the living room, it's either already gone or his choice of spots isn't obvious enough."

"There's nothing here that shouldn't be, unless it's on top of the refrigerator. I haven't gotten to that yet."

Trahern looked. "Nothing up here." He ran his finger over the top and held it up for her to see. "I'd guess no one has touched it in a while. Maisy would have ripped into the cleaning service for that."

"She was something, wasn't she?" It was nice to share her memories of Maisy with someone who understood. "I never met a tougher woman or one with a bigger heart."

Blake smiled. "She scared me to death. In all my years of fighting with blades, I've never seen her equal with a knife."

She knew he was exaggerating, but the affection in his voice was real. "Yeah, I remember the first time you hugged her. I thought we were going to need an ambulance for her."

"Yeah, well, I only did it for the cookies."

Right. Maisy had stuffed him with sweets from the first night, and seeing Trahern actually reach out to someone had surprised them all. His gesture had been a major turning point. She wondered if *he* knew that.

"We'd better start on another room before we run out of time." He walked out, leaving her to follow.

Blake's cell phone vibrated for the third time in less than fifteen minutes. He sighed and pulled it out of his pocket, expecting it to be Jarvis, but the number had a Seattle area code.

"Bane, this better be good. I told you I'd check in when I had something worth reporting."

The woman's voice on the other end of the line sounded amused. "If you can't tell the difference between me and Devlin, Trahern, I'd better have the Handlers there ship you back home."

"What's the matter, Doc, don't you have enough bone-headed Paladins there to keep you busy?" He did *not* need a mother hen checking on him. Not with Brenna listening to every word, despite pretending that she was engrossed in feeling up the couch cushions.

Laurel just laughed at him. She'd been way too happy since she and Devlin Bane had hooked up. It was enough to make a grown man sick—and a little jealous.

"If Devlin can't keep you busy, why don't you

go play with your pet Other? Or has someone shown the good sense to kill him?"

He knew she wouldn't appreciate that little comment, but too bad. He was born and bred to hate Others. It galled the Seattle Paladins that she'd taken one in, like a mongrel dog that was more likely to bite her than appreciate the gesture. All because the shifty bastard had saved her life.

"Leave Barak out of this. You know you're supposed to check in with me regularly, Blake Trahern. I haven't heard from you in almost two days."

"I've been busy."

"That's no excuse. The only reason the Handlers in St. Louis aren't haunting your footsteps is that I promised them you'd keep in touch with me."

All traces of good humor were gone from her voice, reminding him that she was fully capable of handling the worst of the Paladins, including him.

"Fine. I'll call in."

The silence on the other end of the line spoke volumes. Finally, she sighed. "How are you feeling?"

"Fine."

"Blake . . ." The warning was clear.

Not for the first time, he cursed the existence of cell phones. "The barrier near here has been going up and down like a damned yo-yo, so how do you think I feel? I'm not as attuned to it as I used to be, but I can still feel enough to make me edgier than normal. Considering I haven't had more than one full night of sleep in almost a week, I'm doing all right. At least I haven't killed anybody." Honesty made him add, "Though I've come close a couple of times." They both knew his ability to control his temper was crucial to his continued existence.

"I'm glad to hear you're hanging in there, Blake." She must have been satisfied because she changed the topic. "How is your friend's daughter doing?"

Blake caught a movement out of the corner of his eye. "Look, Doc, I've gotta go. I'll check in tomorrow." He disconnected the call before Laurel could do more than sputter.

"Was that one of your Paladin friends?"

"No."

Brenna gave him a disgusted look. "You want me to trust you, but you make it hard when I can't get an answer to a simple question."

"When I did answer your questions, you didn't believe me." Turning away, he made a pretense of checking out the judge's rack of CDs. He was being a jerk, but he didn't want to explain his relationship with Laurel Young. How safe would Brenna feel if she found out that his doctor was afraid for him to be out on his own because of the very real risk that he'd cross the line into murderous insanity?

"I thought you'd like to know that I finished going through the dining room. Do you want to do your old room while I check out mine?"

"Fine. We should leave in half an hour or so." He probably owed Brenna an apology, but she was already gone. Maybe it was for the best. Laurel's call had reminded him of all the reasons he should keep Brenna at arm's length. That kiss in the car had been a monumental mistake—one he'd give almost anything to make again.

chapter 6

Blake headed for his old bedroom on the floor below. There wasn't much that he felt sentimental about, but this room was the first real haven he'd ever known. His early years had taught him not to get attached to anything that anyone bigger, meaner, or stronger could take away.

A wave of familiarity washed over him as he entered the room. Nothing had changed. When he'd left for Seattle twelve years ago, he'd packed only his clothes and a few books. His remaining possessions were exactly where he'd left them.

When he'd completed his training as a Paladin, he had been given his choice of places to be assigned. Seattle had topped his list for two reasons. First was the city's proximity to both major fault lines and volcanoes, which promised a lot of action. At the time, the adventure had appealed to him.

More important, Seattle was as far as he could get from Brenna. He'd been eighteen, a mere four years older than her. But the difference in their levels of experience was a vast chasm.

At fourteen, she had been sweet, gentle, and incredibly brilliant. Her big green eyes had looked out at the world with equal curiosity and innocence. And all too often, those same eyes followed his every move.

Blake had already seen more ugliness than most people experienced in a lifetime. He had walked away from the Nichols' house not because he didn't care if he hurt them, but because he cared too much.

And now here he was, right back where he'd started.

A few well-chosen curse words relieved the urge to punch the wall. When he started searching, the first thing he noticed was that the bedspread was on crooked. It could be another case of the cleaning service not doing its job properly, but he didn't think so. Despite the unused air of the room, someone had felt the need to search it.

Whoever it had been, they must have been getting desperate if they had wasted their time looking through his old high school yearbooks. On the other hand, if they had wondered what his relationship was to Brenna, now they knew. It didn't really matter, though. Dr. Vega and his staff all knew his name; they would have given it to the police once Brenna disappeared from the hospital.

He slid his hands under the edge of the mattress and lifted. Nothing. The same went for the dresser drawers and the nightstand, which left only the closet. As soon as he opened the door, a flash of memory made him grin. He'd had one hiding spot that even the most determined of snoops would have been unlikely to find.

He yanked the spare blanket and pillow off the shelf and then tossed the few items of clothing on the bed. Next he lifted out the shelf and the hanger rod, allowing him to pry away the board that acted as their support. He'd installed hinges on the board so that it would open easily, revealing the small hidden space he'd built into the wall.

He used to keep his ready cash and a box of condoms in there to prevent Maisy from finding them when she cleaned his room. He'd never told anyone about his handiwork, but the judge must have discovered it because there was a large envelope rolled up and tucked inside the hole.

He dragged a lamp into the cramped space to get a better look: there was always the chance that whoever had searched the room had left him an unpleasant little surprise. He studied the envelope without touching it, but couldn't quite make out the writing. No guts, no glory. He yanked the envelope out and let it drop to the floor. When nothing exploded or started ticking, he picked it up.

It was addressed to "Blake Trahern" in a familiar scrawl. He started to rip it open, but changed his mind. If this was the judge's last message, then Brenna deserved to be with him when he read it. Maybe her father's own words would help convince her that Blake had been telling her the truth and she was in grave danger.

He quickly returned everything to the closet in case the previous searchers took another run at the house. When the room was back to the way he'd found it, he went looking for Brenna. It was time to get the hell out of Dodge. Once they were settled in a new hotel room, they could learn what the judge had uncovered that had cost him his life. Knowing he'd been the one to get his friend involved made Blake sick.

He took the steps upstairs two at a time, the need to be gone riding him hard. He found her standing outside her father's room, tears streaming down her face.

"Brenna?" He'd been wondering when the reality of her father's death would finally hit her.

She didn't respond immediately, but finally she turned toward him. "I feel as if I should knock first. How stupid is that?"

She placed her hand on the doorknob. "One of

us needs to search his room. I guess that would be me." When the door swung open, she gasped, "Dear God, what happened?"

Blake pushed past her into the room. It looked as if a tornado had unleashed its full fury. Books were torn and scattered across the floor. The mattress was half off the bed and the dresser drawers had been upended. Whoever had searched this room had done so in a fit of rage.

Brenna rounded on him, the tears replaced with indignation and determination. "I want to hurt whoever did this, Blake!" She balled her hands up in fists. "I want to hurt them bad!"

So did he. He would hunt the bastards down and kill them with his bare hands—but not before they suffered for ripping Brenna's life apart. Judge Nichols had known all along that either of his careers could bring someone's fury down on his head. But Brenna had made no such choice, and for that the bastards would die.

He placed his hand on her shoulder. "Brenna, I don't know if it's any comfort or not, but they didn't find what they were looking for."

"How do you know?" she asked.

"Because we were right. He left the files in a place where one of us could find them." He held out the envelope, giving her a chance to recognize her father's handwriting.

If anything, she looked even more depressed as

she traced Blake's name with a finger. "You mean he left it where *you* could find it. Not me."

Damn, he hadn't thought of it that way. "That only means he'd ferreted out my secret hiding place."

"He addressed it to you, Blake." Her eyes were sadder than anything he'd ever seen.

Damn it, he'd probably considered the material classified, not for the eyes of anyone outside of the Regents. Even from the grave he was shutting his daughter out.

The only way Blake could ease Brenna's pain was to get her out of this house, where she was surrounded with memories. "We need to go. Get your things."

He took her arm and muscled her out of the room. Maybe the shock would put some spark back into her.

Glaring up at him, she snapped, "I don't take orders from anyone very well, least of all from you."

"Too bad. We've been here too long already." The condition of the judge's room seriously bothered him. If this madman were to return right now, there's no telling what he'd do. Blake could survive almost any kind of attack, but Brenna was far more vulnerable. Picking her up, he tossed her over his shoulder.

"Blake Trahern! Put me down right now!"

He ignored her fists pounding on his back. A single suitcase was sitting outside her bedroom door. "Is this all you're taking?"

"Figure it out for yourself, you big jerk!"

It took him a bit of juggling to hold onto the envelope and snag the suitcase before heading down the stairs. She'd given up fighting him, but he knew that there'd be hell to pay the minute he set her free. A motion outside the front window caught his eye.

"Bloody hell!" He set her down. "Brenna, we've got company. Take your suitcase and this," he said, shoving the envelope at her. "Do you still have the car keys?"

She nodded as she saw the car pulling up out front. "Those are the two detectives who interviewed me in the hospital."

"They're probably the ones who trashed your father's room. Go out through the kitchen and don't look back. I'll make sure you get clear and then follow if I can."

"But—"

"*Go* Brenna!" He tossed her his cell phone. "If I don't catch up with you five minutes after you reach the car, or if you hear gunfire, get the hell out of the area. When you're sure you weren't followed, call Devlin Bane in Seattle and tell him what happened. He's listed in my numbers. You can trust him."

She was smart enough to look scared and was already moving toward the door. "Don't make a target of yourself for me, Blake. If anyone is going to rough you up it's going to be me for hauling me around like a sack of potatoes."

"I'll look forward to it, babe." He grinned and kissed her hard and fast before she could sputter a protest. Then he turned her toward the door. "Now get out while there's still time!"

She looked back right before she stepped out of the door. "Keep safe, Blake."

He waited in the kitchen doorway, where he could keep an eye on both the front porch and the backyard. Brenna had taken his orders to heart and was crossing the yard at a full-out run. He'd give her another forty-five seconds to get completely clear before following her, knowing it was going to be close. The detectives were already out of their car and walking up to the porch.

A glance out back told him that Brenna was struggling with the gate. "Come on, honey, you can do it. It's just nerves making you clumsy."

It took her two more tries to get it open, but he'd buy her all the time she needed to get away, even if it meant using up another one of his lives. At the sound of a key in the front lock, he drew his gun.

•   •   •

"Damn it, Trahern, answer your phone." Jarvis paced his office forward and back for the fifth time in as many minutes.

An automated voice came on the line telling him that the party he wished to reach was currently unavailable. Disconnecting, he kicked his wastebasket, scattering wadded-up papers across the floor as it bashed into the wall. The small act of violence pleased him, although he'd have to pay for a new wastebasket. The Regents were usually generous in providing Paladins with all they needed, but repeated wastebasket abuse was frowned upon.

He was due back in the tunnels in two hours. The chance of getting good cell phone reception near the barrier was almost zero. He slipped his hand into his front pants pocket and fingered the blue stone, liking the smooth feel of it but hating the puzzle it represented. An internet search had turned up nothing similar in color or characteristics, confirming his suspicion that it had come across the barrier. The only question was why, and his gut feeling was that Trahern knew the answer.

No one had mentioned specifics, but something had happened in Seattle recently that had the Regents upset. The absence of facts didn't keep anyone who'd caught wind of the rumors from speculating long and loud about what had happened. Hell, somebody had even hinted that the Seattle Paladins had adopted one of the Others as a pet. He had laughed when he'd heard that one. When it came to their enemies from the dark side, Blake Trahern was a cold-blooded killer. He'd be the last one to leave an Other walking around in one piece. That had to be one of those urban myths that developed a life of its own.

Maybe he should try Trahern's number again. As he brought up his list of contacts, someone knocked on his door. Slipping the phone back in his pocket, he called, "Come in."

A familiar but unwelcome man appeared in the doorway. What was Ritter doing hanging around the Paladin command post? The man was a Regent and normally kept to their fancy office building in St. Louis. Whatever he wanted, it couldn't be good. Jarvis didn't stand up; no point in making the man feel welcome.

Leaning back in his chair, Jarvis steepled his fingers and stared at his guest. "Mr. Ritter, what brings you this way?"

Ritter sat down. "I heard the fighting had been particularly bad and wanted to check on the men. Judge Nichols used to keep abreast of the Paladins on a day-to-day basis. His death has left an immense hole in the organization." The man shrugged slightly as if to show his distress at his fellow Regent's untimely death. "I thought it wise to pick up the slack."

The last thing they wanted right now was a Regent snooping around. "I'd be glad to e-mail you a copy of my daily personnel report, sir." Anything to keep him out of their way.

"That would fine, Jarvis, and I appreciate the thought. However, until someone is appointed to assume Judge Nichols's duties, I feel a strong Regent presence is needed to remind the Paladins that all is well with the organization. We don't want you to feel that no one is concerned with your welfare."

His smile raised Jarvis's hackles. The man had all the sincerity of a jackal. With Trahern on some kind of vengeance quest, Others dropping mysterious blue stones in the tunnels, and minor earthquakes coming in swarms, a nosy Regent was the last thing Jarvis needed.

"Do you know when the new Regent will be taking office?" he asked.

Ritter picked a small piece of lint off the cuff of his suit jacket before answering. "The Board of Regents is hard at work on that very issue, but the progress is slow. Many of my fellow Regents were badly shaken up by the attack on Judge Nichols, wondering if they could be next. Until we know why he was singled out for assassination, none of us feel particularly safe."

"I thought the police were investigating his judicial cases for suspects." Not that he believed for one minute that they'd find that some crazed ex-con had gone after the judge as payback.

Ritter sat back in his chair and stared up at the ceiling for several long seconds before meeting Jarvis's gaze. "This is not for general broadcast, Jarvis, but there are indications that all is not right within the organization. I, for one, find it highly suspicious that a guard was murdered in Seattle. As I understand it, Trahern was involved in that situation. Now we have a murdered Regent here in St. Louis, and who should show up at the hospital but Blake Trahern. Then there is the matter of Ms. Nichols's disappearance under questionable circumstances. I would think the police would be greatly interested in any information you might have on their current location."

Jarvis flexed his hands to relieve the achy need to lunge across the desk and choke the life out of Ritter. Any hints that Trahern had killed the Regent were inexcusable, unless the man had solid facts to back up the accusation. And if they *had* concrete proof, they would have had every Handler in the area hunting him down to execute him on the spot.

There was something slippery about the way Ritter always talked in hints and innuendo between bouts of glad-handing everyone in sight.

Right now he stared at Jarvis, like a spider

watched potential prey to see which way it was going to jump.

Jarvis gave Ritter an impassive look. "I don't know anything about Trahern's current location, nor do I know where Ms. Nichols is at the moment. However, you do know that Blake Trahern and Judge Nichols go way back. I'm sure you have friends who would come support you in your time of need, too."

He glanced at his watch and stood up. "I hate to be rude, but I have to get a move on. I'm due back in the tunnels in just over an hour."

Ritter reluctantly rose to his feet. "I hope you have a quiet night of it." He went to the door but paused before crossing the threshold. "Need I remind you, Jarvis, that your duty is first and foremost to the Regent organization as a whole? If Trahern is involved in something that would jeopardize our mission, you are obligated to make sure that he is stopped. Do I make myself clear?"

"Yes, sir. I am very clear on my duties." Jarvis kept his gaze level with Ritter's. "Now, if you will excuse me."

He turned his back and pretended interest in a stack of folders on the shelf behind his desk. He waited until he heard the click of the door closing before returning to his desk, holding off dialing Trahern's number again in case Ritter pulled some juvenile stunt like walking back in pretending to have forgotten something, just to see if Jarvis had immediately called Trahern to report in.

No, he'd be more the type to order Jarvis's office bugged. Well, he could go right ahead and try. Some of the best computer geeks in the area were also Paladins; he'd give them a heads up about his suspicions. Playing cat and mouse was the sort of thing they lived for.

Calling Trahern would have to wait until he was on his way to the tunnels, and he hoped his friend wasn't in over his head. His gut feeling was that there was something seriously wrong, but that Trahern wasn't the cause. His cold-eyed friend might just be the cure, God help them all.

Blake had told her to give him five minutes after she ran for the car. That deadline had come and gone. She put the key in the ignition and the engine roared to life.

Putting the car in drive, she pulled away from the curb, hoping that Trahern would materialize. Fear for him left a sick taste in her mouth. What had happened? Had he been captured? Was he lying bleeding or dead somewhere?

She pushed the buttons that lowered the windows in case Blake saw her and yelled to get her attention. But as she passed by the road leading to the alley, the only noise she heard was several popping sounds—gunshots! Oh, Lord, they had come from the direction of her home. Blake's orders had been very specific: she was to leave the area and call his friend in Seattle.

A smart woman would do as he said, trusting that he would be able to save himself. But how could she live with herself if she left him to die without trying to help? Images of Blake laying dead or dying in the yard were enough to have her backing up and turning into the cross street. The tires squealed, making her curse. So much for sneaking up on them.

More shots rang out, giving her second thoughts, but there was no turning back now. The alley was too narrow to do more than drive straight-arrow down the middle. She slowed as she approached the gate. She'd left it open, hoping to save Blake a second or two, but he was nowhere in sight. What if he was trapped in the house? Should she park and go back inside? No, she'd only provide another target for the shooters and complicate the situation.

Craning her neck, she tried to catch a glimpse of what was going on. There was a flicker of motion at the kitchen window, but it was gone too quickly to make out who it was. Were the two detectives trying to bring Blake to bay in the kitchen?

The car nosed beyond the fence on the far side of the yard, and two houses down a man stumbled out from behind a garage, waving his arms to get her attention. His sudden appearance startled a scream out of her, causing her to slam on the brakes. The car stopped inches from where Blake swayed, a blossom of bright crimson on his shoulder. She threw open her door to climb out.

He stumbled to the car and growled, "Get back inside! They're only a few seconds behind me."

He nearly fell into the car, wincing in pain. Sweat poured down his face as he tried to staunch the bleeding with his bare hand. "Get us out of here!"

She peeled out.

Where to go? A hotel was out of the question until she got the bleeding stopped and him into a clean shirt. Even cheap and sleazy motels frowned on their customers bleeding on the sheets. That thought had her giggling, an indication how close she was to hysteria.

As she drove, she kept a wary eye on the rearview mirror, watching for anyone who might be following them. So far, the road was empty for several blocks.

When she reached a major thoroughfare, she remembered the small park where she'd changed clothes. It would give them privacy while she assessed his injury and applied first aid.

If he didn't wake up soon, she'd call someone for help—either Jarvis or the friend in Seattle he'd mentioned. Devlin Bane was too far away to be of immediate help, but maybe he could tell her if she could trust Blake's care to Jarvis.

Blake moaned quietly as they went around a corner, and she saw the entrance to the park a short distance ahead. She crossed her fingers that no one else had chosen that moment to take a trip down lover's lane. Luck was with them; the park was deserted. She followed the narrow road around to the solitary picnic table and parked.

Blake stirred and tried to open his eyes. "Where?"

"We're paying another visit to your favorite picnic table, Blake." She got out of the car and ran around to the other side. "I wanted to hear more about your youthful adventures."

She wasn't sure, but she thought he might have smiled. He mumbled something that sounded like splinters, which was way too much information. She tugged on his good arm, trying to get him out of the car.

"Come on, Trahern, I need to see how bad the wound is."

He blinked up at her. "Doesn't matter. I'll heal in a day, two at the most."

"Nobody heals that fast, big guy."

"We all do. Ask Jarvis or Devlin Bane." He got a funny look on his face. Leaning closer to her, he whispered, "You know, everybody thinks I'm the big bad ass, but Devlin could take me out that fast." He tried unsuccessfully to snap his fingers to demonstrate.

She braced herself against the open door and tried again to tug him up out of the seat. "You can tell me all about how tough you are when we have you sitting down on the Blake Trahern Memorial Picnic Table."

He had the audacity to laugh at her. "Jealous, Brenna? We could give the old picnic table a quick spin if you'd like. I'm up for it." His inadvertent double entendre cracked him up again.

"Sorry, but my idea of a good time doesn't include having someone bleed all over me. Come on, big guy, get out of the car."

It took all her strength to muscle him up out of the seat. He tried to help, but his height made it hard to keep her balance when he leaned on her for support.

When at long last they reached the table, she eased him down on the bench. "Stay there."

She ran back to the car to get the first aid supplies they'd bought to bandage her arm. A few gauze pads and some surgical tape didn't seem like a lot in the face of all that blood on his shirt, but it would have to do. He was already unbuttoning his shirt one-handed when she came back, but his attempts to help were more of a hindrance.

She set her supplies on the table and then

eased his shirt off his shoulder. Too bad they couldn't just throw it away, but it could cause them both serious complications if someone were to find it and report it to the police. His T-shirt, now more red than white, was going to be harder to remove.

"Give me your knife." She ripped several strips off his shirt to hold the dressings in place.

She successfully avoided looking directly at his wound until she finished stripping off his shirt. Most of the blood had soaked into the shirt, and she wiped the rest off as best she could, revealing a deep groove along the top of his shoulder. It had to be agonizing, but he seemed supremely indifferent to the pain.

"I'm going to wash it first." She poured some bottled water on a couple of gauze pads and dabbed at the wound. Blake grabbed her wrist and forced her to press harder.

"You can't hurt me, Brenna. Paladins have a high tolerance for pain."

She would have believed him more if his lips weren't pressed together so hard that they were white along the edges. But he was right; she wasn't doing him any good with her half-hearted efforts. She poured some water on the open wound, causing him to hiss in pain. After wiping away the dried blood, the area was as clean as she could make it. She applied a thick smear of antibiotic ointment.

Then it was only a matter of covering the wound

with more gauze pads and taping them in place. When that was done, she rooted through his duffel for another shirt. Pulling it on without jarring his shoulder took some effort and care. When he tried to help her she batted his hands away.

Afterward, she gathered up the bloody shirts and the scraps of paper she'd torn off the gauze. Maybe she was catching his paranoia, but she wouldn't leave any obvious signs that the two of them had been in the park.

"All right. Let's get you into the car."

He lurched to his feet, almost oversetting both of them. "Sorry," he murmured as he leaned back against the table for balance.

"Don't worry about it."

Maybe she was grasping at straws, but his footsteps seemed to be more sure as they slowly returned to the car.

When she had him settled in the front seat, she reached across him to fasten his seat belt. Heat was pouring off his body, but wasn't it too soon for infection to have set in? She hoped so, or she'd have to call for medical help. And anyone who saw the bullet wound would have to report it to the police, which they didn't want—not until they figured out who were the good guys and the bad guys.

After she was behind the wheel, she wondered why the two police at the house hadn't caught up with them. Several shots had been fired; had he killed them? God, she hoped not.

"Blake, how did we manage to shake the police so easily?"

He turned slightly and opened his eyes. Their silver gray darkened when he saw the real question in hers. "I shot their tires. They shot me." He turned away to stare out the window, his face all hard lines and edges.

"I'm sorry all of this happened, Blake. It seems like you're getting sucked further and further into my problems."

He rode in silence for a few minutes. "It doesn't matter. I would have killed them if it had been necessary, without second thoughts or re-grets."

His words shocked her right through to her soul. "You don't mean that."

He sighed, his eyes bleak but unwavering. "Honey, I've killed so many times that two more bodies wouldn't even be noticed. It's what I do. It's who I am."

When he looked away this time, she was relieved.

chapter 7

Brenna drove west on Highway 44 for some distance before picking a random truck-stop motel. The place was swarming with semitrucks and cars, so the employees should be too busy to pay much attention to them.

After paying for the room with cash, she drove their car around to park in front of their room. She'd asked for a first-floor room on the back side of the motel so their car couldn't be spotted from the highway.

It took her several tries to wake Blake up enough to get him out of the car, and she saw that he'd started bleeding again.

"Come on, Blake, we've got to get you bandaged again."

He pushed her hands away. "It won't kill me, and if it does, I won't stay that way long." He turned those hard gray eyes on her. "But if I do die, or pass out to the point you can't wake me, tie me down. Chains would be best, but enough rope will work. Wait in the car until Jarvis gets here. He'll know what to do."

"What are you talking about, Blake? I'm not going to tie you up." The idea horrified her.

"Promise me, Brenna. You have to do this or you won't be safe."

"You'd never hurt me." She was surprised by the strength of her belief.

"I wouldn't be me anymore." He shuddered, his eyes the cold, hard gray of marble. "Now promise me!"

He was so agitated, she worried that he'd make the bleeding worse. "I promise."

With that nonsense settled, he hauled himself up out of the car. She barely got him inside the door before he started to sink to the floor, but she managed to shove him to the nearest bed before he collapsed. She pulled down the covers, took off his shoes, and covered him up.

Winded, she sat on the other bed to catch her breath and think. It had been hours since she'd eaten, and the truck stop café was bound to have something deliciously full of cholesterol and salt. Blake wasn't going anywhere soon, and she had to keep up her strength to help him. She picked up her purse and walked out, locking the door behind her.

Inside the noisy café, a gum-popping waitress led her to a booth in the back, right past two tables full of state troopers. One of them offered her a friendly smile, which she returned. Even if there had been an alert sent out by the St. Louis detectives, they'd be looking for a couple, not a woman traveling alone.

There was always the chance that one of them would recognize her, but if she left now she'd only draw more attention to herself. She sat down and discreetly checked their table. When she was satisfied that they weren't interested in her, she studied the menu.

A middle-aged waitress appeared, coffeepot in hand. "What can I get you, hon?"

"I'll have the bacon cheeseburger and fries, with an iced tea. I'd also like a bowl of soup to go, and two pieces of pie."

"I'd recommend either the apple or the cherry."

"Make it one of each." Brenna handed back the menu.

"I'll be right back with your drink."

When the waitress returned with the iced tea, Brenna took a quick gulp. Rats, one of those fruit-flavored varieties. Whoever got the mistaken idea that raspberry and tea went together? Still, the cool glass felt good to the touch, soothing her tightly stretched nerves.

In the silence, Blake's words came back to her.

She had worried that he was dead when they hadn't heard from him for all those years. But if he were to be believed, her father had known all along where he was and hadn't told her. To make matters worse, the two of them had belonged to some secret organization, one that had claimed her father's life and now threatened Blake, as well.

She felt betrayed by both men. Unexpected anger washed over her, surprising her with its intensity. The decisions that they had made without consulting her had thrown all of her hopes and dreams into chaos. She had planned to spend this summer researching her latest book. Instead, here she was on the run with a wounded man who thought he was immortal.

Her temper faded as her eyes drifted back to where the state troopers where finishing up their late dinner. All her life, she'd been taught to respect the law and those who wore the badge. Most of them were good, honest people who could be trusted to enforce the law fairly. That was why her reaction to Detective Montgomery and his partner Detective Swan bothered her so much.

From the first moment, she'd sensed something was wrong with their approach to solving her father's murder. Were her gut instincts totally out of kilter? She trusted Blake—who talked like a crazy man about not dying and needing to be chained down. The two detectives wore badges, yet she didn't want to be near them at all, especially until she and Blake found out what was in the envelope her father had left him.

The waitress returned with her burger and fries. Picking up the hamburger, Brenna leaned forward to keep it from dripping grease on her blouse.

The taste of charcoal-broiled beef filled her senses, reminding her how long it had been since she'd eaten. She slowed down, not wanting to wolf down her food. But she couldn't afford to linger too long, with Blake alone and wounded. He'd likely sleep soundly for several hours, but his earlier ramblings about dying and chains had shaken her up.

A sudden vibration startled her into almost dropping her burger. Wiping her fingers on the napkin, she reached into her front pocket and pulled out Blake's cell phone. She'd forgotten all about it. Should she answer the call?

Flipping the phone open, she read the number. The area code wasn't local and the name showing with the number said DOC—most likely someone he knew back in Seattle. The only one he'd told her to trust was a man named Devlin Bane. Still . . .

She pushed the answer button. "Hello."

The woman on the other end of the line sounded cautious. "May I speak to Blake Trahern, please?"

"May I ask who is calling?"

"Dr. Young. And you are?"

"Brenna Nichols."

The coolness in the voice melted slightly. "I'm sorry about your father, Ms. Nichols. I know Trahern thought a lot of him."

"Thank you, Doctor." She fumbled for what to say next. Maybe this woman knew Devlin Bane. "Would you know Devlin Bane by any chance?"

"Yes, I do. Why do you ask?"

"Would you ask him to call me?"

The freeze was back. "Why do you need Devlin? And why didn't Blake answer his phone himself?"

She had to trust someone. Glancing around to make sure that no one was paying attention, she dropped her voice and went for broke. "Dr. Young, Blake was shot today trying to get us away from the police investigating my father's death. He told me if I needed help, I should call Devlin Bane."

"Is he hurt badly?" There was no mistaking the worry in the doctor's voice.

"The bullet caught him high in the shoulder. I don't know much about bullet wounds, but I think it was more bloody than dangerous. I cleaned the wound and wrapped it. He's sleeping right now."

"Ms. Nichols, listen to me very carefully. I want you to call Trahern's friend Jarvis and tell him what you just told me. He can be trusted to get you any help that you might need. You should be all right for now, but if Trahern acts at all strange, get as far from him as fast as you can. Do you understand me?"

Brenna frowned. "Explain yourself, Dr. Young."

"I can't."

Annoyed, Brenna softly warned, "Listen, Doctor, I don't appreciate you trying to scare me away from Blake. He's already tried that with some ridiculous story about Paladins. I've known Blake since he was a teenager. He'd never hurt me, so there's no use in trying to tell me different. Now if you'll excuse me, I'd like to finish my dinner."

She disconnected the call. Her food had grown cold while they had been talking, but it didn't matter. The conversation had left her stomach unsettled. Catching the waitress's attention, she signaled that she was ready for her bill and the take-out food.

When the phone buzzed again out in the parking lot, she ignored it. After locking the motel room door, she turned on a lamp near Blake's bed. As far as she could tell, he hadn't moved while she'd been gone.

"Blake, wake up. I've got some soup for you."

When he didn't immediately respond, she tried again, louder, and reached out to touch his arm. He bolted upright, knocking her back into the other bed. He shook his head, his eyes wide-open and crazed looking. His hands were fisted and ready for battle. She fought down the urge to run for the door, sensing that to do so would only make him worse in some way.

"Blake, I'm sorry. I didn't mean to startle you." And scare herself, either.

His expression was completely blank, his eyes unfocused. She wasn't sure if he knew himself, much less her. She tried to talk him down.

"Blake, it's me, Brenna Nichols. You were shot earlier today, trying to protect me from two detectives at my father's house. You remember. You gave me your phone and the keys." The urge to run was riding her hard, but she held her ground. She'd done enough running the past few days.

"We're at a motel. I went to the café to get something to eat and brought you some soup and apple pie. I got myself cherry pie, but we can trade if you want. I like both, but you should eat your dinner before it gets cold."

He remained motionless, but she could almost see the adrenaline surging through him. There was still no recognition in his eyes as he stared at her. The potential for violence hung heavily in the room—at any second he could strike out, not even knowing what he was doing. Maybe she should head for the door, but she knew she couldn't out-distance him.

As frightened as she was, she sensed that he

was horribly lost. How could she abandon him when he needed her the most? An angry Blake Trahern she could handle, but one lost and hurting made her want to wrap her arms around him to show him he wasn't alone.

The cell phone chose that minute to start vibrating again. Maybe someone on the other end of the line could help her.

"I'm going to answer your phone now, Blake. It might be one of your friends calling." Please, God, let it be a friend near enough to be of some help.

A quick glance at the screen told her that she was about to meet Devlin Bane. She brought the phone up near her ear and pushed the button. "Hello, this is Brenna Nichols."

Evidently Blake's friend was another one who didn't waste time with small talk. "Ms. Nichols, this is Devlin Bane. Dr. Young asked me to call you. She said Trahern has been wounded."

"That's right." She kept her voice level and her eyes on Blake.

"Is he still sleeping?"

"Not anymore."

Bane's response was short and pithy, reminding her of Blake in tone and word choice. For some reason, she found that comforting.

"How do his eyes look?"

"A little wild."

"No, what color are they?" His voice was grim.

"Color?" What kind of weird question was that?

"I don't ask frivolous questions. Answer me."

She didn't much like his tone of voice or attitude, but if he could help Blake, she'd put up with it. "Silver gray."

A sigh of relief came over the line. "That's good. That's very good. What's he doing now?"

"He's sitting on the bed, looking like he can't quite figure out where he is."

Across the room Blake stirred slightly, sitting up straighter as he blinked and focused his gaze on her. In a matter of seconds all the confusion melted away, along with much of the tension in his body.

"Uh, I think he's back, Mr. Bane." Although from where, she had no idea and didn't want to ask.

Blake held out his hand for the phone; she got up to hand it to him and she sat on the edge of his bed. Blake ignored her while he held the phone to his ear.

"Bane, what the hell do you want?"

He kept his eyes averted, as if seeking privacy, but she wasn't going anywhere. She wished she could hear the other side of the conversation because Blake was only answering in monosyllables. Finally, he disconnected the call and set the phone on the bedside table.

"How long was I out?"

"Close to an hour."

His expression bleak, he asked, "Did I hurt you?"

The renewed tension in his body told her the importance of her answer. "I'll tell you the same thing I told Dr. Young: you would never hurt me. I don't understand why everyone—especially you—has a hard time believing that!"

He stared down at her with those silver eyes that had been so cold a few minutes ago. Now something stirred in their depths, something that sent delicious shivers of warmth through her to settle deep within her.

Oh, Lord, he was going to kiss her again. She suspected he didn't want to, noble fool that he was, but whatever shimmered between them was stronger than either of them could fight. She reached up to stroke his cheek with a feathery touch, liking the slight roughness of his day-old beard, then moved on to trace the straight slash of his mouth.

He slid his good arm around her shoulders and pulled her close. Surprising herself, she shifted to straddle his lap. His eyes widened and warmed. No one had ever accused him of being slow. His arms wrapped around her, pulling her against his chest so tightly that there was hardly room to breathe. She didn't care.

"Brenna . . ."

The way he said her name was a sigh or perhaps a prayer. She closed her eyes and laid her
head against the strength of his chest, soaking in
his warmth. Blake ran his hand up and down her
spine, each time closer to her bottom. It was a
strange sensation, teetering on the edge between
cuddling and passion, her body growing warm and
liquid as his touch became more daring.

She pressed a kiss against the pulse point at the
base of his neck. He rewarded her by sliding his
hand down her bottom, squeezing gently.

Feeling bold, she kissed her way along his jaw-
line to his mouth. In the space of a heartbeat, the
air around them crackled with heat lightning, a
storm about to break. There was no place to take
shelter from the power flowing around them, but
she didn't care. It was right and necessary to find
healing in each other's arms.

As soon as their lips met, his tongue surged into
her mouth, staking his claim. She wiggled closer,
cradling the hard response of his body against the
center of her own need.

He tasted of darkness and a power unlike anything she had ever experienced. For the first time,
she believed that he was something beyond mortal
men—something dark that others feared, and
rightly so. But when he wrapped her in his
strength, blocking out the light of the world, she
learned that his night had a warmth and sweetness

of its own. Like the moon, he was changeable and moody, but the pull of his strength drew her like nothing she'd ever known.

Blake fell back across the bed, letting her sprawl along the length of his body. She put her hands on his chest and pushed herself up to see his face in the dim light. Once they crossed this line, there would be no going back.

"I don't want to hurt you." She wasn't talking about his shoulder.

"You can't." That was a lie, and they both knew it.

She tugged his T-shirt up, wanting to feel the warmth of his skin, knowing touch spoke more truth than words could. Her eyes closed as she concentrated on the pure pleasure of skin-to-skin conversation. Blake lay still and let her explore, as the damp center of her body rubbed against the hard ridge of his desire, making her ache for the moment when they both stripped away the last vestiges of civilized behavior.

"I want you."

His voice was deep and rough in contrast to the gentleness of his touch as he reached up to fondle her breasts. She leaned into his palms, his caress soothing and inflaming her.

"Then take me, Blake."

"Brenna, we . . ."

She shushed him with a fingertip. "No more talking. No more reasons why we shouldn't."

He grabbed her finger and kissed it, sucking gently on the tip and sending hot need straight through to the center of her. She wanted him to use that wonderful mouth for other things than warning her off.

"I want you. I want this." She rocked against him again. "I need this."

"I'm not a forever kind of guy, Brenna. You know that." Then he stole her breath away with a lingering damp kiss on her palm.

"I'm not asking you for anything you can't give me. Just tonight. Just us."

Pulling her shirt off over her head, she flung it on the floor. Then she guided Blake's hand to the clasp on her bra. His eyes were molten silver as he flicked it open and freed her breasts. The calluses on his hands rasped against their sensitive tips, making them feel heavy and full.

In a quick move, he rolled so that she was on her back with him stretched out beside her. Starting at the curve of her neck, he nibbled his way down to her breast, suckling hard and then soothing her with the tip of his tongue. Each tug and touch sent another flicker of heat between her restless legs. His hand followed that same path, using his long fingers to stroke her through her slacks.

She needed them both to be naked, but when she reached for his zipper he snagged her hands and anchored them over her head. Her protests died on her lips as he tugged her zipper down instead, then slid his hand inside the waistband of her panties. His touch was more than she could bear and yet not nearly enough to satisfy, especially when he only teased her a bit.

"Blake!"

He almost smiled, obviously enjoying her frustration. But then he slid one finger deep inside her. It was a step closer to heaven, but not there yet. Her whole consciousness narrowed down to the hot length of the man beside her. When he finally released her hands, she fisted them in his hair and tugged his face down for a long, sweet kiss. She flicked her tongue in and out of his mouth, mimicking exactly what she wanted from him.

She whispered her previous demand again. "Take me, Blake. Now."

"I'm not a gentle man, Brenna."

"I'm not asking to be coddled." She reached for his zipper again; this time he didn't stop her.

He was going to hell and he knew it, but right now he didn't give a damn because he was going to get a glimpse of heaven on the way. All the dreams he'd had about bedding this woman had been only shadows of the reality. Right now he thought he might die of the pleasure of her determined hands trying to undo his pants. Normally the zipper on his jeans worked just fine, but he was so swollen with need that they were a tight fit.

Finally he sat up and shucked off his jeans himself, enjoying the wide-eyed look on her face when she saw the full length of him. He was a big man all over, but she didn't seem the least bit intimidated. On the contrary, she shimmied out of her own pants and then parted her legs in invitation. He should take it slow, letting her body adjust to him, but that wasn't going to happen. Not with this heat raging between them.

He wanted to plunge into her wet warmth and ride her hard, her legs high around his waist and her nails digging into his back. Her woman's scent was driving him crazy as he knelt between her ankles. Even so, he took the time to kiss the arch of her foot and then laved the sweet curve at the back of her knees. She lifted herself in invitation, hurrying him along the journey to the apex of her legs. He studied the beauty of her body and let the tip of his tongue trace his upper lip to warn her of what he intended to do next.

Her eyes darkened in anticipation.

He lowered himself to stroke her inner thigh with his tongue. Short little laps had her panting, until he finally reached his goal. She tasted of all things female, pleasing him that she wanted him as much as he wanted her. Her hands dug into the mattress.

"Blake! I can't . . ."

He smiled against her. "Oh, yes you can, and will." Then he eased two fingers inside her as he tongued her small nub, until he sent her screaming over the edge of pleasure. Kneeling, he used the last bit of his sanity to hold back for a few seconds. Surrounded by the halo of her dark hair, her face was flushed with pleasure. He could have stared at her beauty for an eternity, but then she smiled and held her arms out to him.

"Blake Trahern, I'm tired of telling you. *Take* me."

And so he did.

He wasn't sure if his heart or his lungs would give out first. She'd urged him on and on until nothing was left, but even now, in the shattered aftermath, he was reluctant to pull out of her body and let sanity return. Pushing himself up on his elbows, he looked down at the woman who had rocked his very soul.

"Did I hurt you?"

She gave him a sexy, cat-in-the-cream smile. "Do I look like I didn't enjoy myself?"

He had to admit she looked pretty damn satisfied. If she'd been any other women, he would have been reaching for his jeans and planning his escape. But this time was different.

"Don't think so hard, Blake." She reached up to cup his cheek with her palm. "Tomorrow will be time enough to worry about what comes next."

Already his traitorous body stirred with the desire for a repeat performance, and he rocked against her as he leaned down to kiss the end of her nose. Her mouth curved up in a delighted smile as she ran her hands down his back to grab his ass and squeezed.

"Why, Mr. Trahern, I do believe you've fully recovered your . . . composure."

He liked her teasing, although he wasn't sure how to respond to it. Nothing in his life experience had prepared him for a woman who played in bed. When he couldn't find words, he settled for turning control of what came next over to her. Wrapping his arms around her, he flipped them both over so that she was on top, their bodies still joined. Her shriek of surprise quickly changed into a moan of pleasure.

"I like this," she purred, rocking back and forth gently.

So did he. In a life filled with ugliness and death, this moment shone brightly with beauty and warmth, giving him a glimpse of what his life might have been if he'd been born purely mortal.

Brenna could tell herself that tonight was enough, but he knew better. A woman like her wouldn't fuck a man just for old times' sake. No, she had some kind of strong feelings for him, ones that would be better directed toward someone who could stick around to build a white picket fence and hold her every night.

But if tonight was all he could give her, he sure as hell was going to make it memorable. He surged upright, deepening his penetration as he kissed her sweet mouth and used his hands to enjoy the ample bounty of her breasts. Judging by the small noises she made in the back of her throat, his three-way assault had her skating close to the edge, taking him with her.

Then the vixen slowed the pace, sliding up until she almost lost him before easing back down, then they both sighed with the sweetness of their shared connection. It only took two more times to break his control. Growling his frustration, he tossed her onto her back. Her eyes were alight with triumph as he thrust deep inside her again and again until her body convulsed in the ultimate pleasure. One more stroke was all it took for him to join her, pouring out his seed with a shout of joy.

Brenna wasn't accustomed to waking up with a man's hand on her breast or his morning erection pressed tightly against her bottom, but she decided that she liked it. She liked it a lot. Enough to see what happened if she wiggled a bit. She quickly found out that a sleeping Paladin woke up ready and able to finish what she'd started.

"Good morning." The growl of his voice against her shoulder felt delicious.

Trahern kissed the back of her neck as he lifted her leg up onto his. The feel of him stretched out behind her as he slowly pushed deep inside of her was the best wake up call she'd ever had. Neither of them felt the need to hurry, savoring the last few minutes before the sun claimed the sky.

Then Blake's cell phone started vibrating, rattling around on the bedside table. A second after it finally stopped it started again, casting a definite pall on the moment.

It had to be either Jarvis or that Devlin Bane.

"You'd better answer that, don't you think? They're only going to keep trying until you do."

With a muttered curse, Blake reached behind him for the phone. He pushed the button and snarled, "Trahern." He listened without saying a word. After what seemed to be an eternity, he spoke again. "Fine. We'll be there after lunch sometime." He disconnected and tossed the phone onto the other bed.

He seemed to hesitate a bit, but then rolled away from her. "Jarvis has something we need to see."

So much for their early morning cuddle.

Brenna tugged the sheet back up to cover herself, suddenly feeling exposed. "All right. Do you want to shower first or shall I?"

"Go ahead. I need to call Devlin."

The warm haven of the bed had definitely chilled, but her pride made her walk naked and unashamed to the bathroom. Inside, she leaned against the counter, wishing that she knew better how to handle an awkward morning after. Her body definitely felt the aftermath from the most vigorous night of lovemaking she'd ever experienced; Blake had held nothing back. And she hadn't wanted him to, not when she knew in her woman's heart that once her life was back to normal, he'd be gone. This time when he walked away, it would be for good.

At least she hadn't blurted out anything stupid, like how much she didn't want him to disappear from her life again. It wasn't something he was ready to hear. Besides, what would they do? Exchange Christmas cards? Somehow she couldn't quite picture that happening.

A knock on the bathroom door yanked her attention back to the moment. "Yes?"

"I was wondering if you were okay. I didn't hear the shower running."

Lord, how long had she been standing there feeling sorry for herself? "I'm fine—just a little slow out of the gate this morning."

She quickly turned on the water and stepped in before it had time to warm up. The sudden blast of cold water startled a small squeak out of her. Trahern must have been waiting outside of the door, because just that quickly, he yanked the shower curtain open.

She shivered and blushed. "Sorry, I wasn't expecting the water to be so cold."

He adjusted the faucet handle until the water was hot before stepping into the tub with her and closing the curtain behind him.

"Turn around."

His abrupt order made her want to refuse, but being there with him was a lot better than each of them being alone in separate rooms. She all but melted when he started washing her back with long slow strokes.

"Spread your legs."

She had to hold onto the wall to support herself as he started at her feet and worked his way up. The combination of warm water rushing down her skin and his heated touch had her aching for more.

"Face me."

His expression was deadly serious as he again lathered up the washcloth and used it to drive her crazy, paying particular attention to her breasts and other sensitive areas. Well, two could play at this game.

She took the washcloth from him. "Turn around."

She loved the power he'd surrendered to her as she learned each curve and muscle of his strong back and solid legs. His numerous scars hurt her heart, so she kissed each one, wishing she'd been there to ease his pain. He flinched each time, but didn't protest.

"Face me."

Hmm, her ministrations had had a profound affect on one part of his anatomy. Ignoring it for the moment, she soaped his chest and let the shower rinse it clean. Kneeling to wash his legs put her at eye level with his erection. She worked up a lather with her hands and gently fisted him and was immediately rewarded with a moan. The sense of power it gave her was heady stuff. Cupping him gently, she slid her fingers up and down his length several times, not sure which of them was enjoying it more.

Then she leaned forward and licked him. His breath caught as he rocked toward her in invitation; she smiled and took him in her mouth. Before she could establish a rhythm, however, his big hands clasped her arms and lifted her to her feet.

"We're short on time, Brenna."

For a painful heartbeat she thought he was refusing what she was offering, but he reached past her to turn off the water and said, "That means we'd better get down to business."

He swung her up in his water-slick arms and stepped out of the tub, then he carried her to the bed and tossed her down so that she landed on her stomach.

"Blake Trahern!" She started to turn over, but he stopped her by snaking his arm around her waist and pulling her to her knees in front of him.

Then he thrust inside her, ending all coherent thought as he pumped hard, his belly slapping against her backside. His hands held her hips steady as his powerful thrusts drove in deep. Nothing and no one had ever taken her with this primitive abandon. She chanted his name, using that single word to tell him how much she wanted this.

He leaned over her and used one hand to squeeze her breasts almost to the point of sweet pain. She wiggled her hips, letting him know without words that she wanted more. His hand followed the curve of her waist down and over her stomach to the nest of curls between her legs, to stroke the damp heat he found there. Lightning struck, sending ecstasy rippling through her. Then Trahern shouted out his own release, and they collapsed in a tangled heap.

He moved away too soon, taking his warmth with him again, but this time, he offered her a hand up off the bed and gave her a quick kiss. "We'd better finish that shower and get dressed. Jarvis will be waiting."

She followed him into the shower, but this time he was all business. Time to get back to the real world.

chapter 8

*B*lake dressed and left to order breakfast for the two of them. As Brenna brushed her hair in front of the mirror, she saw Blake's bandage in the wastebasket by the dresser. What was it doing there? When had he peeled it off?

She'd entirely forgotten about his wound. Closing her eyes, she pictured him getting dressed a few minutes ago. He should have been favoring that shoulder, but he'd moved as if there was nothing wrong with it. And there was no wound crusted over with dried blood; only a fresh scar where the bullet hole should have been. How could that be? Her own cuts, although days older, looked much worse.

She dropped onto the edge of the bed as her world rocked. Could his wild claims possibly be true? Could he be everything he claimed to be: a Paladin who died and lived again, and healed from wounds that would prove fatal to anyone else? If that was true, then his kind really did fight a secret war against invaders from other worlds. Not only that, but her father had been a part of Blake's world, living a double life she hadn't known about.

Her mind refused to accept it, but her heart told her otherwise.

The urge to move, to run, to deny everything had her up and packing. She stuffed her personal belongings back into her suitcase. It took a couple of tries to close the zipper, but finally her bag was sitting on the floor by the door. Then she perched on the edge of the bed to wait for Blake to return.

She was glad he wasn't back yet: she needed time to come to terms with what had happened.

Last night, she'd taken a lover who wasn't completely human.

He knew the minute he stepped back into the room that something had changed. Brenna had accepted the food he'd handed her with a quiet thank you, but she hadn't looked at him directly since his return.

Something was definitely wrong. It was in the tense set of her shoulders and the sideways looks when she thought he wasn't watching. Her bag was sitting by the door as if she'd been ready to bolt before he returned.

She'd been so vocal in her approval of their love-making, but now she had withdrawn to someplace that didn't include him. They'd both acknowledged that last night had been special, something to revel in and then walk away from. Perhaps this was just her way of doing that, but he didn't like it. Not one damn bit.

"What's gotten into you?" Besides him, last night, but he wisely kept that snide remark to himself.

She jumped, as if she thought he was going to attack her. Had she finally accepted what he'd been telling her?

She still hadn't answered, so he crossed the narrow room and crowded her.

"What happened to convince you that I'm a Paladin?" He stood over her with his legs apart, a warrior's stance. He wouldn't apologize for what he was.

At least now she was looking at him—or more accurately, his shoulder. "Your wound isn't just healed; it's already just a scar."

"That's part of the Paladin package, honey."

She glared at him, not appreciating his attitude. Too damn bad; he was what he was. But that didn't mean that he liked the way she was looking at him, as if he'd suddenly turned into a monster. She was the first person outside of the Paladins that he'd trusted with the knowledge of what he was, and now she was throwing that trust right back in his face. If it wouldn't have frightened her even more, he would have hurled her suitcase across the room.

He hated, really hated, the fear in her eyes.

"And just how does one become a Paladin?"

Now she sounded like a snooty college professor, which he didn't like much better. He was proud of what he was; he'd thought she would be, too.

"One doesn't *become* a Paladin; you're born one. The doctors in Research could tell you more, but I doubt that you'd find it very interesting."

Her chin came up. "Is Dr. Young one of those doctors?"

What was that odd note in her voice? "Yeah, she is. How do you know about her?"

Brenna concentrated on cutting her bacon into very small bites. "She called earlier. Since I didn't know if she could be trusted, I asked her to have your friend Devlin call."

He was no expert on women's emotions, but he was pretty sure that was jealousy in her voice. While that pleased him on some selfish level, now wasn't the time to put more strain on their relationship.

"Devlin is the top dog among the Seattle Paladins. Dr. Young is our Handler: that means she puts us back together and decides if we've got enough humanity left in us to live. She and Devlin are lovers." He shook his head. "None of us saw that coming."

Brenna looked puzzled. "What's wrong with them being lovers?"

"It's never happened before in all the history of the Paladins. Handlers and Paladins have no emotional involvement. That makes it easier when the Handler has to decide to put down a Paladin for crossing the line."

Her eyes were wide with shock. "What line?"

"Damn it, Brenna, haven't you been listening?" He spoke slowly and clearly, as if explaining something to a small child. "Paladins live and die repeatedly, becoming more like the Others with each death, until they finally wake up stark raving mad and have to be put down like a vicious animal. We travel that path at different rates, but eventually we all get to the same destination."

Brenna stared up at him as one emotion after another flitted across her face—shock, horror, the worst of all: pity.

"Why, Blake? Why does it have to be that way?"

He shrugged. "Genetics. Dr. Young thinks she can change that, but I'm not holding my breath. It's been fun, though, watching everybody scrambling to decide if it's okay for a Paladin to hook up with his Handler. Devlin doesn't give a damn what anyone else thinks, and Laurel Young can go toe-to-toe with the best of them."

"She's your Handler, too?"

"Yeah, she is." And one of these days he was going to cause Laurel Young a whole lot of pain when she had to grab that needle full of toxins and shove it in his arm. They'd all seen how devastated she was the first time she'd ended a Paladin's life, even though he'd been a complete stranger. None of the Seattle Paladins liked the idea that their final death would hurt her deeply, especially Devlin's.

However, Devlin's progress toward becoming like the Others had evidently slowed down. No one knew why, but all of Research was interested in finding out. Devlin didn't think much of being considered a lab rat, but if it meant saving some of his friends from certain death, he'd put up with a few extra needle pokes and tests. Besides, it gave him an excuse to hang out with his woman right under the nose of the higher-ups. Devlin was just perverse enough to enjoy that.

Brenna had shoved her breakfast plate aside, having eaten only a little of her meal. She seemed to have run out of questions for the moment, so he concentrated on finishing his own bacon and eggs. They had a long way to drive to meet up with Jarvis, so it might be awhile before they'd have a chance to eat again. Although his body did heal quickly, it would take another couple of days to recoup the energy he'd lost to the healing process.

When he was done, he made quick work of

packing up. If he stayed in the area much longer, he'd have to stop and buy more clothes. He'd left Seattle in such a hurry that he'd thrown only the bare minimum into his duffel. One T-shirt had been lost to yesterday's gunshot, and Brenna hadn't returned the one he'd loaned her. Not that he'd ask for it back. He rather liked the idea of her sleeping in his shirt—unless he had another chance to keep her naked in his bed.

Like that was going to happen again anytime soon.

Ritter stared out of the hotel window and cursed. Where the hell were Trahern and Brenna Nichols? His two buffoons with badges had reluctantly admitted to a run-in with them at her house, and the stupid bastards had made two major mistakes. First, they let Trahern shoot out their tires so they couldn't follow him. And second, they shot Trahern himself. They had no idea what a Paladin was, and he saw no need to enlighten them.

The fools would find out soon enough the next time their paths crossed his. By all reports, Trahern was as bad as they came, volatile and a remorseless killer. With luck, the Paladin would dispose of the two cops and save him the trouble.

Right now, he'd give anything to know where Trahern had gone to ground with the Nichols woman. What had they found in the house that two police searches had missed? There was no proof that they had located anything, but it seemed unlikely that they would have been on their way out of the house empty-handed.

Damn, he hated puzzles. If Nichols had found enough incriminating information to come after him, then why was Trahern still running instead of coming after those responsible for the judge's death with guns blazing? Maybe they'd gone to ground until Trahern recovered from his wound, if the detectives really had gotten in a lucky shot. That gave him maybe another twelve hours to locate the fugitives and get that information before they could act on it.

The same genes that endowed them with long life and recuperative powers also gave Paladins exceptional intelligence and logic. Not much got by them when it came to their life in the trenches, and something had happened in Seattle to arouse the suspicions of Trahern and his pal Devlin Bane.

If that idiot guard, Sgt. Purefoy, hadn't already died for his incompetence, he would have taken great pleasure in killing the little shit himself. Not only had Purefoy failed to take out Bane and throw the Seattle Paladins into disarray, but his actions had led Trahern to involve the judge in their problems. Nichols had been a top flight Regent, honest and hardworking. God, he'd hated that man. How could anyone associate with criminals day in and day out and still be such a straight arrow?

It was such an irresistible scam. He'd managed to get word across the barrier that those who wished to cross into this world could do so at a price. When the barrier failed, a few blue stones would change hands, and those whacked-out bastards were home safe. Only a select few guards knew about the deal he'd made. And every one of those filthy Others faced death at the point of a Paladin sword, their bribes merely padding his pockets.

Which reminded him, the latest payment was late. He'd checked his bank balance online, and it didn't reflect any transfer of funds from his customer. Since he was taking all the risks, the least the bastards could do was be prompt with the money. He had police to bribe, hands to grease, and tracks to cover. As soon as he dealt with the little problems of Trahern and that Nichols woman, he'd tie up a few loose ends and disappear.

Judging by Trahern's medical records, he was but a breath away from insanity and turning Other. If someone were to arrange a nasty death for Ms. Nichols, it wouldn't be hard to convince the Regents and Ordinance that the unstable Paladin needed to be put down—especially with the death of two detectives tied into his case. Yes, that would be the crowning touch. With all the death and mayhem, his own disappearance would go unnoticed until it was too late.

But first, he needed the judge's information, to contain the damage. He wasn't worried about it incriminating him; once he disappeared that didn't matter. But if Nichols had managed to trace the chain of guilty parties beyond Ritter, there wasn't a place on earth that would be safe enough to hide in. And what good was amassing a fortune if he didn't live to spend it?

The silence in the car was so thick, Brenna could hardly breathe. She turned her head to watch Trahern's hands on the wheel. They were masculine hands, large and strong, with calluses that she now knew came from swinging a sword. The idea should horrify her, but now that she was over the initial shock of learning who and what he really was, all she could think of was how those same hands had felt last night as he had made love to her.

The sex had burned hot and hard and a little rough, but she'd felt wholly cherished in his arms. Even now, she relished the memory of being the sole focus of all that intensity.

Big, tough guy that he was, he would probably deny it, but she knew her reaction had hurt him this morning. Surely he could understand her shock, though. After all, normal men didn't get shot in the shoulder, sleep for a couple of hours, and wake up strong enough to make love three or four times before the sun came up.

To top it all off, she wished they could do it all again. Her wayward thoughts had her shifting in her seat, which caught Trahern's attention.

"What's wrong now?" He didn't bother to look her way.

"Nothing. I'm fine." She wasn't fine and wasn't sure she ever would be. "How much farther?"

"Another fifty miles or so."

They rode on in silence for another handful of minutes. Her stomach was muttering something about it being long past time for lunch. According to the last sign they'd passed, another town should be looming on the horizon.

She was about to mention it when Blake said, "I thought we'd stop in the next town. We need to talk."

That sounded ominous.

"When are you going to open the envelope my father left for you?" She looked directly ahead, not wanting to see his reaction.

"There's a small roadside park a few miles before the compound where Jarvis is waiting for us. I was going to stop there after lunch."

"Is it another one of your trysting spots?" she sniped.

He kept his attention on the road's sharp turns,

but there was a particularly irritating look on his face, as if he found her question entertaining.

"I know the park's there because I've driven past it often enough. There are plenty of picnic tables I never got around to trying out." He smiled, just a little. "We could add another table to my list, if you're interested."

She was interested all right, but sex alfresco had never been one of her fantasies. At least, up until now.

Food helped. Coffee hot enough to scald his mouth also helped, and even yesterday's stale cake helped. Anything that kept him too busy to think about the woman sitting across from him in the booth. How could Brenna have spent the night in his arms, burning up the sheets, then look at him like something she'd found under a rock? It pissed him off royally. That, and having to admit how much her attitude hurt him.

Hell, he knew he wasn't completely human, but most of the time he didn't feel all that different. Back in his training days, a Handler had said the genetic difference between a normal human being and a Paladin was less than one half of one percent. Of course, that small percentage was alien DNA, a legacy from a few Others who had managed to cross the border and insinuate themselves into the population of this world. Their genetic makeup, combined with human, made their offspring different from both the parent stocks in important ways.

Some of the differences were good: longer life, the ability to heal, sharp intelligence. But they were more than offset by the downside: every Paladin, without exception, became more and more like the Others as time went on. It was ironic that he'd spent a lifetime fighting his distant relatives.

"Slow down, Blake, before you choke on your food. We've got plenty of time."

Easy for her to say. But time was running out for both of them. He figured the two St. Louis cops were paid dupes, just as the guard had been back in Seattle. It was the man jerking their strings who interested him.

Closing his eyes, he imagined the pleasure he'd take from slicing the bastard into little pieces. That wasn't his usual way of doing business. The Others he fought died quickly, if not painlessly. This time, he planned on savoring it.

"Uh, Blake? I don't know what you're thinking about, but it can't be pleasant." Brenna's eyes reflected worry and maybe a touch of fear again.

Damn, it was bad enough she thought he was some kind of alien creature, without scaring her on top of it. He dragged his attention back to the present and picked up the bill. "Let's go. I don't want to keep Jarvis waiting."

She reached across the table to lay her hand over his. "Can't we talk first?"

"About what?" He didn't move, enjoying the warmth of her hand on his.

She waved her fork in the air. "I don't know, whatever people talk about. The weather? The last book you read?"

He glanced out the window. "It's hot outside."

Brenna rolled her eyes and sat back. "Well, so much for that subject. What have you been reading lately?"

He hesitated, not wanting her to read more into his answer than was necessary. "One of your books."

"Really?"

"Yes, I told you back in the hospital that I'd read all but the newest one. What's the matter? Do you think we're some kind of primitive life form that can't read?" He held out his hands. "We've got opposable thumbs and everything; with special training, we can even turn the pages for ourselves."

Brenna surprised him by laughing. "I wish you could see your face, Blake."

Rather than taking offense, he took pleasure in seeing her smile again. It felt damn good to see her enjoying herself, even if it was at his expense.

"Seriously, though, I'm just flattered that you'd buy my books and read them."

He shrugged. "I like the way you bring history down to how it affects an individual. Most of the time, we only see it from a distance."

Her eyes lit up with pleasure. "That's one of the nicest things anyone has ever said about my work. Some of my coworkers at the university sneer because I write for public consumption rather than for some dusty old scholarly magazine."

She took his hand in hers again, tracing the line of calluses built up from hours of hefting a sword. "I'll have to send you an advance readers' copy of the next one. It will be coming out in just over eight months.

His good mood plummeted. If his test results were to be believed, there was a damn good chance that he wouldn't be around in eight months. He pulled out his wallet and laid down enough money to cover the bill.

"Time to head out."

Brenna's smile faded. "Fine with me. Are we still going to stop on the way?"

"Yeah, I think we should." He glanced at the black cat clock on the diner wall, its tail swishing off the seconds. "I'd better give Jarvis a call and let him know that we'll be later than I thought."

"I'm going to stop in the ladies' room. I'll meet you at the car."

She walked away a little too quickly; he watched until she disappeared into the forbidden territory of the women's restroom. What was she going to do in there that had her glancing back at him so guiltily?

Hell, was she going to do something stupid like write a message to the police on the mirror with a lipstick? He tried to remember if he'd seen her wearing any but came up blank.

No, it was more likely she was going to make a phone call. But to whom? She hadn't mentioned any close friends since they'd been on the run. He made a mental note to find out more about her private life when things slowed down. Not that he wanted too many details; it would only make it harder to walk away when the time came. He didn't want to be able to picture her apartment or that college where she worked. Or worse yet, anyone she might be dating.

That thought had him walking toward the restroom, with no idea of what he was intending to do. The realization that he was overreacting brought him up short, and he veered off toward the front door. No matter who it was she called, the two of them would be safely underground in the tunnels before anyone could track them down.

She followed him outside only a moment or two later. He'd been expecting her to drag her feet, giving her mysterious white knight time to come charging to her rescue, but she climbed right into the car. When he started the ignition, though, she put her hand on his.

"We need to stop across the street."

He turned his head to see a Super Wal-Mart surrounded by swarms of arriving and departing customers. "Why?"

She looked away. "I need to pick up a prescription."

"You should have told me if you were in pain. We would have stopped yesterday and gotten you something."

"I'm not in pain." Her cheeks flushed pink.

"Then what?"

"I need my birth control pills." She glared at him as if daring him to say something.

But at that moment, he couldn't have strung together two coherent words. Good God—birth control hadn't even crossed his mind last night. How many time times had they . . . ? Not that it mattered; once without protection was enough. Twice was asking for it. And four or five times . . .

If he offered to also buy a box of condoms, would she think he was assuming that they'd pick up where they left off this morning? But if she'd missed several doses, she'd be at risk to get pregnant. As he waited for a break in traffic, he tried to decipher his reaction to the situation.

Shouldn't he be in a panic? The last thing either of them needed was for her to get pregnant by him. She'd been raised by a single parent, but her father had been an exceptional man. Blake didn't want Brenna struggling to juggle parenthood and her career without a husband there to help. An image filled his mind of a small boy with light gray eyes showing off an impressive tower of blocks to his proud mother. Then with a fiendish grin, he knocked them down, giggling at the noise and destruction.

"Blake, it's not that big a deal. Lots of women take birth control pills for medical reasons." She sounded disgusted now.

"Medical reasons?"

"Don't ask. I need the pills. Is that all right with you?" There was a little temper in her words.

She didn't want the pills because she was having trouble resisting his dubious charms. No, she just needed them. Disappointment was swift and bitter. That didn't mean he wouldn't pick up the condoms—just in case. It might be too late already, considering last night, but he wanted to be prepared.

Jamming his foot on the accelerator, they burned rubber across the street. He took the first spot he found and followed her into the store. She wasn't going to like it when he bought the economy-size box of condoms, but he'd learned years ago to always be prepared.

The Ozark countryside rolled past Brenna's window with beautiful tree-covered hills and sparkling rivers. This had always been one of her favorite places to take a leisurely drive. For her last book she'd spent hours roaming the area, tracing the paths of women who had come before her, raising their families in log cabins throughout the Ozarks.

With Trahern at the wheel, the drive was anything but leisurely. They flew past a mileage sign, warning her that the roadside park he'd mentioned was only a short distance away.

She was still trying to deal with that little episode at the store. Just as she was about to pay for her prescription, Blake had set a large box of condoms on the counter, leaving her no choice but to pay for both with the money he'd given her.

It really hadn't hit her until that moment that they'd been playing with fire, having unprotected sex. Even if she'd only missed a few days of her pills, they were at risk until her new prescription took effect. Her hand strayed to her stomach. She'd always wanted children but had planned to find a husband first, in the ordinary way.

Blake Trahern was anything but ordinary. He leaned more toward extraordinary. How would she explain to a child what he did for a living? *Honey, Daddy will be late tonight because he and his friends have to kill alien invaders.* She wanted to giggle, though there was nothing funny about the whole situation.

Blake slowed for the turn into the park and

then stopped. She reached for the envelope they'd tucked under her seat and held it out to him. He accepted it, his silver eyes looking grim.

"Don't you want to read it first?"

She did, but it wasn't addressed to her. "No, you go ahead."

He nodded and climbed out of the car and came around to her side to open her door for her. When he held out his hand, she accepted it without hesitation. No matter who or what he was, he was still the man who had held her in his arms and made her feel safe.

The small park, which offered a panoramic view of the rolling Ozarks to the west, was deserted. Trahern chose a picnic table at random, sat down on the top, and stared at the envelope in his hands, a strange expression on his face.

Rather than hover, she walked the short distance to the restroom to wash up a bit. The splash of cold water on her face felt good. She leaned across the sink to study her face in the mirror. She was tired, and it showed in the dark circles under her eyes. Even so, she felt better than she had two days ago. Too bad she couldn't borrow some of Blake's spooky ability to heal.

To give Trahern some privacy, she next walked over to read the small marker that explained the park had been built in memory of one of the founding families in the area. When her life got back to normal, their story might provide the seeds for another book. She loved delving into the past and finding a way to bring it back to life in the minds of her readers.

Blake walked up beside her. She shivered despite the heat, wanting to lean against his oak solid strength, but resisting the temptation.

"He asked me to give this to you." The legal-size envelope had her name on it in bold letters. "I'll share the rest of it with you when you're ready."

He started to walk away, but she reached out to him. As soon as he stopped, she dropped her hand away from his arm. She knew she was giving him mixed signals—wanting him close, not wanting his alien nature. Maybe it wasn't fair, but not much in her life was, right now. "Don't go too far."

He turned to watch the road, staying close by.

Her fingers shook as she opened the envelope. It hurt to know her father had been so sure of his potential death that he'd felt it necessary to write down his last thoughts to her. Unfolding the paper, she blinked her eyes clear of tears so that she could see the words.

Dear Brenna,

I'm sorry if you are reading this because it means that something has gone horribly wrong. There's always the potential danger from an irate defendant, but that goes with the territory of being a judge. I accepted the risks and trusted the law to protect the two of us.

What I never told you was that my love for the law caused me to take on another role, becoming a member of a secret group called the Regents. Although it is imperative that they operate under the radar of everyday, ordinary people, I will trust you with the truth.

Our world is in constant danger from invasion from another world. I know this sounds like some crazy sci-fi story, but I swear to you it is the truth. However, our world has also been blessed with a class of warriors, straight out of one those fantasy books you always loved, whose job is to fight unto the death to stop the Others in their tracks. Our old friend Blake Trahern is one of these amazing Paladins. I knew it from the first time he was dragged into my court.

If you are reading this, I am dead and you are with Blake. I would trust him with my life and, more important, I would trust him with yours. I am proud of the man he has become and want you to tell him so.

I love you, Brenna Marie. You have been the light of my life. I'm sorry I won't be there to walk you down the aisle or to hold my first grandchild. Think of me on those days, and know your old man wishes he was there beside you.

Again, trust Blake to keep you safe. I fear for both of you until he and his friends root out the corruption that threatens to bring down the Regents. If that were to happen, the whole world will suffer.

Love,
Dad

All the grief she'd been holding back finally came crashing down on her. As her heart shattered, tears blinded her, leaving her groping for something solid to hold onto. Then the world tilted—and she fell to the ground.

chapter 9

*B*lake caught Brenna's collapse from the corner of his eye. Son of a bitch! He barely managed to break her fall. He scooped her up in his arms, carried her to the nearest table, and settled her in his lap. At first she fought him, trying to break free, but he wasn't about to let her go.

Burying her face against his chest, she sobbed, her tears burning hot through his thin T-shirt. He wished like hell that he had the right words to comfort her, but all he could offer was the sanctuary of his arms for as long as she needed him to hold her.

The hurricane of her pain tore through them both. His own grief was as intense as hers, but he lacked the release of tears. It felt as if she was crying for the both of them, even if she was unaware of it. Judge Nichols had been Blake's personal savior. Without him, he would have died over and over in the streets years ago. The man had given Brenna life, but he'd given Blake hope: a much rarer gift in this world.

He was grateful that they were alone when the dam broke; anyone who stumbled across them would have been shocked by the intensity of Brenna's tears. But finally, slowly, she grew quieter, and he gently stroked her back, hoping it brought her some peace.

She mumbled against his chest that she was finished now, and he crooked a finger and gently lifted her chin. Her face was blotchy and her eyes swollen and red from her tears—he'd never seen anyone more beautiful in his life. With more gentleness than he'd known he possessed, he slowly lowered his lips to hers. She met him more than half way.

Their sweet kiss brought him the comfort he craved. He tucked her head down against his shoulder and rested his chin on her hair. Her hand found its way up to his face. He closed his eyes and enjoyed the soft caress before turning his face to kiss the palm of her hand.

"Thank you, Blake. I didn't mean to lose control like that."

"Don't sweat it. I'm surprised it didn't happen sooner." He gave her a quick squeeze to tell her he was glad to have been there when it hit.

She angled her head to see him better. "My father wanted me to tell you that he trusted you with his life and with me."

Her words stabbed right into his chest. He had put the man at risk, and it had cost the judge his life.

Evidently Brenna could read him better than anyone else. "No, Blake. This was not your fault. You didn't plant that bomb. If you hadn't alerted my father that something was wrong, someone else would have. And you know there was no way he would have kept his nose out of things."

He wasn't convinced, but her words helped ease his guilt. Another kiss was definitely in order, though if they kept that up, he might very well want to try out this picnic table. He doubted Brenna would be up for that, even if he was. Literally. The idea had him smiling.

"Blake Trahern, I do not trust that look." When his grin widened, she figured it out on her own. "No. No way." She sat up in his lap, which only made her more aware of his body's reaction. "I will not get naked with you out here in broad daylight."

Did that mean she would get naked when it got dark? He hoped so. He moved her beside him; the distance would help him concentrate on the matters at hand.

"We need to get going before Jarvis sends out the troops. I promised we'd be there by three at the latest."

"I'm ready." Then she realized that she'd dropped her father's letter. She scrambled off the table to retrieve it and handed it to him. "I think he meant for you to read this, too."

He quickly scanned the letter. At least the judge had told his daughter good-bye and that he'd loved her. She might not appreciate it now, but later she would draw some comfort from that little bit of closure. But if the man had suspected he was in danger, why in hell hadn't he called? He knew Blake would have come and brought along trust-worthy friends. Together, maybe they could have prevented this whole disaster.

There must have been no time.

He handed the letter back to Brenna. "He was a good man who took his oath seriously. The world is a poorer place without him."

"Thanks, Blake. That means a lot coming from you."

They returned to the car.

"What else was in the envelope?" she asked.

"A computer disk and some spreadsheets. He wrote a note that I could trust Jarvis, and should get his help deciphering the information on the disk and the printouts." There had also been a let-ter for him—one he wasn't ready to share with her and perhaps never would.

"Then we'd better get moving."

"Sounds like a plan." He turned the key in the ignition and left the small park in their dust.

• • •

Jarvis swore. If that damned Regent called or stopped by one more time, he was going to do something they'd both regret. But it might just be worth it, considering what a total prick the man was.

He hated Ritter's expensive haircut and hand-tailored suits. Even more, he hated the way Ritter sneered at his jeans and scuffed shoes. Screw him! The Regents paid the Paladins handsomely, but Jarvis didn't spend it on clothes. The bloodstains were too hard to get out.

His phone rang.

Checking his watch, he realized that it might be Trahern. He snatched up the receiver. "Jarvis."

He listened to what the guard at the entrance told him. "Would you repeat that?"

The second time didn't make him any happier. What the hell was Trahern thinking? Why couldn't he have stashed the Nichols woman at some local hotel? Obviously the idiot was thinking with the wrong part of his body. A blind man could see that Trahern had it bad for Brenna Nichols, even if he didn't want to admit it.

Still, nobody, but nobody, brought civilians into the Center. The place had security that rivaled the Pentagon, but leave it to Blake to do the unexpected.

"I'll come down myself."

He took his time, knowing he would draw more unwanted attention to the breach in security if he rushed down to the gate. He'd rip Trahern's head off when he got him and his unwanted companion back to his office.

The guard stood with his gun aimed squarely at Trahern's chest. Jarvis scowled in disgust. Only a head shot would have stopped Trahern from entering the compound if he wanted to. The only reason he'd held back was because that would have put Brenna Nichols at risk.

Trahern saw him before the guard did. "Can't say much for your hospitality, Jarvis."

The guard remained stationary, but his stance was more relaxed. "Sir, Blake Trahern has clearance to enter, but the woman does not. She claims to be Judge Nichols's daughter."

"That's exactly who she is, so you can stand down. I'll take responsibility for the two of them."

He waved them through the security arch, ignoring the warning alarm that Trahern was packing weapons. Every Paladin set the alarms off regularly.

"Glad to see you up and about, Ms. Nichols." He didn't miss the way she stayed close to Trahern; evidently Blake had convinced her to trust him. Lucky bastard.

"Follow me and we'll go to my office." He

quickly got them into an elevator, getting her out of sight before the nosy Regent found her, and pressed the codes that would take them deep into the Earth.

When the elevator settled on the lowest level with a gentle bump, he was the first out of the door. The gods were smiling on him, because the immediate area was empty.

"We're in the clear, so hustle."

Before they reached the end of the corridor, though, Trahern grabbed his arm and he angled his head to the side. Someone was coming down the hallway to the right. The three of them backed away, taking refuge in a weapons closet. Brenna looked horrified, although not surprised, at the sight of all those swords and axes. How much had Trahern told her?

When the two guards passed by without incident, the three all but ran the short distance to Jarvis's office. When the door shut behind them, he took a deep breath and let it out. They were safe for the moment.

"What's so damn important, Trahern, that you'd be crazy enough to bring her here? You know the rules. If anyone finds out what you've done, they'll slap you in chains and turn you over to the Handlers." He crossed his arms over his chest.

Trahern's eyes turned to silver ice. "The judge was killed by one of our own."

Jarvis glanced at Brenna. "And she knows who and what we are?"

"*She* can answer for herself." Brenna moved to stand beside Trahern. "I know what Blake's told me. And my father told me to trust him."

"What about me?"

"You, too." She nodded. "Despite the wild stories I've been hearing, it was my father's wish that I trust you two to find out who killed him."

Jarvis turned his attention back to Trahern. "I assume you've got some proof that one of our own is behind the attacks."

Trahern held out an envelope. "According to the judge, it's all in here. That's what got him killed. I figure it will kill us, too, if we aren't careful. Are you in or out?"

Jarvis didn't have to even think about it. "In." He took the package.

"We've got to go back in."

Detective Swan took a swallow from his over-size soft drink. They were parked in the alley behind the judge's house. "No matter what that Mr. Knight says, we have to at least act like this is a normal murder investigation. If we don't give the lieutenant something soon, he's gonna be riding our asses. He's under a lot of pressure from the top to get this case solved."

"Tell me something I don't know." Montgomery wadded up the last of his burrito in a napkin and tossed it back in the bag. He should have known better than to eat spicy, greasy food when he was this tense. He kept a bottle of antacids in the glove box, but if they didn't get a handle on this situation soon, he'd have worse than a case of heartburn.

"We've been through that damn house so many times, I feel like I live there." He leaned back against the headrest and closed his eyes. "We need to find that guy Brenna Nichols took off with, not to mention her. She knows more than she told us at the hospital."

Swan laughed. "We already know who killed the judge. Knight wouldn't be greasing our palms if he weren't the one who wired the bomb into the ignition of the judge's car. The real questions are why he did it and why this Trahern fellow is sniffing around."

Montgomery added, "And why Brenna Nichols took off like a scared rabbit. If she didn't have something to hide, she would have asked for police protection like anyone else would have."

Yeah, that was a definite puzzle. But the one Swan was interested in solving was the identity of Mr. Knight. If that was the man's real name, he'd eat his badge for breakfast. So far he hadn't been able to get the guy's prints, but the man had to slip up sometime. When he did, Montgomery would coerce his buddy in the lab to run the prints ahead of the pile of cases waiting.

"Let's run a check on Trahern's bank card again," he said. "The man can't be made of cash. At some point either he or the woman is going to have to hit an ATM or a bank. When they do, we'll know where to start looking."

Swan wolfed down the last of his tacos. "You check those. I'm going to call a few more rental agencies and see if I can come up with what kind of car he has now."

"Good idea."

He liked it when his young partner came up with an idea on his own. Swan might have the makings of a good detective yet, but Montgomery wouldn't be around to find out. Either he was going to retire with the money that Knight paid him, or he was going to dig a hole to hide in when Knight decided he and Swan were no longer of use.

"Let's head for the office."

The thought of seeing their commanding officer had Montgomery reaching for the antacids again. He was going to need another bottle soon.

Brenna looked cold. He should have thought to tell her to bring a jacket. Paladins didn't notice the constant chill of the tunnels, but humans didn't tolerate the low temperature as easily. He upped the thermostat in Jarvis's office a few degrees.

How much longer was Jarvis going to be gone? He was tired of pacing the room, while Brenna sat dozing in a chair. The bruises from the explosion were fading rapidly, but the dark circles under her eyes reminded him how much she'd been through the past few days. He reached out to run a lock of her hair through his fingers, wishing there was something more he could do for her.

He'd certainly played his part in turning her world upside down—both in bed and out. He'd carry the memories to his grave of how damn good she'd felt underneath him, panting his name as he pushed them both over the edge.

She'd made him feel warm and human again. If Jarvis hadn't been due to come back at any moment, he'd have given in to the temptation to kiss her awake and convince her to try out the top of Jarvis's desk. Would she find it a cut above a picnic table? Somehow he doubted it.

He frowned just as she shivered again, reminding him again how unsuited she was to his world. With a muttered curse, he stripped off his outer shirt and draped it over her.

Her eyes opened and she gave him a sleepy smile. "Thanks. Are you sure you don't need it?"

"If I did, I wouldn't have given it to you."

She frowned and then closed her eyes, shutting him out. He knew he was snapping at her, but this constant waiting was eating at him. Maybe he should have explained that Paladins quickly adapt to the ambient temperature, from severe cold to severe heat—but she already looked at him like a particularly interesting bug. The last thing he wanted to do was give her any more examples of how strange he was.

She snuggled down in the chair, wrapping his shirt closely around her. He thought she was going to drift to sleep, but she opened her eyes again. "How long will he be gone?"

"Wish I knew. If he doesn't come back soon, I'll go looking for him. He won't freak too much if I go wandering, but you'll have to wait here."

"Why was he so upset about me being with you?"

"I broke my vow of silence when I told you about the Paladins and Regents. In doing so, I outed Jarvis, too, without asking him if that was all right."

She sat up straighter. "What's the big deal about all this secrecy? You guys don't sound much different than any other special operations troops."

"They don't fight with swords, for one thing. Then there's the little matter of us being almost impossible to kill. And if we do die, we come back. When the Paladins were first organized into a fighting force against the Others, society had an unfortunate tendency to crucify anyone who was different. We went underground, both literally and figuratively, because that's where our battles were. The less anyone knew about us or the Others, the better."

Jarvis picked that minute to come back in. "Sorry I was gone so long."

"No problem. I was just giving Brenna a short lesson in the history of Paladins and why we keep a low profile."

Jarvis yanked out his chair and dropped into it, propping his feet up on his desk. "While you're at it, do you want me to print out a roster, so she can expose all of us at the same time?"

Brenna sat upright; righteous indignation making her ready to do battle. Although it would have been amusing to let her rip into his friend, there wasn't time for a debate.

"I had to tell her about us so that she'd know what we're up against. She's an intelligent person. Once she understands our situation, she'll protect our secret." He glanced over toward Brenna. "I trust her."

That pronouncement had Jarvis's boots hitting the floor and Brenna staring at him with her mouth open.

Finally, Jarvis shook his head as if to clear it. "Well, that being the case, let's go."

"Where to?"

"The tunnels."

He picked up a pad of paper and scribbled a message on it. Blake read it upside down from across the desk.

We think our computer server is being monitored. My boys have set up shop down in the caves where we can control who has access to our system. A couple of them have been working on the judge's disk and spreadsheets. We've also rigged my office to interfere with any unwanted ears. I can only run the equipment for short times to avoid arousing their suspicions.

"Okay, let's go."

Brenna slipped on his shirt and followed them to the door.

"Do caves bother you, Brenna?" Trahern asked. If she was claustrophobic, they definitely had problems.

"I don't know. I've never been in one."

Jarvis looked incredulous. "You grew up in the state that has about the most caves and caverns in one place in the world! How did you manage to avoid visiting Onondoga or the Meramec Caverns?"

She shrugged.

"Well, get ready, woman. You're about to see one of the best unknown wonders of the world."

Jarvis led them back to the elevator and keyed in his identification.

As the elevator slid farther into the depths of the Earth, Blake stood close to Brenna in case the depth of their destination bothered her. She leaned against the elevator wall and closed her eyes. It had already been a long day for them both, and it didn't seem likely to end anytime soon. He was used to going long periods of time without adequate rest, but for her sake, after Jarvis showed them what they'd gotten from the disk and spreadsheets, he would ask if there was room for them in the underground quarters.

They reached bottom with a soft *whoosh*. When the doors opened, Brenna stepped into the cavern, her eyes full of wonder. The barrier ran along the far wall; its shimmering light lit the caverns with a soft glow. Closing his eyes, Blake let the energy of the barrier thrum through him and soaked up some of its power. He knew the instant that Brenna spotted it. She latched onto his arm and pointed at the natural wonder as if he couldn't see it for himself.

"It's beautiful."

So was she, taking in all the amazing wonders in front of her.

"Can I touch it?"

"Only if you like playing with high voltage wires. It packs quite a punch, which is why the Others only cross if the barrier comes down."

"I wish I had a camera." Realizing what she'd just said, she made a sound of disgust. "I'm sorry; I didn't think."

She glanced at Jarvis. "Studying the history of people and their daily lives is what I do. Writing a history of the Regents and the Paladins is the sort of thing that we historians would give our right arm for."

Jarvis nodded, accepting both her apology and her explanation. Trahern could understand why the history of the Paladins would appeal to a scholar, and he thought about all those file cabinets of records stored below the Center in Seattle. Most women wanted sparkly jewelry or a night out on the town, but Brenna would prefer a week among the dusty old files. Like that was ever going to happen.

Jarvis led them through a labyrinth of tunnels, some narrowing and twisting, others wide open with wonderful views of the big cavern where the barrier pulsed and glowed. When they reached a bank of cubicles built in one of the lesser caverns, Trahern was reminded again how strange it looked to see high technology surrounded by the ancient rock.

A Paladin he didn't recognize sat hunched over a keyboard, his fingers a blur. Jarvis waited until the man sat back to let the computer do its thing before making introductions.

"Blake Trahern and Brenna Nichols, this is

John Doe. Oddly enough, everybody who works here is named John Doe. If we had time, we would love to do a statistical analysis of something like that happening." He grinned.

If the man was surprised to hear that his name had changed, he gave no sign of it. "I was sorry to hear about your father, Ms. Nichols. He was a good man."

"Thank you, Mr. Doe. That means a lot to me."

The Paladin turned back to the computer and let his fingers dance over the keys. They watched in silence for several minutes. Finally, Trahern had had enough.

"Jarvis, is there a place we could get some shut-eye? We've been on the road all day and last night wasn't exactly restful." Brenna's face flushed bright pink. Son of a bitch, he'd worded that wrong. "I got shot yesterday coming out of the Nichols's house. It wasn't bad, but it hurt like hell."

Jarvis frowned. "Do you need a Handler to take a look at it?"

"No, Brenna did some rough first aid, and she talked to Devlin Bane and Dr. Young. They told her what to do."

His friend looked suitably impressed. Studying Brenna with a thoughtful expression on his face, he told her, "You're holding up quite well, considering you've been shot at, kidnapped from the hospital, and trapped all night with a wounded Paladin. I know battle-trained guards who wouldn't have borne up under that kind of strain."

"Thank you . . . I think." She gave him a puzzled look, as if wondering if he were serious.

"And yes, Trahern, I can fix the two of you up with a room just down the hall. The accommodations aren't anything to brag about, but the sheets are clean and there's plenty of hot water." He reached for a telephone. "I'll have your bags brought down."

A single room. It probably had two beds, since the rooms were meant to house Paladins needing a break when the barrier acted up, but even that would be too close. How was he supposed to sleep, knowing she was only a few feet away? He closed his eyes and remembered again how it felt to have their bodies joined, and to hold her in his arms when passion left them both exhausted and exhilarated. His body reacted immediately and he shifted his position, trying to hide it.

Brenna turned her head to meet his gaze. Those eyes of hers saw way too much, because she immediately blushed again before turning away. But she didn't demand separate sleeping arrangements.

Jarvis hung up the phone and motioned them to follow him. "I wish I could offer something a little farther away from the barrier, but I don't think it will bother you much, Trahern. You're more acclimated to the one in Seattle now."

That was true, but he could still feel the soft hum of this one purring through his blood. The longer he was near it, the more he would feel its fluctuations and mood swings, unless he had something else to occupy his mind. He suppressed the urge to grin. Brenna wouldn't appreciate him bedding her just so he could ignore a throbbing wall of energy.

She'd given him a glimpse of paradise burning up the sheets with him, only to snatch it all away just because he'd healed overnight.

And now he was going to spend a long night, lying awake wanting her, when what he needed was some serious sleep.

He tapped the mysterious Mr. Doe on the shoulder. "If you find out anything worth knowing, wake me up no matter what time it is."

Mr. Doe looked past him to Jarvis before nodding. Trahern resented Jarvis outranking him, but Devlin Bane was the same way in Seattle. No one had cast a vote, electing them the leaders, but they'd both earned the respect of their fellow Paladins. Trahern would just have to live with the pecking order.

"I'll get you settled so I can get back to work." Jarvis led them into one of the side tunnels that branched off to the right.

The three of them walked in silence, Brenna still shivering despite Trahern's shirt. He'd put his arm around her for the warmth of his body, but he wasn't sure how she'd react. The last thing he wanted was for her to shove him away in front of Jarvis or the others. In private he'd put up with her hot and cold moods, but that was the limit of his patience.

Jarvis unlocked a door and tossed Trahern the keys. "As I said, it's nothing fancy, but it's safe. If you need me for anything, push zero on the phone by the bed and then tell them to page me. Since cell phones don't function worth crap this close to the barrier, the land line is your best bet."

"Thanks, Jarvis." Brenna entered the room, then stopped and looked back. "I've been meaning to ask, is Jarvis your first name or your last?"

"Yes." The arrogant bastard walked off down the hallway laughing.

Trahern followed Brenna and looked around. There weren't two beds. Only one—and it was a double. He glanced at the floor; limestone would be cold and miserably uncomfortable to sleep on. He'd had worse places to sleep. Maybe.

"They're quick with their service." Brenna pointed to her suitcase and his duffel in the corner.

"Probably anxious to get us under lock and key before anyone else finds out that we're here." He picked up his bag and set it on the heavy metal dresser on the far wall. "I'm going to call to get you another blanket. It's almost impossible to warm this place with that huge, open cavern out there."

"Okay, if you think we'll need it."

She closed the bathroom door behind her, leaving him wondering what she'd meant. Did she think one blanket each was enough, or that they'd both be warm because they'd be sharing the blankets and the bed?

He reached for the phone. "Can we get another set of blankets? Ms. Nichols doesn't handle the cold as well as we do."

There, let them think what they would. No one but him and Brenna would know their sleeping arrangements. Either he and the limestone would make a night of it, or he'd be curled up next to Brenna, breathing in her warmth and that sweet scent that was uniquely her. He wouldn't take anything for granted, but a man could always hope.

Brenna leaned over the sink to get a better look at her face. Her bruises were almost gone now. Even the cut on her arm was healing nicely. Her teeth were freshly brushed, and her hair smelled clean and hung in loose curls around her face.

Did she have the courage to walk back into the room and crawl into that bed with Trahern? She'd thought about making a bed on the stone floor, but rejected the idea. He'd rocked her world with his lovemaking, and she wanted to see if he could do it again.

Taking a deep breath, she stepped into the bedroom only to see Blake making himself a cozy little nest on the floor. Either he wasn't interested in sharing her bed, or he wasn't taking the chance that she'd refuse him. Well, they'd see about that.

"I'm done. Your turn."

He gave her an odd look at her cheery announcement, then gathered up his shaving kit and sleep sweats. As soon as she heard the shower turn on, she spread one of Trahern's blankets on the bed for extra warmth, then kicked the rest of his pallet under the bed.

That done, she turned off the ceiling light, leaving on only the dim bedside lamp. She'd need its shadows to hide her embarrassment as she tried to lure Trahern to her bed.

Before she could chicken out, the shower shut off. It was do or die time.

She turned back the covers and crawled between the cold sheets. Her nipples immediately budded up hard, making them ache worse for Trahern's big hands to warm them. Should she strip off the T-shirt and panties she'd put on after her shower? No, it would be bad enough if Trahern chose to sleep on the floor without the added humiliation of having to put her clothes back on again.

The bathroom door opened. Oh, Lord, what had she done?

chapter 10

*I*t didn't take Trahern long to notice his pallet was gone. His silver eyes immediately sought her out, seeing the pillow on the bed she'd placed beside her.

"If we share that bed, I won't stay on my side, Brenna."

"I know that." She wished he'd quit being so darned noble.

"I'm still a Paladin and everything that means. Nothing has changed."

Why didn't he just shut up and make love to her?

"I know that, too."

"Then take that T-shirt off."

Something in the gleam of his eyes warmed her heart and gave her courage. Blake Trahern, Paladin and warrior, wanted her as much as she wanted him. Damp heat pooled between her legs, and her breasts ached. Eventually he'd walk away, but right now that didn't matter.

She peeled the shirt over her head and tossed it on the floor. She couldn't wait for him to take her breasts in his hands and suckle them with that wonderful stern mouth of his. Just in case he wasn't getting the idea, she cupped her breasts and lifted them up, ready to demand his immediate attention.

His expression softened almost to a smile. "First take off your panties. I want nothing to be in my way."

The vision his words created had her squirming even as her panties joined the T-shirt on the floor. But two could play at this game. "Your turn."

He immediately stripped off his shirt and sweats, leaving him gloriously, beautifully naked. Her body wasn't the only one wanting more than hot looks and a striptease.

"Come here, Blake. Now." She held out her arms. "I feel empty."

He strode toward her, a warrior claiming his rightful prize for the night. When he pulled back the covers and climbed in, the blast of cold air was quickly replaced with the heat of his body.

"Tell me what you want, Brenna."

When she lifted her breasts again, he obediently placed a wickedly hot kiss right on her nipple. She reached for his hand to replace hers, and he smiled as he gently squeezed. Closing her eyes, she moaned with pleasure as he rubbed his whiskery skin against her tender flesh.

He stopped. "I should have shaved."

Brenna ran her fingers along his cheek. "I like how it feels. Now kiss me."

"Yes, ma'am."

He sprawled on top of her, pinning her head down on the pillow as he complied with her order. His tongue demanded entry, telling her that she may have begun this dance, but he was going to lead. She licked her lips, inviting him in, while parting her legs to nestle him against the very heart of her.

It felt so good to have him in her arms again, feeling his powerful strength. As their tongues tangled and mated, he reached down to lift her legs high against his hips. She locked her ankles across the upper curve of his backside, wanting him to take her hard and fast.

The rumble of his laughter rolled through her. "In a bit of a hurry, are we?"

"I *want* you, Blake." Did he understand that she meant more than just sex? She hoped so.

With two hard thrusts, he was deep inside her. For the first time all day, she felt warm enough. Then he rolled over, taking her with him. When she raised herself up, he pushed up even more deeply inside of her, making her feel stretched and full.

His hands cupped her breasts and squeezed as she rocked forward. He suckled each one in turn, driving her crazy. She repaid him by rocking up and down quickly, squeezing him with her inner muscles. He moaned. She smiled and did it again.

His eyes glittered up at her, warning her that retribution would be swift and pleasurable. After a few more up and down slides, she was suddenly on her back, her legs on his shoulders as he kissed his way down her belly to the empty ache between her legs.

His hot breath sent chills through her as he tongued her slick folds, fanning the flames of her needs, his pursuit of her pleasure relentless. But she didn't want to reach her climax without him.

"Please, I need you back inside me." She turned over and pushed herself up on her knees, offering herself to him in the most primitive position she knew.

"Lord, woman, you make me crazy." He slid his hand between her legs, stroking her and slipping a finger deep inside her. She buried her face in the pillow, overwhelmed with sensations.

"Brenna." Her name sounded like a prayer as he moved against her slowly, letting her adjust to the new position. Holding on to her hips, he thrust faster and more deeply, reaching for that ultimate joy that only his body brought to hers.

As the universe shattered, they both cried out

in release and then collapsed. When sanity slowly returned, Blake pulled her into his arms for a sweet and gentle kiss.

Then he turned off the bedside light and curled around her, an unspoken promise to hold the darkness at bay.

He'd been awake for almost an hour, but he was in no hurry to leave the warmth of the bed. He loved feeling the curve of Brenna's backside snuggled up against him.

She stirred and stretched. "Good morning."

"Yeah, it is." He planted a kiss on her cheek as he ran a hand down her back, tracing the curve of her hip. "How'd you sleep?"

She turned to face him and smiled. "Just fine."

He wrapped his arm around her waist and pulled her against him, letting her feel how fine he felt himself. Sliding her hand down between them, she admired the length and breadth of his desire with her fingers.

Pure physical pleasure burned through him as he claimed her lips with his own. He'd love to finish what they'd started, but she had to be a bit sore from their activities during the night. It took all the strength he could muster to break off the kiss. He tugged her hand back up and away from temptation.

"How about I find us some breakfast?"

"Sounds good."

He sat up and reached for the phone. While he waited for someone to answer, Brenna rose to her knees and leaned against his back. Jarvis answered just as she started nibbling on Blake's ear.

"Stop that!"

"Stop what? I haven't done anything." Jarvis's voice held a hint of laughter.

Blake caught Brenna's wandering hand and held on tight. "I was wondering where we could get a meal around here."

"Come back to the main cavern and take the elevator up to the second level. Any of the John Does can point you in the right direction."

"Thanks."

"If you hurry, you can eat and still make the morning workout."

"Sounds like fun. I'll be there."

He hung up the phone, then captured Brenna's hands in his own. "Listen, wench, I have to save my strength to show Jarvis which of us is the better swordsman."

"I could tell him how good you are," Brenna said with a sultry laugh, eyeing a certain part of Trahern's anatomy. "After all, I have first hand knowledge about your ability with a sword."

"Yeah, but then he'd want to prove you wrong, and I'd have to hurt him." He tugged her off the bed. "Let's get dressed. I seemed to have worked up quite an appetite."

That set her giggling. "So have I. Are you sure we can't send for room service?"

"Somehow I can't imagine Jarvis wearing a waiter's uniform and holding his hand out for a tip."

Brenna started pulling clothes out of her suitcase. "Can I come watch the two of you?"

Trahern pulled his T-shirt on over his head. He wasn't sure Brenna was ready to see the Paladins ply their craft, even if they were just practicing. "I'll have to ask Jarvis. He might prefer it if we kept you out of sight."

He watched as she pulled on the shirt he'd loaned her the day before, liking how she looked with his shirt on. She might want to keep it permanently, but he wanted it himself because it would carry her scent. He'd cherish that small reminder of her when he returned to Seattle.

"Ready?"

"Sure thing."

"As long as she stays out of the way, I don't see why she can't watch."

Brenna gave Jarvis a bright smile. "Just stick me in the corner. You'll hardly know that I'm there."

Jarvis arched an eyebrow. "Honey, you're the

only woman in the whole complex. You'll be noticed."

He opened a door to reveal a large gym. Men were already scattered around the room, most either stretching their leg muscles or going through a series of graceful moves. They were all over six feet tall and in prime condition, yet in her opinion, Jarvis and Trahern stood out in the crowd. She'd never seen so much eye candy in one place!

She settled herself on a stack of gym mats and leaned against the wall to watch. Over the next few minutes more men, all Paladins she assumed, walked in. At Jarvis's command, they chose weapons from a rack of swords.

Trahern stripped off his shirt and tossed it to her. She watched as he picked up a sword, then checked its grip and the blade. He returned it to the rack and chose another, swinging the second blade several times before he was satisfied. She couldn't tear her eyes away from the flex and play of his muscles as he swung the sword. Even if she didn't know what he did for a living, she would have recognized him as a warrior. When he glanced in her direction, she blushed, knowing she'd been caught staring.

He winked at her on his way to join Jarvis. The two men held up their weapons in a mock salute, then proceeded to dazzle her with a display of grace and power as they sought to get the best of one another. They seemed an even match, first one and then the other gaining the upper hand.

She soon realized that the rest of the men had ceased their workouts to watch Jarvis and Trahern, too. From the grins on their faces, they were enjoying the show as much as she was. Both men were dripping sweat, and their fierce expressions and determination to dominate held everyone riveted.

Their fighting styles differed greatly. Jarvis was quick and moved with a dancer's grace, while Trahern used his size and strength more. Finally, at some invisible signal between them, they stopped and backed away from each other.

Jarvis held his hand out to Trahern. "Damn, man, you've improved with age."

"Yeah, well, you still move pretty good for an old man."

When some of the other Paladins laughed, Jarvis turned on them. "Any of you want to see what this old man can do?"

Most of them held up their hands and backed away, but a few held their ground.

Jarvis nodded. "Trahern, you want to help me whip this bunch into shape?"

"Sounds like fun." He moved up to stand with his friend. "How many shall we take on at a time? We don't have all day."

"You're right. How about all of them at once?"

Then the fight was on, with Blake and Jarvis standing back to back and taking on all comers. Brenna watched with her heart in her throat, mesmerized by the beauty of what they did, yet terrified that someone would slip and draw blood.

Trahern and Jarvis gradually whittled down their opponents until only the last four remained. She would have thought both men would be showing signs of exhaustion by now, but Trahern actually picked up speed, forcing the two men he faced to back down and surrender. Jarvis accepted that as the challenge it was and quickly vanquished his remaining foes, as well.

The entire room erupted in a round of applause for the victors. Jarvis and Trahern both grinned and handed their swords off to the nearest Paladins.

"Damn, I've missed that." Jarvis slapped Trahern on the shoulder. "You might not be much on style, boy, but nobody can beat you for strength or sheer cussedness."

Trahern sneered at his friend. "Watch who you're calling boy, old man. But much as I hate to admit it, between you and Devlin, I've learned from the best."

Brenna didn't have adequate words to describe what she'd just witnessed. She'd watched enough sports to know what a well-trained athlete was capable of, but nothing compared to the beauty and deadly grace of these men with their weapons.

And her lover was the best of the bunch. As she handed Blake his shirt, she didn't quite know what to make of that.

"You're not sleeping." Brenna raised her head up to look at him. "Is something wrong?"

"It's the barrier. I can feel it." He turned onto his back and crossed his arms under his head. "The longer I'm here, the more sensitive to it I become."

She traced a lazy circle on his chest with her fingertip. "Is it a good feeling?"

"More like a vibration that feels either right or wrong. Like a melody that falls into discord for a few notes. It jars rather than soothes."

"What does it sound like when it goes down completely?"

"Like a scream for help. When that happens, every Paladin in the area grabs a sword and runs for the barrier. Some of us have an ability to help reestablish it. The rest of us hold back the invasion."

She shivered. "Why do they try to invade, since they know you'll be waiting for them?"

"A good question; one that we've never found a satisfactory answer for. When most of the Others come across, they're almost mad with battle fever. They'll charge against overwhelming odds. We try damn hard to keep that kind from making it to the surface, because they'll kill anything that moves."

"And the rest?"

"Lately, some evidently thought they were buying their way across, using some kind of blue stones that don't exist in our world. We either force them back or kill them."

"And the few that do make it to the surface. What happens to them?" Her eyes were huge in her face.

"If they're crazy, eventually we find them. The others disappear into the general population and make a life for themselves."

Her hand on his chest stilled. "They've inbred with humans, haven't they?"

"Yeah, near as we can figure."

"Are their children different in significant ways from normal human children?" She snuggled closer. "Is there any way to pick them out?"

He didn't want to answer, but he wouldn't lie to her. "Not on the outside."

"But on the inside?"

Staring up at the ceiling, he captured her hand with his and kissed her palm. "They have some special abilities. One is recovering from mortal wounds."

It didn't take her long to connect the dots.

"The mix of their genes with human produced Paladins."

"Yeah, lucky us."

She snuggled closer. "So, tell me if I'm right about this. Their gift to your genetic makeup lets you come back from wounds that normal humans can't, but only for so long. After that, something changes."

He told her the brutal truth. "We become like the worst kind of Other, ready to kill anything that moves. That's why when we're injured or killed, they strap us down on steel tables with heavy duty chains. Depending on how we do when we wake up, they either feed us or kill us. Nothing in between."

He half expected her to move away. Instead, she moved her body over his to sprawl over his chest. Then she kissed him on the mouth softly, until she teased his lips apart and her tongue darted in to find his. The kiss was long and wet and the sweetest gift anyone had ever given him.

He wrapped his arms around his woman and held her as close to his heart as he could get. For the first time in his life, he faced the shadows that made up his world without feeling alone.

Deep in this cavern, it was impossible to gauge how long she and Blake had been asleep. Brenna shifted slightly, feeling a bit stiff and sore. That shouldn't surprise her; she and Trahern had given each other a good workout last night. She hadn't been a total innocent before, but she'd never had a lover who came close to the way Trahern made her feel.

"What are you smiling about?" Blake's voice rumbled through his chest where her head lay.

"How do you know I'm smiling?" Without a window, the room stayed dark unless one of them turned on a light.

"I can feel it." He lifted her chin to plant a kiss on her mouth.

"I'm smiling because of you and—well, all of this."

He rolled onto his side, hooking his leg over hers. "So you like this, do you?"

She punched him lightly on the arm. "You don't strike me as a man who needs to go fishing for compliments. You must have women howling at your door."

"There haven't been all that many. Paladins aren't generally the marrying kind, so women tend to shy away from us. Any woman can do a hell of a lot better than someone who kills for a living."

Tears filled Brenna's eyes as she thought of generations of Paladins, living to fight with no love or compassion in their lives to compensate. It broke her heart to know how that must feel. If it were up to her, Blake would never forget that the woman in his bed cared about him.

She was about to give him a very specific demonstration of that when a klaxon went off outside the door, loud enough to wake the dead. Blake all but shoved her aside as he lurched out of bed, kicking his feet free of the blankets. He felt his way to the door and flipped on the overhead light. Brenna sat up, blinking against the sudden brightness. "What's going on, Blake?" She tried not to feel hurt about his rough treatment.

"The barrier. It's down." He was already jerking on his jeans and shirt. "They don't sound the alarm unless it's bad. I'll be back when I can."

He might be in the room still, but she knew he was already gone. This was what he'd been trying to tell her. As long as the barrier was in jeopardy, he had to fight.

He opened a small closet in the corner and hefted a sword, checking its balance. How convenient: loaner blades. He tried two more before closing the door, then he left without a backward look.

The horn outside kept blaring; what should she be doing? Certainly not huddling under the covers. Throwing back the blankets, she walked across the floor and headed into the bathroom. She turned on the shower to heat up while she brushed her teeth.

The chill of the room kept her moving at a brisk

pace as she showered, dried off, and dressed. She ran a quick brush through her hair after toweling it as dry as possible.

But now that she was dressed, there was nothing left for her to do but make the bed and straighten out her suitcase. She hesitated before doing the same for Blake, wondering if rifling through his duffle was a bit too personal. Then she laughed at herself. She knew the man well enough to have hot sex with him all night, but not well enough to fold his shorts without asking first?

But then their current situation was only temporary. Sure they enjoyed sharing some hot sex between the sheets, but Trahern had been clear that they weren't going to spend the rest of their lives together. If she was going to protect her heart, she needed to set some limits.

The klaxon shut off; the sudden silence almost as much of a blow as the loud horn had been. Once the ringing in her ears stopped, she could hear other sounds all too clearly, sounds that had her nerves shrieking and her stomach roiling. There was no mistaking the clang of steel against steel out in the cavern and the screams of pain as someone went down, bleeding and perhaps dying.

Trahern had said the Paladins would all likely survive an attack, but she wasn't convinced. Healing quickly was one thing; resurrecting the dead something else entirely. The noise grew louder, then just as quickly faded into the distance. Their room was only a short distance up a tunnel that led to the main cavern; there was no telling how close the fighting had come.

She took a deep breath and slowly turned the doorknob to take a quick peek. Her senses were immediately assaulted by the noise and smell of battle. The sickly, acrid scent of blood—and lots of it—carried through the air. The smell made her want to shut the door and hide, but a man was moaning in pain close by.

Blake would probably be seriously angry with her for leaving the dubious safety of their room, but she had to know if she could help. The immediate hallway was empty. She all but ran toward the cavern, knowing she was risking far more than a long lecture from Blake or Jarvis. As she neared the end of the tunnel, the noise grew louder as swords clanged and men yelled in two languages. One she recognized as her own; the other was more guttural and hard on the ears.

She edged forward until she ran out of wall. One look out into the cavern, and she knew she would never be quite the same again. Due to television, no one was ignorant of the horrors of war, but that was only a pale shadow of what it was like firsthand. It seemed like a scene straight from hell, all chaos and cacophony.

The Others were easy to spot since they were

dressed in black and gray, which matched the uniformly dark color of their hair. Their skin was almost unnaturally pale, standing out in stark contrast.

The Paladins wore mostly jeans and shirts; a few were in sweats, and one was bare-chested and wearing flannel pajama bottoms. The fighting seemed to ebb and flow, with first the Others gaining ground, then dancing back as the Paladins relentlessly pushed them toward the barrier.

There were bodies on the floor, a few Paladins, but far more Others lying contorted in pain or death. She frantically searched the cavern for Trahern Finally, she spotted him standing back-to-back with Jarvis. Each of them swung a broadsword in huge arcs, keeping a circle of determined Others at bay. Several of their brethren had already fallen before the Paladins' blades, but still they came.

Yesterday she had watched them do this in practice; now it made her sick and afraid. Though Blake had been telling her the truth all along, nothing he'd said had prepared her for the horror of it all.

She wanted to scream, but fought it back. The last thing the battling men needed was the distraction of a hysterical woman. What could she do to help? She might be crazy for even wanting to try, but only someone totally heartless wouldn't want to ease the suffering before her.

She finally spotted a badly wounded Paladin only a few feet away, crawling in her direction, leaving a trail of blood behind him. For the moment, the fighting had moved in the other direction. Without giving herself time for second thoughts, she charged out into the cavern and grabbed the man by the arm to drag him to safety.

"If I help, can you stand?"

He nodded, grimacing in pain. It took them a couple of tries, but finally he was on his feet and leaning far too much of his weight on her shoulders. Together they managed to walk the short distance to the tunnel, and when they were out of sight of the cavern, she eased the wounded Paladin onto the floor.

"I'll be right back."

She ran to her room and scooped up the rest of the clean towels. She found a first aid kit in the weapon closet, and grabbed her leftover medical supplies before running back to her patient.

He was where she'd left him, his face dripping with sweat despite the chill in the air. She knelt beside him and opened the kit. The supplies inside seemed hopelessly inadequate for the open slash wounds on his arm and leg: the leg of his jeans was already soaked in blood, as was his shirt.

"I'm going to cut away your jeans."

He bit his lower lip and nodded.

She used bandage scissors to uncover the large

gash in his upper thigh. The ragged slash had laid his leg open to the bone. He had to be in agony, but he only moaned as she picked out the threads of denim stuck to the wound and cleaned it as best she could. Then she applied clean gauze and wrapped the leg with surgical tape to hold the bandage in place.

By comparison, the wounds on his arm seemed minor. She focused on stopping the blood that kept welling up from the cuts, and it gradually slowed as she got them bandaged. To her amazement, as soon as she got the last bit of tape in place, her patient pushed himself up off the floor.

"What are you doing?" She couldn't believe he could move, much less stand.

He nodded toward the cavern. "It's not over yet. Thank you, whoever you are." After planting a quick kiss on her cheek, he was gone.

She stared after him as he limped away, leaving her with a pile of bloody towels and the scattered remains of the first aid kit. What should she do next? Wait until the next bloody Paladin came within reach? What good did it do to patch them up if they were just going to dive right back into the thick of things? No doubt it was a question that people like Dr. Young had been asking themselves for years. Brenna gathered the mess in the hallway and retreated to their room.

Witnessing the battle, even for such a brief

time, was a huge piece of the puzzle that Trahern had been trying to help her understand. Paladins healed quickly. Paladins fought Others. Paladins weren't completely human. They lived solitary lives near fault lines and volcanoes, keeping the battles they fought hidden from the rest of humanity. The list went on and on.

He was proud of what he'd become, and understandably so. On another level, though, deep down inside him, he was convinced that he was losing his hold on his humanity. But no man treated a woman the way he had treated her, both in bed and out, without having pretty strong feelings for her. And if he cared about her, then there was hope for him. She refused to believe otherwise.

Sitting on the edge of the bed, she did what women had been doing for an eternity: she waited for her man to come back from the war.

chapter 11

*T*rahern surrendered his sword to the armorer. "Sorry about the condition of the edge; I blocked a couple of blows from a battle ax with it."

The resident weapons man ran his hand along the blade. "It did its job; that's all that matters. I'll restore it tomorrow."

"Thanks for the loan. I left mine in Seattle."

"No problem. From what I hear, they were damn glad to have you swinging it out there today." The man turned to put the sword away. "And I know at least one of the guys is grateful to that woman of yours."

The temperature in the room dropped ten degrees. "Really? How's that?"

Something in his tone—or maybe it was the way his hands clenched into fists—warned the armorer that he'd unwittingly blundered into dangerous territory. He backed away from the counter and closer to the sword behind him.

"Seems she found him bleeding on the cavern floor and pulled him into one of the tunnels to patch up his leg and arm. She did a bang-up job because he returned to the fight. Last I heard, the Handlers were fussing over him, but he's going to heal without having to die first, thanks to her."

"I'll pass along the good news to her."

Trahern forced his hands to relax, despite the sick fear in his gut. What in the hell was Brenna doing out in the cavern? The woman must be crazy, because he knew she wasn't stupid. What if she'd been the one to catch a sword blade across her leg or arm? She could have bled to death before he'd even known she was hurt.

He'd planned to stop in the showers and clean up before returning to their room, but to hell with that now. If she'd seen the battle, it wouldn't come as a surprise to her that he was covered in blood.

Battle always left him testy and buzzed, and he had planned to leave Brenna alone for the rest of the night since he felt like a ticking bomb. But if she couldn't be trusted to stay put, she was a danger to herself and to others if the barrier went down again.

He left the armorer, anger and adrenaline sizzling inside. Cleanup in the cavern was already under way, with the Guard standing watch as the dead and wounded Paladins were turned over to the Handlers. The bodies of the Others were already gone. He'd never asked what was done with them and didn't care.

When he reached their room, he didn't bother knocking.

Inside, Brenna sat on the edge of the bed, her hands folded in her lap. Judging by the pallor of her skin, her brief skirmish with his reality had left her badly shaken.

Good. She *should* be scared.

He walked straight into the bathroom to take a badly needed shower. At that moment, he didn't trust himself not to hurt her—not intentionally, but because battle fever still bubbled through his bloodstream.

Before the door shut completely, Brenna forced her way into the room.

"Don't." It was as much warning as he could muster.

"Shut up, Blake. By now you should know I don't respond well to orders."

She lifted his T-shirt, torn and splattered with blood. Her expressive face showed no fear, only concern for his new bruises and a couple of shallow cuts. Her hands felt so damn gentle as they checked him for further injury, their touch a healing balm to more than just his wounds. He closed his eyes. Already he could feel the battle fever fading away, to be replaced by something that burned just as hot from a different source altogether.

He caught her wrist to stop any further explorations before he lost control. "I need a shower."

She gave him one of her temptress smiles. "Do you need someone to wash your back?"

His good intentions died a fast death. He still planned on giving her hell for risking her life, but that could wait until later. Right now, she'd be lucky if he didn't take her against the wall with no finesse or foreplay.

"I'm not in the mood to be gentle." He released her wrist, giving her one last chance to back away.

She didn't hesitate. Raising up on her toes, she wrapped her hands around his neck and pulled him down to meet her halfway for a hungry, hot kiss. Their tongues dueled for supremacy, but it didn't matter which one dominated. Both burned with a fire that only one thing would quench.

He stepped back long enough to undo the front of her jeans and slid his hand deep inside. Damn if she wasn't already damp, all the invitation he needed. He yanked her jeans and panties down to the floor; Brenna smiled and kicked them free, spreading her legs in invitation. He knelt down to lift her leg over his shoulder. He smiled at the hungry expression on her face as she dug her fingers into his shoulders, waiting for him to do more.

"Please, Blake!"

He leaned closer to the curls at the juncture of her legs and kissed the inside of her thigh. Using the lightest touch he could manage, he slowly stroked his fingertips up her leg, stopping just above her knee.

Brenna tangled her fingers in his hair and forced him to look up. "I never thought you were a tease."

"Honey, I'm a lot of things you don't know about." He trailed his fingers up the back of her thighs to cup her bottom and squeezed, bringing her tender folds closer. As Brenna trembled, he tongued her gently, but she was poised right at the brink of climaxing, so he backed away, much to her audible frustration.

He rose to his feet and tugged her hands down to the buttons of his fly.

As she teased and rubbed the front of his pants, he pulled her against his chest to nibble the warm pulse at the base of her throat. She worked the buttons open, one by one, until at last he was free. She cooed with delight as she cupped him and caressed his hard length. If he let her continue, everything would be over long before he'd run out of ideas of how to torment her.

Tugging her hands away from his body, he lifted her against the cool tile of the bathroom wall. With a single thrust, he melded his body to hers. He pistoned inside of her, driving them both beyond the limits of sanity. His breath was ragged as he burned off the last of his adrenaline, loving the way she panted and clung to him, digging her nails into his shoulders.

Before he lost complete control, he withdrew from her body. She clearly wasn't happy when he set her down, but he'd led her out to the bed in the other room.

"Sit down."

For once, she did as he wanted without arguing. Kneeling between her feet, he stripped off her shirt. He loved the curve of her breasts peeking over the edge of her bra and showed his appreciation with quick little kisses. Once again, it wasn't enough for his demanding lover. With a flick of his fingers, he undid the front clasp of the bra and it joined her shirt on the floor.

She tugged his mouth down to suckle her breasts. He knew he should be more gentle on her delicate skin with his callused hands, but judging by the little sounds she was making deep in her throat, she didn't mind in the least.

"Lie back, Brenna." Once again, he lifted her legs onto his shoulders, spreading them wide. "You are so beautiful."

She knew he was exaggerating, but she was too overwhelmed by the way he was pleasuring her to argue. This time the touch of his tongue was harder, more demanding, as he breathed his heat right at the center of the inferno he was building inside her. He combined his kisses with sliding his fingers deep inside her. Better, but still not what she wanted. Her body needed more, much more, to fill her up inside.

He picked that moment to run his tongue over her sensitive nub in the same rhythm as he stroked his fingers. Her body tightened, waiting for that one final touch that would send her flying . . . But once again he stopped just before that happened.

"Blake Trahern!"

He laughed, sounding all too male and satisfied with himself. Just to further frustrate her, he took his own sweet time in putting on a condom. Then, with a predator's smile, he crawled up her body, taking time to plant hot, wet kisses on her nipples before nibbling his way up to her mouth. He poised right at the entrance of her body. She thrust her hips up, encouraging him to take her. He kissed her on the tip of her nose and finally, with several sharp thrusts, buried himself in her body.

He slowly pulled almost all the way out, leaving her feeling bereft. When he plunged in again and again, pleasure streaked straight through her. She chanted his name like a mantra, his thrusts picking up speed as he pounded his pleasure into her. Then she captured his mouth again, her kiss matching the rhythm of his thrusts.

Her legs locked around his waist as he rode her

hard, until finally he slipped a hand between them to rub his fingertips over the center of her need. She threw her head back and keened her joyous satisfaction. The sweet sound drove him over the edge, and his body poured out his release.

It took a while for the world to right itself. He loved the feel of Brenna laying limp in his arms, their bodies still joined.

Unexpectedly, she giggled. "I guess that answers the question of whether you're all right."

He laughed loud and long. When he caught his breath, he told her, "I can't remember ever being more all right. Damn, woman, you sure know how to make a man feel welcome."

He planted a final kiss on her mouth before gently withdrawing from her body. "I still need that shower."

"I'll join you."

He wasn't about to argue. There was a world of possibilities involving hot water and soap-slicked skin.

Cocooned in the warmth of the bed, Trahern took a deep breath. "You shouldn't have come out of the room until you knew it was safe."

She'd been expecting this lecture ever since Blake had returned, looking grim and cold to the soul. Though he was right, she didn't regret the frightening glimpse into the hell he lived with on a daily basis. How could anyone live, knowing his life would be full of battles and pain?

"I can't promise I won't do it again." She looked him in the eye. "And I won't have you trying to protect me from the parts of your life you think I can't handle." She poked him in the chest to emphasize her point.

He sighed. "Brenna, the Paladins' secrets have been safe from the outside world for generations. If we were to start broadcasting our existence, there's no telling what would happen. At the very least, the military would want to get their hands on us. We can't afford to be defending ourselves on another front. There are few enough of us as it is."

"Fine," she snapped, then scooted as far away as the bed would allow. How dare he lump her in with everyone else? "Keep your secrets from the outside world. But, considering everything we've been through in the last few days, I hardly consider myself to be part of that group."

He immediately wrapped his arms around her and pulled her back against him, spoon style. "Damn it, Brenna, don't twist my words around. I was just trying to say that I'm not used to sharing myself with anyone. Men who have served with me for years don't know me as well as you do."

That admission went a long way toward assuaging her anger. "I'm not asking for more than you can give, Blake, but knowing the truth is what enables me to cope. You don't have to hide who and what you are from me. Even when you leave, your secrets will be safe with me."

The shrill ring of the phone prevented any more conversation. Blake reached over her to pick up the receiver. "Trahern here."

Judging by the sudden tension in his body, it wasn't anybody he was glad to hear from. A few seconds later he slammed the phone down and rolled away from her. The chill in the room had nothing to do with the limestone cavern that surrounded them.

"Blake?" She put her hand on his bare shoulder.

His only answer was a heavy silence, but at least he didn't try to shake off her touch.

"I can't help if I don't know."

She moved closer, draping her arm over his chest and sharing her warmth with him. Slowly, some of his tension drained away. After a bit, he finally spoke.

"Jarvis said Mr. Doe has made progress on your father's disk and spreadsheets."

That was good news, wasn't it? So there had to be more. She settled in to wait him out. Finally, she gave up and prompted him to speak. "And?"

Trahern lunged to his feet. "And I have to go take a bunch of fucking damn tests!"

"Tests? Why?" She held her breath, not sure how to help when he was like this.

He took a long breath and then another one. "There was an incident back in Seattle, involving a Paladin from outside the region."

"What happened to him?" she asked.

"He turned Other with no warning at all and had to be put down." Trahern's eyes held the chill of a winter sky.

She focused on Trahern. "What's that got to do with you?"

In a burst of anger, he kicked his duffle across the room. "Because of him, every time I fight, I have to report to the nearest Handler and let them run tests."

"What kind of tests?"

He started pacing. "The kind, little girl, where they decide whether I'm still human enough to live or if I must die. Right then, right there, no quarter given."

Sympathy wouldn't help him. Temper might. She left the bed to confront her angry, hurting Paladin. "So what are you worried about?"

Stunned didn't do the look on his face justice. He stared at her as if she'd just grown a second head. "I just told you what happened to that Paladin in Seattle!"

"I'm sorry he died, but he's not you." Right now she was more worried about the man in front of her. She hadn't thought that anything frightened Blake Trahern, but obviously the tests did.

"Died is such a nice, sanitary way to put it." He glowered down at her. "They held him down, kicking and screaming, as they shoved in a needle of toxins to kill him permanently, the same way they would any other dangerous animal. Laurel Young was the one wielding the needle. It almost destroyed her, too."

He ran his fingers through his hair. "Now, fool that she is, Laurel spends most of her waking hours trying to find ways to hold off the changes that are part of our basic nature. Because one of these days, it just might be her lover who gets the needle."

He walked into the bathroom and slammed the door.

She noticed he didn't lock it. For the moment, she'd allow him some privacy, but if he didn't come out soon, she'd go in after him.

So Laurel Young's work was the only thing standing between him and that needle he was so afraid of. As well as Brenna herself. She would fight tooth and nail to protect her man, just as Laurel Young was doing. She might not have the medical knowledge that his Handler had, but they did have one thing in common: both of them cared too deeply about the Paladins to want them to suffer.

And it was time to show Blake Trahern that she

meant to fight for him. She knocked, and when he didn't answer, she pounded louder.

"Blake Trahern, I need to get dressed, so quit hogging the bathroom. We've got to get through those tests so we can find out who killed my father. You can't do that hiding in there."

The door swung open. Blake clearly hadn't appreciated her last remark. Too bad.

Brushing past him, she reached for her toothbrush. "So what do you say we get the tests over with? Then we can concentrate on the important stuff."

"So your father's death is more important than mine?" His voice was as glacial as the silvery cold gray of his eyes.

She looked him over from top to toe and back again, letting her eyes linger in certain spots along the way.

"You're talking to the wrong woman if you want sympathy. I can personally testify that you are very much alive. If you'd been any more alive in that bed, I'm not sure I would have survived the experience." Then she gave him a gentle shove. "Now go get dressed and give me some privacy. While you're at it, make up your mind: tests or talking to Mr. Doe first."

She shut the door behind him, hoping that she'd gotten through to him. Blake would pass their damn tests with flying colors. They'd have a major fight on their hands if they thought they could get anywhere near him with that awful needle. She might be sleeping with the big oaf, but that didn't mean she was blind to his faults. He was hardheaded, bossy, egotistical . . . and so very sweet when she least expected it.

Maybe he'd had problems with his past tests, when he was alone, but now he had her. He and the rest of his supersecret friends would just have to accept that things had changed.

Blake closed his eyes and willed his body to relax. A mob of half-crazed Others armed with swords didn't scare him as much as the tangle of wires that connected him to the fucking machine that beeped and whirred and mapped out his thoughts in squiggles of ink. A soft touch on his hand reminded him that Brenna was sitting beside him, breaking his concentration on all things hateful.

He still wasn't sure how she managed to bulldoze her way past the Handler and his boss to get into the room. She'd done it with smiles and assurances that Dr. Young would back her up, and damn if Laurel hadn't done exactly that. In fact, she had told them that if Dr. Crosby, the local Handler, didn't allow Brenna into the room, she would go over his head and deny him access to her patient.

"You're frowning, Doctor Crosby. Is there some

problem?" Brenna squeezed Blake's hand. Her palm was damp, a sign she wasn't as calm as she wanted everyone to believe.

The doctor shook his head. "Not that I can find, anyway. It's just that these results don't correlate very well with Mr. Trahern's previous tests."

Brenna immediately jumped to her feet, almost knocking the poor man to the floor as she put herself between him and Blake. For the first time in hours, Blake felt like grinning.

"Then do them again, Doctor. Blake's just fine, and I won't have you and that blasted machine saying otherwise."

The doctor straightened his lab coat, trying to restore some dignity. "You misunderstand me, Ms. Nichols. However, I won't discuss my findings with either of you before I share them with Mr. Trahern's Handler back in Seattle." The doctor looked more puzzled than worried. What was going on?

Trahern joined the discussion. "They're my results, Doc. You can tell me, and anything you have to say, Brenna can hear."

"I'll tell you what. Have Ms. Nichols disconnect you from those electrodes. I'm sure you can show her how to do that. Meanwhile, I'll make a quick call to Dr. Young. By the time you come into the lab, I should be ready to discuss the results with you." He bolted out the door before they could argue.

"That seemed odd." Brenna stared at the door. "Is that a normal reaction for a Handler?"

Blake sat up and started pulling off the electrodes himself. "I don't know if anything they do is normal or not. But Laurel Young always looked slightly sick when she watched my results come out of that damn machine."

Brenna reached over to remove the last electrode. She let it drop down on the bed, then cupped his face with her hand. "Well, it couldn't have been too bad if he's letting you walk out of here on your own."

Blake turned his face to nuzzle her palm and then tugged her down onto his lap. She giggled, then sighed as he turned his attention to kissing her good and proper.

She slapped his hand away when he tried to do a little exploring. "Come on, Blake. We've got other things to do right now."

"Not me." But he let her escape when she pulled away.

"Let's go see what the doctor says."

He noticed that she held his hand as they returned to the main lab room. If she drew some comfort from his touch, he was glad. No one else had ever turned to him for comfort. The sensation felt strange, but a good strange.

The doctor, still on the phone, held up a finger for them to wait. "I'm not sure this is wise, Dr.

Young, but Mr. Trahern and his fiancée are standing here. I'll put you on speakerphone."

Fiancée, huh? So that was how Brenna got by the normal security. She was obviously going to bluff it out, gazing at the telephone as if it were the most interesting thing she'd ever seen. He squeezed her hand as they waited for Laurel to explain what had the local doctor's knickers all in a twist.

"Trahern, is that you?"

"Yeah, Doc, it's me."

"Let me be the first to congratulate you on your recent engagement." There was just enough sarcasm to make her local counterpart give him and Brenna the evil eye.

"Thanks. I can hardly believe it myself." He'd pay for that one later, judging from the look Brenna shot him.

"Let's hope she knows what she's getting herself into."

"I can speak for myself, Dr. Young. And, yes, I knew just what I was doing."

"I suspect that is true, Ms. Nichols—but back to the matter at hand. Blake, it appears that you and Devlin have become a bit perplexing for the Regents. I was reading the tests from here as Dr. Crosby ran and reran the scan, and they're not only better this time, but they are markedly better. Just like Devlin's."

No wonder Laurel sounded happy. If Bane's tests weren't a fluke, then maybe there was hope for them. Blake figured she'd be using him for a guinea pig, too, when he got home to Seattle, but he wouldn't put up much of a fight.

"I suspect you have some celebrating to do, Mr. Trahern. And congratulations again. I also suspect your Ms. Nichols has something to do with all of this."

Before he could respond, a chill ran up his spine: the barrier again. It wasn't as bad as earlier, but bad enough. "Gotta go, Doc, but thanks for the good news. I'll let you know how things turn out here."

He was already dragging Brenna along in his wake, hitting the door out of the lab at almost a run. Maybe it would have been wiser to leave her with Dr. Crosby, but the doctor would have his own preparations to make if there was more fighting.

"What's wrong?" Brenna asked.

"The barrier." It was hard to get even those words out, with the need to fight burning in his veins. "I'll get you to safety first."

"But—"

"Not now, Brenna. I have to."

She planted her feet and dragged him to a stop. "I know that, you nitwit. Let go of my hand and *go*. Surely I can find my way back to the room by myself."

"Even if you could, you don't have the security codes." He'd throw her over his shoulder again and carry her to their room and lock the door if that's what it took. "Don't get stubborn with me right now."

"Fine."

They reached the elevator, and he keyed in the numbers that Jarvis had given him earlier. He supposed they were supersecret, but he didn't give a damn if Brenna did memorize them. The elevator was slow in coming, but it was unlikely that he'd been the only Paladin caught above ground when the barrier dropped. Despite his best efforts, he could barely control the surges of adrenaline in his blood. Those good test results wouldn't be worth a tinker's damn if he didn't maintain until he had a sword in his hand.

At last the elevator arrived. When they were safely inside, he started counting off the seconds until they reached the caverns below. At the bottom he instinctively shoved Brenna behind him until he knew exactly what they were walking into. The doors slid open to reveal a cluster of Paladins, armed and ready to fight. They turned to check him out. Although he didn't know half of them by name, they all recognized him from the previous fight.

"Is the corridor clear?"

The closest man nodded. "Yeah. The barrier was only down for a few seconds, but it's weakening again." His grin turned feral. "If you hustle, you should be back in time for the party."

"Sounds good."

"I can find my own way." Brenna tried to tug free of his grasp.

"We've already settled that argument."

He picked her up and loped down the passageway, knowing that she'd peel a strip off his hide later for embarrassing her. Served her right, for telling the medical staff she was his fiancée. He opened the door to their room and dumped her on the bed. His mistake was in laughing when she squealed. Her temper came boiling out, and she was on him like a tiger.

For a woman a fraction of his size, she packed a mean punch. He jumped back out of reach, rubbing his jaw. "Damn it, Brenna, that hurt."

She glared up at him until she realized that she'd actually left a bruise. The fight all melted away as she stammered out an apology. "I'm sorry. I didn't mean to . . ."

He didn't help her mood by laughing again. "Yes, you did, and I probably deserved it. But you said you could handle being around me even when the need to fight is riding me hard."

The look she shot him was pure disgust. "You just wanted to show off in front of your friends. Well, go on out and play." Then she added, "And be careful."

He yanked her against him for a kiss guaranteed to keep her hot and bothered until he returned and could pick up where he'd left off. "Stay inside. I can't concentrate if I have to worry about what you're doing."

She nodded, then buried her face against him and held on for a long hug. "I meant what I said, Blake. Promise me that you'll be careful."

"I will, honey. And after this little fracas is over, we'll concentrate on solving your father's murder so your life can get back to normal."

She looked pretty fragile as he picked out another sword from the closet and left the room. As he pulled the door shut, he had to wonder if he'd ever find the strength to walk away from her permanently.

Ritter watched the readouts and frowned. Now was not the time for the barrier to go up and down like a damn yo-yo. However, at least he now knew that Blake Trahern was somewhere around here. Not that he'd found out from those two buffoons he'd been paying to find him. No, he'd accidentally stumbled across a medical report on Dr. Crosby's desk when he'd stopped in for his monthly inspection of the medical facility.

He couldn't show any interest in the report, considering how secretive all the Handlers had become with their patients' records. He could remember a time when Handlers considered themselves to be little better than zookeepers.

Not any more, though. One of the Handlers out in Trahern's home territory of Seattle was even rumored to be practically living with one of the Paladins. The idea made his skin crawl. What was wrong with the woman, that she'd accept a mutated freak for a lover?

He drove to the street gate of the facility, wishing he didn't have to go down into the caverns. But confirming that Trahern was down there with his old buddy Jarvis would mean that the judge's daughter was close by, too. She must be holed up in a hotel nearby; it was doubtful that either of the two Paladins would like her being out of sight any longer than necessary.

The sword-wielding troglodytes did have a powerful sense of loyalty, he had to give them that. Once he'd taken care of Trahern, then he could go after Jarvis for failing to report his friend's whereabouts; he'd risk out-and-out rebellion among the local Paladin population, but who cared? As soon as those few loose ends were cleaned up, he'd be gone without a trace.

The new identity he'd recently purchased would get him out of the country. Once he reached his initial destination, he'd pick up the paperwork for his permanent new identity and then there'd be no stopping him.

Faking his own death would be a bit trickier. But by the time the police got back the reports showing the body really wasn't his, it would be too late. He'd be soaking up the sun and spending the money he'd collect in a few days, once he made final delivery of the stones.

He keyed the security code into the gate and waited to be identified and allowed through. With the facility on full alert, it took longer than normal: the guards had more on their mind than allowing a Regent rapid admission. Finally, though, the gate rolled back and the guard waved him through.

"Sorry for the delay, sir, but we're in lockdown again."

"Quite all right. Maintaining security is our priority, especially when we're under attack."

The guard's reaction was unusual. "You'd think so, wouldn't you?" He cursed, then spat. "I guess it all depends on who you know."

He started back to the guardhouse, but Ritter called, "Why? What's happened?"

The guard dropped his voice, careful to keep his eyes away from his coworker who stood inside watching them. "As long as I've worked for the Regents, we've been under strict orders that all of our facilities were strictly off limits to civilians."

There was only one civilian Ritter could think of who might have gained access, with the help of two of her father's friends, but he was careful to keep his excitement from showing. "As far as I know, that hasn't changed."

"See, that's what I've been saying. But because it's Jarvis and that cold-eyed bastard Trahern, everybody's been turning a blind eye to her being here."

The last thing he wanted was an irate guard sending ripples of discontent up the chain of command.

"Oh, you must be referring to Ms. Nichols, the judge's daughter." He leaned toward his window and lowered his voice, forcing the guard to step closer to the car to hear. "We okayed her to be brought in. Until we know who murdered her father, it's imperative that she be protected. We'd do no less for any member of our extended family who was in danger through no fault of their own." That drivel ought to appeal to a loyal member of the Guard.

The man was smart enough to look doubtful, which was all right. If he were too easily fooled, they would have fired him years ago. "If you say so, sir."

"I appreciate your caution, Sergeant. Once I'm inside, I'll double check with Jarvis to make sure that Ms. Nichols is not being allowed full access to the facility." He put his car back in gear and drove inside the fence, rearranging his plans.

● ● ●

The battle was just a small skirmish, enough to get everyone stirred up but not enough to work off the rush of battle fever. Unlike the others, Blake had a warm and hopefully willing woman waiting back in his room to help take off the edge.

"If she sees you smiling like that, she'll bar the door." Jarvis fell into step beside him. "After that display earlier, you'll be lucky if she doesn't use that sword on you while you're asleep."

Blake smiled wolfishly. "It was worth the risk."

"Man, you've got it bad." Jarvis shook his head in disgust. "So are you moving back here, or is she going to Seattle with you?"

Blake stumbled to a stop. "What the hell are you talking about?"

"Unless you've been sleeping on the floor these past few nights, I have to think you two have been sharing more than body heat. She's not the kind of woman to take that sort of thing lightly, which means she wants you. Personally, I can't imagine it—but I've never understood women very well."

Trahern's sword clattered to the floor as he pinned Jarvis against the rough rock wall in a chokehold.

"You know what your problem is, Jarvis? You never know when to shut the fuck up! What we've been doing or not doing is none of your damn business!" He landed a solid punch to Jarvis's gut.

His friend came back fighting, kicking Blake in

the knee and following up with a quick jab to his kidneys. Blake cursed Jarvis's entire family as he blocked another punch and used his opponent's momentum to send him crashing to the floor. Jarvis rolled up to his feet and came charging right back. Blake took great pleasure in throwing him a second time, but then Jarvis managed to send him flying back against the tunnel wall, knocking the air out of him.

The door down the hall flew open. "Blake Trahern! Jarvis! What do you two think you're doing? Isn't fighting the Others enough, without you turning on each other?"

Blake held up his hands, signaling his withdrawal from the fight.

Jarvis got in one last cheap shot before he, too, ceased fire. He wiped a trickle of blood off the corner of his mouth. "I'm sorry, Brenna, but he started it."

"Like hell!" Trahern roared.

She rolled her eyes in pure disgust. "You both sound like a pair of eight-year-olds."

"Aw, gee, Mom. We're sorry."

Jarvis's wisecrack didn't amuse Brenna, but it cracked up Blake big-time. He couldn't remember when he'd spent as much time laughing as he had over the past few days. It didn't exactly feel natural for him, but it did feel good.

Maybe some of that got through to Brenna, because the lines of disapproval framing her luscious mouth softened enough for him to risk grabbing her up for a hot kiss. She made a token effort of pushing him away, but then sighed and gave in. When he set her back down on her feet, she stayed right beside him, her arm around his waist.

"Oh, for Pete's sake, take it inside, will you?" Jarvis pretended to look ill. "I was going to ask you two to come with me to talk to Mr. Doe about his findings, but now obviously isn't the right time."

Brenna frowned. "Can we get something to eat first? We missed lunch, and I know Blake must be hungry."

Jarvis, bastard that he was, started laughing. "Honey, what he's hungry for has nothing to do with food. But I could use a break myself." He glanced at his watch. "I'll meet you in an hour."

Then he walked away, still laughing.

Brenna waited until she thought he was out of hearing before saying, "Well, that was embarrassing. He thinks we just wanted time to have sex."

She underestimated the highly developed hearing of a Paladin, but Blake figured she probably missed the slight falter in Jarvis's step as he turned the corner. "No, he knows that we both need to eat. He just figures we'll have sex first."

Brenna's face flushed bright pink, but she didn't deny it. Rather than give her time to think of reasons why they shouldn't, he swept her up in his arms and carried her inside, kicking the door closed.

This time, when he tossed her down on the bed, he joined her. Neither of them gave much thought to food for some time.

chapter 12

Mr. Doe had made a major breakthrough in tracing the names and numbers that her father had left behind. His fingers clicked over the keyboard as he tapped into the world of cyberspace, the same rapt expression on his face that most computer geeks had. But most gamers didn't keep a sword propped against the corner of the desk in case its owner needed to charge into a battle.

"Okay, see here?" He pointed to the screen. "These numbers don't make sense, unless someone has had their hand in the till."

"How much money are we talking about?" Trahern leaned over the man's shoulder to study the spreadsheet, and his lips moved as he added some figures in his head. "Holy shit! No wonder people are dying."

When the phone on the desk rang, Jarvis snatched it up. "What? Oh, hell. Where is he now?"

Blake moved away from the desk, putting himself between Brenna and the unknown threat. Several of the others adjusted their positions at the same time. She wondered if any of them realized what they had just done. Probably not, their need to protect was so second nature to them.

Jarvis hung up. "One of the Regents is on his way down. Evidently one of the guards up top snitched about Brenna being here."

"Is it too late to hide her?" Trahern's eyes had turned glacial.

"Probably. The bastard was already inside the gate and on his way to the elevators before anyone thought to warn me." Jarvis muttered something obscene under his breath. "Guys, pretend to be doing something useful. If he walks in and we're all brandishing swords and glaring at him, he just might suspect that something's wrong."

Blake waited until several of the others had moved away before asking, "Do you think he's involved?"

Jarvis frowned. "I hate to point fingers until we know more, but I wouldn't be surprised. He's been poking around here more in the past week than he has in years. He's also shown a lot of interest in your whereabouts, all in the guise of heartfelt concern over his late friend's daughter. I've never had much use for the smarmy bastard—but that doesn't mean he's guilty."

"Can we prove anything?"

"Not yet," Mr. Doe said. He hit a few keys, and the spreadsheet disappeared into a swirl of bright colors that settled into a fantasy game. A dragon glided down from a skyscraper to sweep the streets with bursts of green flame. Doe laughed with malicious glee as he manipulated the dragon to chase one unlucky person after another.

"I've never seen this game before," Brenna said, moving in closer to look over his shoulder. Playing fantasy video games was one of her secret vices.

"That's because I haven't finished writing the software for it. I'm still not happy with how the dragon looks when he and the hero duke it out." There was no mistaking the pride of ownership in his voice.

She leaned closer to the screen. "It's so good now, I can't imagine how you can improve on it. I'd love to give the finished product a try."

Clearly pleased, Mr. Doe nodded. "I'll send you a copy. I'm always glad to get some expert feedback before I take my stuff to market."

She grinned at him. "I'll hold you to that promise. Of course, I might have trouble tracking down one Mr. Doe among so many."

"Don't worry. I'll find you."

The *ping* of the elevator erased the group's good humor. Jarvis and Trahern must have decided to go on the offensive, for they reached the elevators just as the doors were sliding open.

The Regent who had them all in such an uproar looked vaguely familiar, but before she could put a name to his face, the klaxons went off again. Blake and Jarvis shoved the man back into the elevator— none too gently, she noticed—and sent it back up out of danger.

The Paladins all seemed oddly unconcerned about the alarm. John Doe had already closed down his dragon game and was back to studying the spreadsheet. Wait. The barrier wasn't down at all. In fact, it hadn't even flickered.

Jarvis caught the eye of one of the other Paladins and made a slashing motion across his neck. The man hit a series of keys on a computer and blessed silence reigned. Once her head quit pounding, Brenna realized that they'd triggered the alarm to keep the Regent from invading their territory.

Blake joined her at the desk. "In case anyone asks, Jarvis just completed the monthly test of the alarms."

"Really? And did that Regent that the two of you shuffled back into elevator know that it was a drill?"

"No," Jarvis said, shaking his head. "If everyone knew it was a drill rather than the real thing, they wouldn't take it seriously." His eyes twinkled with glee. "Besides, it's our job to make sure the Regents are safe from attack by the Others. If we'd let him stay because of the drill, next time he might not take my order for him to leave as seriously."

"And how long will he stay gone?"

"I programmed the computer to freeze the elevators for thirty minutes."

Mr. Doe broke in. "See these deposits? The individual amounts are different, but the total withdrawal is the same." He ran a finger down the screen. "Here, here, and here."

"Can you tell where the money is coming from?" Blake slipped his arm around Brenna's waist as he leaned closer to the screen.

"I should be able to trace it. Looks like Judge Nichols was on to something."

"But what was the money for?" Brenna asked. And what could possibly be worth her father's life?

"I'd guess it was for these." Jarvis tossed a blue stone onto the desk. It caught the light from the fluorescent lights overhead, casting an intense blue glow across the desk. "Does that look like that blue dust you and Bane found back in Seattle?"

Trahern nodded. "Yeah, except we never found a piece nearly that size. Where'd you get it?"

"In one of these tunnels. It's the only one we've found, but that doesn't mean much. With the swarms of small earthquakes all over the area, the barrier is down as much as it's up. We've been running on little sleep and food, so I can't swear nothing got by us."

"We didn't get enough dust to analyze. Do you have someone in the labs you can trust to keep his mouth shut?"

"I already had it looked at." Jarvis picked up the stone and polished it on his shirt. "According to the report, this stone doesn't exist. Not in this world, anyway."

"What did the lab guy think it was?"

"Some kind of aberrant garnet was his best guess, and even that was iffy. They occur naturally in several colors here, but blue isn't one of them. He wanted to keep it longer to determine what properties would make it so valuable to someone on our side—but while I trust him, I can't say the same about his coworkers. If one of them noticed what he was doing, there'd be no keeping the lid on this."

Trahern frowned. "I know someone in Seattle who might have some answers."

"Who? Devlin Bane? What would he know about it?" Jarvis put the stone into his pocket.

"No, not him." Trahern looked around the cavern, silently reminding Jarvis that they weren't alone. "I don't want to say more about it until I check."

"Which will be when?" asked Mr. Doe.

Jarvis gave him a slight shake of the head. "The rock can wait. Right now, we need to decide what to do about Ritter before he figures out how to override my commands on the elevator, and starts poking his nose in where it doesn't belong."

Brenna reached out to touch Jarvis on the arm. "How much trouble will you and Blake be in, now that he knows that you two let me in here?"

He responded with a gesture that reminded her of Trahern—another big tough guy who could take care of himself against all comers. That didn't mean that they should have to go it alone all the time, though. All the Paladins deserved better than that.

"I'll go pack." She started to walk away, but Trahern stopped her. "What?"

"Where are you planning on going?"

A good question.

"It makes sense to stay long enough to pick up the trail your father left. That will tell us some where to go next."

The klaxons went off again and he yelled to Jarvis, standing three feet away from him, "Tell them to quit playing with that damn alarm! We already got rid of the asshole."

But Jarvis's attention was riveted on the barrier at the far side of the cavern. What had been swirls of stunning bright colors was now tainted with streaks of sickly green and black.

"Son of a bitch!"

Mr. Doe shut down the computer before snatching up his sword to join the rest of the Paladins already forming up in battle stance. Jarvis wasn't far behind him. The need to join them was riding Trahern hard, but he clearly didn't want to leave her alone, either.

She shoved him toward his friends. "Go! I can get back to the room myself."

Before he could respond, the barrier flared brightly and then disappeared. To her horror, a mob of Others came across in a huge, disorganized surge. The clang of steel on steel froze her on the spot as they tried to overwhelm the Paladins with sheer brute force and numbers.

Already, enough blood had been drawn to scent the air with its coppery flavor. She'd be the most help by leaving Trahern free to concentrate on stemming the tide, so she made a beeline for their room.

Blake waited until she was almost into the hallway before turning to face his foes. She thought she heard him bellow out a challenge, but that might have just been her imagination. His voice was one among many, all full of fury and some with pain. Tears burned her eyes as she tried to shut out the horrific sounds. She paused to take one last look back just in time to see Trahern swing his sword in a huge arc, sending his opponent's head bouncing across the cavern floor in a spray of blood.

Her stomach heaved, and she retched up her lunch. Wiping her mouth on the back of her hand, she stumbled down the hall to their room. But once again, the door barely muted the death and dying that was going on such a short distance away. How could Trahern and the others face each day of their lives, knowing this was all that awaited them? No wonder they developed such a hard view of the world.

How could he be so gentle with her and yet deal out brutal death with such relish? A woman would have to be a saint or a fool to fall in love with a Paladin and share that life with him. Since she'd never considered herself to be either one, maybe it was time to start figuring out exactly where that left the two of them.

When fall came, she planned on being back at the university. Blake would resume his life in Seattle, fighting his war as long as he could. She only hoped that after this powerful lust for each other burned out they could part as friends. However, now that he was back in her life again, she wanted to keep him there.

Ritter paced the floor, pausing often to glare at the clock on the wall. The bitch was here; so close he could almost smell her perfume. And when she was almost within his grasp; with whatever information her nosy father had left with her, the damn Others had to attack. The guards had been called down to lend support and wouldn't let him near the cavern while all hell was breaking loose.

They tried to tell him that it was for his own protection, but he knew they figured he'd just be in the way. He tried to convince them that he wanted nothing to do with the fighting, that his concern was for the safety of Miss Nichols, but that had gotten him nowhere. So now he was stuck prowling the upper floors, while everything he needed to finish this mess hovered just out of his reach.

The elevators would only respond to those with battle codes, so he might as well leave and send for his two detectives. It was past time for them to earn their keep.

There was only one road in and out of the compound. He'd direct them to wait for Trahern and his woman to leave; then it would be a simple matter to ambush them. How sad that the innocent Ms. Nichols would be killed in a shootout between her kidnapper and the police. And what a tragedy that the police would die, as well.

Feeling energized, he left the building and headed for his car. The sullen heat of a Missouri afternoon hit him like a sauna, but he didn't care. In seconds he'd be enjoying the comfort of leather seats and air conditioning, while those sons of bitches down in the cavern were fighting for their lives.

Yes, some days things just went right according to plan.

Swan shifted in his seat, stretching his arms overhead and hitting the ceiling of the car. "How long do we have to wait?"

"As long as it takes." Montgomery was getting annoyed with his partner's constant questions. It was like working with a five-year-old.

"Did he say when Trahern and the woman would be coming this way?" Swan looked around at the desolate scenery. "Or even why they'd be coming this way? Hell, there's nothing out here for miles and miles."

Montgomery agreed, but bitching about it every ten minutes didn't help. He needed to take a piss and stretch his legs. "You stay with the car. I'll be right back."

"Where are you going?"

As if he couldn't figure that out for himself. They'd been swigging coffee and bottled water for the past five hours. The only reason Swan wasn't answering nature's call was that he was fifteen years younger. In a few more years, his prostate would have him pissing in the bushes, too.

Unless they ended up in jail for this little escapade, but that didn't bear thinking about. They'd hired on to do a job, and they had to see it through. This whole mess stunk to high heaven, but there wasn't much they could do about it now. Even if he hadn't already spent most of the money he'd been paid up front, Mr. Knight wasn't the kind to accept refunds from an employee who'd developed a distaste for the work.

Although it felt good to walk around outside, the day was hot and getting hotter. At least they'd found a spot along the dirt road wide enough to back the car into the shade of some trees. That was something else that had him puzzled. How had Mr. Knight managed to track Trahern to such a remote spot, anyway?

The road didn't appear on any map Montgomery had looked at. It made sense that Trahern would have looked for a safe hiding place, especially if he needed to hole up until his bullet wound healed, but out here? Sure, it would be easy to guard with only one way in, but that also meant there was only one way out.

He picked a handy tree and took care of business. After zipping his pants, he headed up a small rise to learn more about their surroundings.

As he neared the top of the hill, he crouched

down. Maybe there was nothing on the other side but more miles of rolling terrain and trees, but there was no need to make a target of himself. Making his way from tree to tree, he reached the top of a rocking outcropping overlooking a small valley.

His caution paid off. He could just make out the road twisting through the woods below where it passed through a high, chain-link fence. He worked his way to the right, careful to keep the trees between him and anyone who might be watching from below. His new position gave him a better line of sight, and what he saw made his pulse race.

There was a gate manned by two armed guards in military uniforms. Son of a bitch! It was one thing to take out a loner; and if Trahern's death would bring down the wrath of the military, he wanted nothing to do with it.

He barreled down the hillside. They needed to get the hell out of Dodge while they had the chance. The heat and humidity, combined with a solid dose of fear, had him panting for breath when he reached the car. He yanked open the door and clambered inside. Turning the key, he ground the starter and had to try a second time to get the engine started.

"We are so screwed! We're getting out of here now; I'll explain when we're someplace safe."

When Swan didn't respond, Montgomery

reached over to shake him awake. How could the stupid bastard sleep, with the car bouncing over the dirt road? His hand came away wet, and it took his brain a second too long to realize it was blood dripping from his fingers, then to see the knife sticking out of Swan's ribs.

A sick certainty of his own imminent death washed over him just as the windshield shattered and pain exploded in his chest. His hands slipped free of the steering wheel, sending the car off the road to crash into the trees.

The engine sputtered and died, leaving the woods eerily silent except for the sound of his own labored breathing. A shadow passed over his eyes, but it wasn't the Grim Reaper. Or, maybe in a way it was, since his former employer stood beside the car with a large gun in his hand.

Ritter pointed the gun at Montgomery's left temple, smiling as he pulled the trigger.

"Devlin is coming in tonight." Trahern dropped into a chair and propped his feet up on the other one.

Jarvis looked up from his desk with a frown. "Why the hell is he coming here?"

Trahern figured he was about to piss off Jarvis in a major way and liked the idea. "Because he wants to."

Since he couldn't take his mood out on Brenna, he'd decided to pick a fight with someone else; Jarvis was a handy target, one whose mood matched his own. The Regent had disappeared during the fight, and until they knew what he was up to, neither of them would rest easy.

"I need a better reason than that. Bane may rule the roost out there on the coast, but he's not in charge here." Jarvis pushed his chair away from his desk, as if sensing where the discussion was headed.

"Okay." Trahern laced his fingers together and cracked his knuckles. "I was lonely and invited him to visit."

"I've got enough trouble here without you deciding to have a party." Jarvis's eyes narrowed, his temper already starting to simmer. "Call him back and tell him not to come."

"Sorry, no can do." Trahern smiled nastily. "His plane left an hour ago."

"Damn it, Trahern, I don't need Bane's interference! Go meet his plane and get back on it with him." He stood and leaned across the desk. "You brought this mess here; you can just take it back to Seattle with you."

Trahern's phone call asking for help may have gotten the judge killed, but the blue stone in Jarvis's pocket was proof that the problem *wasn't* just in the Pacific Northwest.

They both knew it, and just that quickly, all the steam went out of Trahern's need to fight. He slumped back in the chair and shook his head. "I'm sorry. I should have talked to you about Devlin earlier, but it wouldn't have changed anything. Once he gets an idea in his head, there's no changing his mind. He has someone he wants to look at the stone."

"One of your lab guys?"

"He didn't say." Trahern had a good idea exactly who would be stepping off the plane with Bane, but he wasn't about to start that fight until he knew for sure.

Jarvis slowly sank back into his chair. He pinched the bridge of his nose and closed his eyes. "Days like these are enough to make me want to retire."

As if any of them ever got to do that. The genes that made them Paladins were so rare, there were never enough of them to go around. In past centuries, the strongest of warriors always had their choice of women, ensuring that a fair number of Paladins were born each year. Modern birth control had changed that.

Which meant Jarvis would retire the same way Trahern would: at the wrong end of a needle.

"Where's Brenna?"

"She's resting. She says she has a headache."

Jarvis's laugh was nasty. "Worn out your welcome in her bed already? I'd say that's a record, even for you."

Maybe they'd have that fight after all. "These past few days have been hard on her. First she lost her father, then everything else that's followed. She must think she's living in an *X Files* episode."

"I suspect she's strong enough to handle anything you throw at her."

"Yeah, right," he sighed.

"I mean it, Trahern. I'll even admit to some jealousy. No woman has ever looked at me the way she looks at you."

"That was before she saw me kill one of the Others." He'd looked back to make sure she'd made it out safely just after he'd separated an Other's head from his shoulders. "Knowing I kill for a living is one thing. Seeing it is another."

Jarvis shrugged. "She'll get over it."

Well, if she didn't, he'd been fine without her for years. He'd be fine again. And if he said that often enough, he might even manage to convince himself.

Before he could wallow in self-pity, Jarvis's phone rang. His friend answered and listened for a few seconds with a seriously pissed off expression on his face.

When he slammed down the receiver, he said, "There's a car parked in the woods down the road. One of the guards thought he caught sight of someone up on the hilltop just outside of the gate and sent a patrol." Jarvis looked grim. "They've got the vehicle in sight now, but they're holding off making an approach until we get there."

He reached into his bottom drawer and pulled out a pair of guns. He shoved one in the back of his waistband and held the other out to Trahern. "Once in a while we get some teenagers looking for a quiet spot to make out, but they never drive this far back."

Glad to have something to do, Trahern accepted the gun. It wouldn't take two Paladins and a squad of guards to run off a couple of trespassers, but they'd make a handy target for his bad mood.

Outside, the sun was starting its slow slide behind the hills to the west. Jarvis had called back the guards, leaving one in position to notify them if anything changed. They kept to the road and were about to cut across country when Jarvis's cell phone rang.

"Son of a bitch! We'll be right there." He took off at a ground-eating lope straight down the center of the road.

Trahern fell into step beside him. "What happened?"

"It looked like one guy was dozing in the car while his buddy was out exploring. Then all of a sudden, the snoopy one came tearing out of the woods, jumped in the car, and took off. The car only went about a hundred feet when someone shot out the windshield, causing the driver to lose control. There was one more gunshot after that."

The guard waited for them just inside the tree line fifty yards down the road. He stepped out of the shadows to make sure they saw him, then faded back into the trees. Until they knew who was shooting, they wouldn't make targets of themselves.

"The car is over there." The guard pointed down the hill toward a stand of pines. "I've been watching since the car was hit, but I haven't seen anyone moving, inside or out."

Trahern had a bad feeling about the whole scene. "I'll circle around wide and come at them from the right. Give me about four minutes to get into position before making your approach."

Jarvis nodded. "I'll take the left." He glanced at the guard. "Hold this position until one of us tells you otherwise."

Then they both moved out. Someone else was out in the woods; Trahern could almost smell the bastard. But whoever it was didn't want to be seen. Was he hoping to use the car as a trap to lure Jarvis or Trahern into his sights? If he wasn't familiar with Paladins, he'd think a bullet would bring them down. If he did know about Paladins, he'd be putting as much distance between him and the car as possible. Depending on how good a shot he was, he could still go for a head shot to take out Jarvis or Blake himself.

Say, someone like their missing Regent.

Trahern couldn't wait to find out; it would feel good to have a tangible target. He slowed his pace, listening for any sounds of his quarry. The dense undergrowth in the woods made it difficult to look for any sign of the shooter. Finally, he found where leaves were disturbed. The trail turned back toward the road. He could see the light of the dying sun glinting off the hood of the car.

Trahern froze and listened. The woods were silent, except for the drone of cicadas and the occasional stirring of some small animal. Nothing that sounded like a man running in full panic, or even walking.

Either the shooter was long gone or he'd gone to ground somewhere close by. Trahern approached the car. Even if their quarry shot at him, Jarvis would have a good idea of where the bastard was.

The car was silent except for the hiss of steam from the ruptured radiator. Neither of the car's passengers was moving. Maybe they'd been knocked unconscious by the impact, but his gut feeling was that they were dead. He crouched down and ran the last little distance, zigzagging between the trees.

The man in the passenger seat was angled toward the window, staring out of sightless eyes. The driver had the back of his head blown off—most likely the second shot the guard heard. Trahern felt, rather than heard, Jarvis moving up beside him.

"Are they dead?"

"Very."

"Recognize them?" Jarvis peered over Trahern's shoulder.

"Yeah. It's the two cops who were investigating the judge's death. The ones who shot me." Trahern backed away from the car and studied the surrounding woods. They felt empty now.

Jarvis gave a low whistle. "Who wanted them dead?"

"I don't think they stumbled onto this road by accident. It's not on any maps, and it's a hell of a long way out of their jurisdiction. I'd guess someone lured them out here, although I doubt the original plan was to kill them. At least not yet."

"You sound like you have some idea of who pulled the trigger." Jarvis looked past the car to study the woods around them.

"Well, we have a Regent missing and now we have two dead cops. Too much of a coincidence for my money."

Jarvis's dark eyes were worried. "Mine, too. I feel like a sitting duck standing here. Let's call for cleanup and get our asses back inside the gate."

"How long can we keep these deaths under wraps?" Trahern asked.

"Long enough. Why?"

"Because it's time to go on the attack. I doubt those two were lily white, but they didn't deserve to die, either. I want to buy us enough time to track down the bastard who was pulling their strings and take him out. He killed the judge, and he killed them. It's payback time."

As they returned to the compound, the only thing Trahern couldn't figure out was why the man hadn't just run after killing the cops. Surely his plan for escape was already in place. The only reason Blake could think of was that the judge's data implicated more than the Regent. And whoever was next up on the food chain must be scary indeed, if Ritter was willing to risk his life to get the information. Good. That meant they had a good chance of rooting out the source of the corruption this time.

chapter 13

*W*hen the click of the door opening woke her, Brenna kept her eyes closed. She'd fallen asleep trying to decide what to do, but still had no answers.

Her stomach churned at the memory of the Other's head separating from his body and flying across the cavern, flinging blood in an arcing spray as it tumbled end over end. She had envisioned the Others as some kind of monsters from a horror movie; instead, they looked human.

Maybe she was naïve. She'd grown up watching one war after another on the nightly news. Was this really any different?

Blake would say so. So would Jarvis and the rest of the Paladins out there. They'd dedicated their lives to protecting the world from the Others, and maybe they were right. But that didn't make it any easier to stomach. She'd give almost anything to be able to return to those days of innocence before she knew about Paladins and the battles they fought.

But she couldn't make it go away; eventually she had to face Trahern. And it looked like that time was now.

The door swung closed. "You don't need to creep around," Brenna said. "I'm awake."

She turned on the light beside the bed and was shocked to see not Blake, but the Regent who'd disappeared up the elevator. He stared at her with wild eyes and a nasty smile, a gun in his hands.

"What are you doing in here?" She yanked up the covers; his cold smile made her skin crawl.

"I'm here to take care of a loose end." He spoke as if that were something people said to each other every day.

She fought the urge to hide under the blankets. "I'm not a loose end, buster. And you'd better get out of here before Trahern gets back. He's the jealous type."

Her captor actually laughed. "Like I'd want to touch you after you've been rutting with that animal."

She sneered right back. "That 'animal' is more man than you'll ever be."

He lunged forward and backhanded her. The pain was almost blinding. She kicked out, aiming for his balls but missed, catching his thigh instead.

Rolling off the bed, she ran for the door, but he was only a half step behind her.

Grabbing her by the hair, he jerked her back, sending her stumbling to the floor. "Don't try to threaten me with the likes of Blake Trahern, slut. He might be harder to kill, but once he's dead, he's vulnerable."

She met him glare for glare. "You're not man enough to kill him, you murdering bastard. Cowards like you kill with bombs because you're too afraid to face your victim. Blake won't have that problem: he'll enjoy gutting you like the pig that you are. And even if you do manage to take him out, there's Jarvis and the others. You won't walk out of this place alive."

"Oh, but that's where you're wrong. They all think I've already left. Right now they're outside, trying to figure out how two St. Louis homicide detectives came to be dead right outside the gates. While they're dealing with that little problem, you and I will collect whatever information your fool of a father left for you to find."

"Don't you dare call my father a fool! He was a good and honorable man."

Ritter looked disgusted. "Call him whatever you like. If he'd kept his nose out of my business, he'd still be alive. Instead, he died in a million little pieces, all for nothing."

The image he painted made her stomach roil,

but she refused to show him any weakness. "At least he believed in something. That's more than you can claim."

"Not true, my dear. I believe in money, and living the good life." He motioned toward the door with his gun. "Once I'm out of here, Ritter of the Regents will cease to exist." He gave her a sardonic smile. "Of course, so will you. Cooperate, and I promise your death will be quick and painless."

"Go to hell." He might succeed in killing her, but she wasn't going to make it easy for him.

"Stupid bitch." He motioned toward the door with the barrel of the gun again. "Get dressed and let's go—now! My patience is wearing thin."

The gun left her little choice but to comply. She turned her back for some semblance of privacy, but could feel his eyes watching every move. Her skin crawled as she dressed slowly, trying to buy time for Trahern and Jarvis to get back. All the while, her mind churned with questions. The two lawmen had obviously been involved up to their necks in this lunatic's plans, but they didn't deserve to die for it. This madman was bent on murdering anyone who came between him and his goal.

Finally, she could delay no longer. Out in the corridor, all was quiet. Once the barrier stabilized, most of the Paladins had retired to their quarters to rest up from fighting.

"I assume your father left a computer disk of some kind."

Ritter could ask all the questions he wanted to; that didn't mean she had to answer. Her reward was a jab in the ribs with the barrel of his gun.

"I'd suggest you show a little more cooperation, Brenna. I can find the information on my own. It will just take longer."

"No, you can't."

"Don't underestimate my abilities. Before Jarvis shoved me back in the elevator, I saw you standing by that Paladin computer geek. He was back out in the cavern working on something when I made my way to your room. I'm sure with a little persuasion, he'd turn over the data to me."

"Paladins aren't corruptible." At least, she didn't think so.

"They *do* have an unfortunate streak of honor running right up their spine. However, I'm quite confident that he'll turn over the files to prevent me from shooting you."

And then this crazy man would shoot him, too. Maybe she could find a way to warn the unsuspecting Paladin of their coming. She deliberately stumbled, hoping the sound of her hitting the ground would carry far enough to catch Doe's attention.

Ritter jerked her to her feet again. "Quit the theatrics, Brenna. He can't hear you. He had headphones on."

So much for her plan. All she'd accomplished were a couple of more bruises to match the one on her face where her captor had slapped her. They were almost at the end of the passage; the brighter light of the cavern was showing just ahead. How could she prevent Ritter from attacking anyone else?

By making a deal with the devil.

She came to an abrupt halt just short of the cavern. "Let me go get the disk."

"Like hell." He pushed her forward.

"You'll stand a better chance of getting away if they never know you were here."

"And if you run out in the cavern screaming for help, every Paladin within hearing distance will be fighting over the privilege to slit me from stem to stern with their damn swords." A glint of fear flashed across his face.

"I won't scream for help."

"And why should I believe you?" He pushed her another few steps down the hallway.

"Because I don't want anyone else to die." Paladins might survive death, but not all of them would come back as the same men they'd been. "I promise you that I'll get the disk and paperwork and come straight back here."

He pushed past her to look out into the cavern. "You're in luck. The computer geek is the only person in sight. You get one chance."

Drawing a calming breath, and then another when the first one didn't work, she straightened her shoulders. As she entered the cavern, she felt the heavy weight of Ritter's gaze right in the middle of her back, as if daring her to betray him.

And she would, if circumstances would allow.

"Something is wrong." Trahern came to an abrupt halt just inside the gate. "I understand why the detectives were killed, but the timing's wrong."

Jarvis gave him a puzzled look. "You've been out in the sun too long, Trahern. The bastard cut bait and ran. It's that simple."

"No, by killing them when he did, he drew us outside the facility. Not only did we find out who his accomplices were, but we know almost for damn certain that he's the one behind the judge's death."

"And while we're out here chasing shadows in the woods, he's . . ." Jarvis looked toward the entrance to the cavern in alarm.

"Shit!" Trahern took off running, his friend at his heels.

If they took the elevator down to the cavern, they might as well hire a marching band to lead the charge into battle. The stairs were safer, even if that meant using up more precious time. There was no telling how long Ritter had been back inside, or what damage he'd already inflicted.

"If he's hurt her—"

"He'll die." There was no special inflection in Jarvis's voice; just a simple statement of fact.

"Tell the guards that we're in complete lockdown. Nobody in, nobody out, unless you personally give the order. Shoot to kill if somebody argues."

Jarvis nodded as he pulled out his cell phone and barked out the orders and codes to confirm the emergency status.

They reached a door leading to a staircase. Before opening it, Trahern asked, "Where will this come out?"

"Next to the elevators on the main floor."

"Is there another way to go? One that will let us approach the cavern from an unexpected direction?"

Jarvis ran through the possibilities. "Yeah, there's a service elevator behind the field quarters. Hardly anyone uses it, so I doubt Ritter knows it's even there." Jarvis led the charge down a labyrinth of hallways.

Trahern pounded after him. The best way to get to the bottom of the corruption in the Regent organization was to capture Ritter alive and wring the truth from him. But if sparing him meant endangering Brenna, the whole organization could go to hell and damn the consequences. Jarvis and the others had better stay out of his way when they cornered Ritter.

As Jarvis punched in the code to summon the elevator, Trahern checked his pistol, wishing he had a sword. Guns were dicey near the barrier; a stray shot could bring it down. It was going to be hard enough to get Brenna clear of danger; adding a charge of Others would be his worst nightmare come to life.

The soft *ping* of the elevator snapped him back to the present. The two of them counted the seconds as they plummeted into the limestone world below, neither inclined to talk. Battle lust was hard to control, and it was critical that he keep his temper and killing instincts under tight rein for Brenna's sake.

"What's the plan?"

Trahern shrugged. "Don't really have one."

Jarvis's smile was wolfish. "I've always wanted to go charging in like Newman and Redford in *Butch Cassidy and the Sundance Kid*. This might be my best chance."

"Neither of us is good-looking enough."

Jarvis laughed, as Blake had intended him to. It helped take the edge off their tension when the fight was upon them; blind rage only got people killed. This wasn't a melee against the Others, but a delicate situation that could go horribly wrong if they weren't careful.

Then Jarvis said, "You know, it would be better if we took Ritter alive."

Trahern looked him square in the eyes. "But if he so much as breathes in Brenna's direction, what say we kill him?"

Jarvis laughed again. "Now we have a plan."

They quickly wound their way toward the main cavern, guns drawn and ready to fire. When they passed other Paladins, Jarvis brought them up to speed while Trahern continued on. The silence ahead bothered him considerably. Either they'd guessed wrong and the Regent wasn't the one they were after, or he'd already come and gone. With Brenna, or leaving her dead body behind?

Trahern's blood ran cold.

Jarvis rejoined him with a pair of swords in hand. Blake swung his through the air to get the feel of its balance. Not as good as his favorite broadsword back in Seattle, but it would do. The familiar feel of a good weapon in his hand further calmed his need for violence. As they grew closer to the barrier, he could sense the Others hovering close by, obviously hoping for another chance to invade. Their proximity had Trahern's skin aching with the need to fight, to kill.

Jarvis held his own sword at the ready, his eyes dilated and wild.

They stopped to listen and heard a soft murmur of voices, one of them Brenna's. Trahern inched forward. She was talking to the computer wiz, but something was definitely off. It was in her posture and the way she stood just a little too far away for normal conversation. Her voice was threaded with tension, as if she had a tenuous hold on her nerves.

Which told him the Regent was close by, near enough to make Brenna feel threatened. So why wasn't she diving for cover and letting Doe protect her? The answer hit him like a kick in the stomach; *she* was doing the protecting.

Son of a bitch! Did she have no sense at all? Even if the Regent got off a lucky shot and killed the Paladin, he'd revive to fight another day. For her, dead was dead. Judging from where she stood, Ritter must be in the passageway to their room.

He eased back and told Jarvis, "He's in the far corridor, and Brenna is square in the line of fire. Can you get someone to circle around that way? We don't want the bastard to know he's in a trap until Brenna and your buddy out there are safe."

Jarvis nodded and retreated down the corridor to make the call without being overheard.

Blake kept a wary eye on the cavern, knowing things could change for the worse in a heartbeat. The Regent had to be aware that his time was almost up; any second now he was bound to run out of patience.

• • •

Jarvis dropped his voice to a low whisper for Trahern's ears only. "I've got two men in position if he retreats. They both know not to make a move unless they hear from one of us."

"Good. I'm going in. He won't be able to take a clean shot at me without showing himself. Don't miss."

"That won't work. From this angle it will be too close. I might hit you instead."

Jarvis was right, and they both knew it.

"If that's the only shot you've got, take it. Once I go down, you should be able to take him out."

"Like hell. You can't afford to die. You might not make it back again."

Blake forced a small smile. "It's got to happen sometime. Today's as good a day as any."

He holstered his gun in the back of his jeans and laid down the sword. "I'm going to walk out as if I don't suspect anything. He probably won't buy the act for long, especially if I get too close to Brenna. And Jarvis—take care of her for me."

"Will do."

"One more thing. If I die, *don't* let Brenna near me in the lab. She doesn't need to see what happens to us. To me."

Jarvis saluted him with his sword, one warrior to another. Then Trahern stepped out into the cavern, prepared to die if that's what it took to save his woman.

With feigned casualness, he walked toward Brenna. If this was to be his last sane moment on Earth, at least he was spending it with her. "Oh, there you are. I was wondering where you'd run off to."

She nearly jumped out of her skin at his sudden appearance. "Go away, Trahern. I'm not speaking to you." But she was; the fear in her eyes spoke volumes.

"You've got to get over being mad sometime, woman. And if I were the jealous type, I'd have to do some serious injury to your computer geek friend here." He strolled toward them, wishing like hell that one of the Paladin gifts was telepathy.

As Mr. Doe spun around in his chair, a series of shots rang out. A splotch of blood blossomed on the front of Doe's jeans' leg as Brenna screamed. Blake charged forward and dragged her to the floor, but not in time. She went down in a boneless heap, holding her arm, blood oozing between her fingers.

Bellowing in rage, Blake charged toward Ritter. Ignoring the stabbing pains in his leg and chest, he chased the bastard down and tackled him. Straddling the panicked coward, Blake wrapped his hands around the man's neck and squeezed.

In a harsh whisper, Ritter begged for mercy. "I've got money! It's all yours if you get me out of here."

"I don't give a flying fuck about your money. You shot my woman, you slimy bastard, and for that you die."

But Blake's fingers refused to cooperate. As he tried to crush Ritter's windpipe, the light of the cavern faded into darkness, and he felt nothing. With the last gleam of his eyesight, he glared down at Ritter. "God damn you—you killed me."

"Blake! Blake!" Brenna's arm dripped blood on his shirt as she tried to revive him, blending with the growing red stain on the soft flannel.

Strong hands pulled her away from Trahern's body, but she fought them off. "No, he's hurt! Get the doctor!"

This time Jarvis wasn't so gentle. "Damn it, Brenna, he's dead. You're the one who's bleeding like a stuck pig. Blake's beyond any help you can give him right now."

Oh, God, he's dead! He's dead, he's dead! His beautiful silver eyes, now a dull gray, stared up at her, empty of life

"Come on, Brenna, we need to get you up to the lab. The doctor will take care of your arm and give you something for the pain." He all but dragged her down the tunnel toward the elevators.

No, they couldn't leave Blake lying on the stone floor in a pool of his own blood! Besides, she'd never told him that she loved him. She'd known that he lived in constant danger, yet she'd let him die without hearing those words.

Jarvis punched the buttons on the elevator and then produced a clean handkerchief to wrap around her arm. "By the time we get that arm stitched up, they'll have brought Trahern in."

"And they'll bring him back from the dead."

The breath of hope was a sweet relief.

Jarvis nodded, but he didn't look as happy as she would have thought.

"What's wrong, Jarvis? What aren't you telling me?"

He kept his eyes focused over her head. "It's true that we can come back, but not forever. From what Trahern's told me, his test results show that he's pretty far gone. It's impossible to guess when the end will come, or why it's different for each of us."

"But his latest results were better," she said stoutly. "What can I do to help him?"

"Pray and keep your fingers crossed."

In the lab, the doctor motioned her toward the examination table as soon as he saw the bloody handkerchief on her arm.

The next quarter of an hour was a blur of white lab coats as the medical staff cleansed her wound and stitched it shut. The doctor asked surprisingly few questions; maybe he was so used to the Paladins' horrific wounds that a bullet wound seemed like nothing.

"That should do you, Ms. Nichols," he said as he clipped the last of the stitches. "Keep the wound dry and clean, and check back with your regular doctor in a week. Be sure to take all of the prescription I gave you. You don't want infection to set in."

"Thank you, Doctor."

Jarvis stepped forward. "She'll have to come back here to have the stitches taken out, Doc. If her regular physician recognized it as a gunshot wound, he'd be required by law to report it. None of us want that happening, especially since the same gun was used to kill a cop today."

The doctor merely shrugged. "Fine, I'll see you in a week. And don't try to be brave: take those pain pills I gave you."

Before she could thank him, the doors to the lab slammed open and John Doe was brought in.

"What the hell happened?" Dr. Crosby asked Jarvis. "I didn't hear any alarms. How many more are coming?"

"It was a random attack. Besides Brenna, there are only two more patients. Jake took one in the leg." Jarvis's expression turned grim. "Trahern was the only fatality."

The doctor motioned for Jake to take Brenna's place on the table. Two of the Paladins carried him over and set him down, then two med techs moved in and started to cut his pants away.

"Hey! These jeans are almost new," Jake complained.

"So what? They've got a bullet hole in them."

"One little hole doesn't matter."

The technicians rolled their eyes but helped him pull the jeans off.

"Brenna, are you going to hold my hand while they stitch up my leg?" He winked at her and tried to smile, though it was a bit shaky.

Jarvis answered, "Trahern finds out you've been flirting with his woman, you'll have more than a hole in your leg."

"Aw, he wouldn't begrudge a man a little bedside comfort."

Jarvis gave the wounded man an incredulous look. "Hello? This is Trahern we're talking about here. If he finds out—and he will, because I'll tell him—he'll have your hide."

The good-natured banter helped to keep Jake distracted from the work being done on his leg. Judging by the sweat rolling down his face, the local anesthesia they'd injected hadn't taken effect yet.

Brenna moved closer and took his hand in hers. His eyes widened in surprise.

She smiled down at him. "Jarvis might be afraid of Trahern, but I'm not. Believe me, he's not so tough. Besides, people who get shot together should stick together, don't you think?" She brushed his hair back off his forehead.

He winced in pain again. "Damn straight."

She could tell when the anesthesia started to take effect because his death grip on her hand loosened. Finally, he let go. Her own arm was starting to throb, so she asked Jarvis, "Can you hand me one of my pain pills?"

He brought her a glass of water and the medicine. "They'll be bringing Blake in any minute. You don't want to be here."

"Yes, I do." And no one was going to push her away until she knew he was on the road to recovery.

"He specifically said that he didn't want you to see him like this."

"Too bad. He can yell at me when he's better."

The doors opened again as a gurney was shoved into the lab with Blake's body on it.

"One, two, three." The doctor counted as they lifted Trahern onto a stainless steel table. "Strip him down."

This time no effort was made to save anything. Even his boxers were cut away, leaving him naked on the cold metal table. Then they brought out a set of chains and began tying him down.

Brenna looked on in horror. Blake had warned her how it would be for him, but the reality was so much worse. "Does it have to be this way, Jarvis?"

"Yes. I told you not to watch, Brenna. This is how it is for us—so either deal with it or get out. I'll be in my office if you need me."

He walked away without looking back, the other Paladins right behind him.

As much as she wanted to escape the harsh reality, Brenna stayed right where she was. She'd gladly face Blake's fury if it meant he was alive and well again.

chapter 14

"You need to leave," Dr. Crosby told her.

"I won't abandon him. Blake needs me."

"May I remind you that this is a medical facility, Ms. Nichols? What I say, goes. Patients, especially dead ones, are not allowed visitors."

Dr. Crosby glared at her impatiently over his glasses. "Young lady, you were wounded yourself and need to rest. We'll send word if there's any change in Mr. Trahern's condition."

"Jarvis said I could stay." She crossed her fingers at the lie, but was pretty sure he'd back up her claim.

The doctor clearly didn't appreciate the challenge to his authority. "He's not in charge of the lab. I am."

The doors behind them flew open and the irate doctor turned his temper on the new invaders, two men and a woman. "I don't know who you people are, and I don't care. Get out of my lab and take Ms. Nichols with you."

He was already reaching for the alarm button, but the closest man caught his wrist before Brenna even realized that he'd moved. Dr. Crosby froze. Considering his captor was almost twice his size and obviously another Paladin, it was the wisest response.

"Sorry, Doc, but the last thing we need is a bunch of trigger-happy guards swarming in here right now." The man kept his voice low, his tone reasonable. "I'll let you go, but please give us a chance to explain before you call for help."

The doctor looked past him to the woman holding out an ID badge. He nodded, but he clearly wasn't happy about it.

The woman said, "I'm sorry about our unexpected arrival, Dr. Crosby; let me introduce myself. I'm Dr. Laurel Young, from the Seattle lab. We've spoken on the phone before. And this is Devlin Bane, a friend of Blake Trahern's, also from Seattle."

Brenna stepped forward. "Dr. Young? I'm Brenna Nichols."

The woman smiled warmly. "Please call me Laurel, and I am so pleased to meet you. I only wish it was under happier circumstances."

Her kindness was almost Brenna's undoing. "They . . . he . . . won't let me stay with him.

They've chained Blake down like an animal, and nobody is doing anything for him." She shot the doctor a venomous look. "Why are you here?"

"I was about to ask that same question," Dr. Crosby said.

"Devlin Bane and my friend are here on Paladin business; Jarvis is expecting them. Since I'm the Handler for both Bane and Trahern, I came along to see how Blake was doing. Now, Doctor, if I could see my patient?" Laurel spoke as if it were the most natural thing in the world for her to invade his domain and take over.

"This is most irregular, Dr. Young. But I would appreciate your expertise with this particular patient," Crosby said. "However, I *am* the Handler in charge of this facility, and I've been treating Paladins since before you were born. My decisions about his care will be final."

Devlin Bane stepped past Laurel to glare down at the doctor, his hands fisted at his side. "That man's chances of making it back this time are close to nil. If having these two women at his side increases those chances by even a hair, they're going to be there. Now are you going to quit being an asshole, or do we need to take this discussion out into the hall?"

Silence hung over the room as everyone held their breath.

Dr. Crosby glanced at Blake's cold, still body and slowly nodded. "I want what's best for my patient, and I know he's precariously close to the end." He turned to face Dr. Young. "Any suggestions you might have will be most welcome."

Bane nodded. "Thank you, Dr. Crosby. Then my associate and I will get out of your way."

"I'll have one of the guards show you the way to Jarvis's office." He pushed the intercom button and requested an escort.

Bane gave Dr. Young a quick kiss. "Call if you need me, no matter how things go. I want to be here for him."

"I will." She looked past him to their companion. "Keep *him* safe."

Devlin looked disgusted. "I said I would. But Jarvis is *not* going to be happy about him being here."

"I know—but Barak will be able to answer questions no one else can." She gently shoved Devlin toward the door. "I have work to do and so do you. I'll see you later."

Brenna and Dr. Crosby had been following the conversation with a great deal of curiosity. Barak bore their scrutiny with mute stoicism. As Barak followed Devlin and Dr. Crosby out of the lab, it finally hit Brenna who—or rather, what—he was. The man was an Other! No wonder Laurel was worried about his safety. Considering Jarvis's mood when he'd left the lab, he was likely to kill first and ask questions later.

Laurel turned to Brenna. "Let's see what can be done for Blake."

Jarvis sat in his office and waited for the door to open. Devlin Bane was on his way down, bringing someone to identify the blue stone. Why the Seattle Paladin thought his man would know more than the local lab boys, he had no idea, but he'd listen to what the man had to say. Then he'd get back to grilling Ritter.

So far, the rogue Regent was holding his own in the interrogation. Jarvis wasn't surprised; after all, the man had obviously been living a dual existence for some time. Well, Ritter could sit there feeling smug and superior all he wanted, but he'd left one little factor out of his equation.

He wasn't in the custody of the police and the standard legal system. Even for a cop killer, there were procedures in place that kept scum like him safe. But Ritter was surrounded by Paladins, men who had lost friend after friend fighting the Others. That one of their own had betrayed them for cold, hard cash wouldn't set well with them.

Jarvis wouldn't let anyone kill the bastard, but Ritter would wish he were dead by the time they had wrung him dry. Trahern especially deserved some time alone with the bastard.

If he came back. Jarvis pinched the bridge of his nose and prayed for his friend's continued existence. He wasn't ready to write his friend off, despite the test results. The Fates couldn't be so cruel—to allow Blake a little happiness, then snatch it away so quickly.

Besides, if there was hope for Blake, then maybe there was hope for Jarvis himself, too.

There was an abrupt knock at the door; no doubt Devlin Bane and his mysterious companion.

"Come in if you have to." He sat back and waited, not bothering to look busy; he wasn't happy about the Seattle Paladin poking his nose in where it wasn't needed or wanted.

The two men entered, and when he got a good look at Bane's companion, Jarvis jumped up and reached for his sword. An Other! As he charged around the desk to attack, Bane put himself squarely between Jarvis and his natural prey.

"Get the hell out of my way, Bane!"

He and Bane were the same height, though Bane had him beat on sheer muscle. That didn't stop Jarvis from trying to get around him to kill their enemy. He almost made it once, which had Bane cursing as he struggled to control Jarvis.

"Why are you protecting that bastard?" Jarvis snarled.

Bane had him by the shirtfront with one fist while his other hand was clamped around Jarvis's sword arm. "Because he saved my woman's life, damn it."

Some of the fight went out of Jarvis, but not all of it. "Explain."

"Put down the sword first. We've got bigger problems to deal with than him."

Jarvis glared at Devlin for another few seconds to show that he wasn't easy to push around, then let his sword arm go slack. Devlin stepped back, careful to keep himself between Jarvis and the Other. Smart man.

Jarvis put his sword down within easy reach and returned to his desk chair. "Answer my question. Why is he here?"

"To see the stone Trahern said you found. Barak will know better what we're dealing with."

Jarvis pulled the blue crystal out of his pocket and laid it on the desk. "Give it your best shot," he said skeptically.

Barak's closeness felt like a burning itch. How many Paladins had this alien killed? He noticed that the Other moved with the same grace as the best of the Paladin fighters. It made him sick to think that they might have something in common besides a driving need to kill each other.

If the Other were human, he would have looked diseased with his pale skin and strangely colored eyes. His face appeared young despite his iron gray hair. Maybe his appearance was normal for his kind—not that Jarvis gave a damn. On *this* side of the barrier, their normal appearance was dead at the end of his sword.

"Do you recognize the stone?"

Barak approached the desk with grave dignity and not even a flicker of fear. Maybe he'd already lost so much that his life held little value for him anymore. He reached for the stone but then hesitated, asking without words if it was all right for him to touch it.

Jarvis nodded. "Go on. Pick it up."

Barak hefted the stone, checking its weight, before holding it up to the lamp on Jarvis's desk. A rainbow of blue-tinted light blanketed the room and the stone took on a glow of its own, one that continued even when Barak shaded the crystal with his other hand.

"It is indeed from my world. We use them for light and to focus energy." He set the crystal back down on the desk. The glow dimmed and gradually disappeared.

Bane reached for it next and held it up to the lamp again. Although the light illuminated the crystal's color better, this time it didn't glow by itself.

"Why does it work for you and not me?" Jarvis demanded.

Barak shrugged. "We aren't the same. The stone knows that."

Jarvis sneered. "You talk as if it were alive. We

have similar crystals in our world, but they don't shine for some folks and not for others."

Barak touched the stone again. "This stone grows, its light getting more powerful as it does. Some of my kind have an affinity for working with it. It is much prized in my world for the light it offers in the darkness."

"Someone in our world has gotten greedy for this little beauty." Jarvis put the crystal back in his pocket.

"I know. They are greedy enough to tell my people that they can buy their way into this world with it. But all that awaits them upon crossing are the Paladins and their swords."

Both Bane and Jarvis ignored that comment. "Why would we want the stuff if it doesn't work for us?"

"I do not know the answer to that question."

Jarvis stood. "I know someone who does. I've got the Regent who killed Judge Nichols and Trahern locked up down the hall. So far, he hasn't had much to say for himself. That's about to change. Care to join the discussion?"

Bane smiled wolfishly and cracked his knuckles. "Sounds good to me. Lead the way."

"What about him?" Jarvis asked, nodding in Barak's direction.

"I'm thinking that seeing an Other cooperating with us might shake up your guest a bit."

Barak nodded gravely. "This man has betrayed both worlds. I want to talk to him myself."

Jarvis followed the other two out the door, wishing that he hadn't just felt a sense of kinship with his enemy.

Blake's hand was cold and stiff as Brenna held it. How could these people chain him down to a bare steel table? Would a mattress be too much to ask for? At least they'd allowed her to cover him with warmed blankets. If Laurel thought it foolish of her to keep changing them as soon as they cooled off, she didn't say anything. But then she was in love with a Paladin, too, so maybe she understood Brenna's need to do something, anything, that might help bring Trahern back.

His leg jerked, the sudden movement startling her.

"Blake moved!" she told Laurel excitedly.

Laurel checked the time and made a note in the thick file she'd been reading for the past hour. "Let me know if it happens again, but don't read too much into it. It could be hours or even days before he really starts to come around."

Brenna gave Trahern's hand a soft squeeze. She didn't care how long it took. Her man was on his way back. Scooting her chair closer to the head of the table, she started to whisper to him. When she'd been unconscious, she'd heard his voice and reached out to it like a lifeline. She would do no less for him. She whispered the three words that she'd held back from him, and would keep repeating them until his silvery eyes opened to the knowledge that she loved him.

"Ms. Nichols, you need to go lie down for a while."

The deep voice startled Brenna awake; she blinked up at Devlin Bane.

"I don't want to leave him alone."

"I know." Devlin's handsome face was all hard angles, but there was sympathy in his eyes. "I'll stay with him for a few hours while you get some rest. He's going to need you alert and strong when he comes back. I promise one of us will come get you as soon as he shows any sign of returning."

Laurel joined them, leaning against Devlin. "The last time Blake was badly injured, it was Devlin who talked him all the way back. You can trust him to take your place for a while."

Brenna's body ached all over, her arm was throbbing, and her head felt as if it were filled with silt. If Blake were to awaken in the next few minutes, she wouldn't have the strength to help him if things got rough. "Is there someplace close by where I can sleep?"

"There's a patient bed through that door. I'll get you settled and then get some sleep myself. Dr. Crosby and I are trading shifts until we know how it's going to go for Trahern."

Brenna looked into Laurel's dark eyes and asked the question that had been hovering in her mind. "Tell me honestly, Doctor, will my being here help?"

Laurel surprised her with a quick hug. "I'm counting on it, Brenna." She glanced back at Devlin. "I have to believe that we can find some way to reverse these changes they go through. Things will look better after a few hours' sleep."

Brenna crawled between the cool sheets on the bed, then murmured a short prayer for Blake and the rest of the Paladins. She was asleep almost before she finished saying amen.

The sound of running feet and anxious voices jerked Brenna out of a sound sleep. Through the closed door, she could hear people talking, but could only pick out an occasional word or two. As she sat on the side of the bed and tried to clear the sleep from her head, though, one thing came through clearly. Whoever was out in the lab was worried, maybe even scared.

That could only mean that Blake was regaining consciousness, and it wasn't going well.

As she entered the lab, she heard an almost inhuman scream and the rattle of chains.

Trahern!

Dr. Crosby, a technician, and some guards surrounded his bed. There was no sign of Devlin Bane, and Dr. Young was across the room on the phone, watching the chaos around Trahern with worried eyes. Brenna cautiously approached the table, trying to see past the white lab coats and uniforms. When she attempted to force her way between two of the guards, they refused to budge.

"Let me through!"

Dr. Crosby spotted her. "What's she doing in here? Someone get that woman out of here now!"

When one of the guards started to carry out his orders, she moved away to avoid his grasp. "I'm not leaving this spot! Dr. Young promised me I could be here when Blake revived."

"Well, she's busy right now, and I'm telling you to leave. This is no place for civilians."

A guard on each side of her managed to catch her arms and all but dragged her to the door. She fought them every inch of the way. What would they do to Blake if she wasn't there to protect him? Tears burned down her face as she tried to break free.

They tossed her out into the hall and then closed the door. She pounded on it with both fists. "Let me in, you bastards! He needs me!"

A shadow fell over her—Jarvis, with Devlin Bane right behind him. She'd never been so glad to see anyone in her life.

"It's Blake. I don't know what they are doing to him, but he's been screaming and they won't let me in."

Laurel Young stepped out into the hallway. "You'd all better get in here before they do something we'll all regret."

The guards tried to block the door. "Nobody in. Doctor's orders."

The combined strength of Jarvis and Devlin sent the two guards flying. Laurel motioned Brenna to follow her while the two men dealt with the guards.

"Dr. Crosby, what is the current status of my patient?" She sounded calm and professional.

Dr. Crosby looked up from the chart he'd been writing in and glared at the commotion near the door. "It's my shift to be here, Dr. Young. There's no need for you to concern yourself with this."

"I beg to differ with you, Dr. Crosby. Blake Trahern is my patient, no matter what city he happens to be in. Now if you'll catch me up on his condition, I'll take over."

Reluctantly, the doctor handed over the chart, clearly not happy about his authority being usurped once again. "Judging from his behavior, Dr. Young, it's clear that he's too far gone to save. If you want the privilege of putting him down your-self, fine. I was just trying to save you that heartache."

Another bloodcurdling scream cut through the room, leaving everyone quiet and shaken. If Brenna didn't know better, she would have thought someone was being tortured.

Dr. Crosby walked away from the table, saying over his shoulder, "I will be making a full report, Dr. Young."

"Do whatever you think is necessary, Doctor. And you can take your techs and guards with you."

Jarvis and Devlin ushered everyone out and then guarded the door.

Brenna was finally close enough to see Blake. Crosby had taken away the blankets, leaving him exposed to prying eyes. She hurried to get another warm blanket to cover him, then took hold of his hand. With her other hand, she gently ran her fin-gertips down the side of his face and whispered his name.

"Blake, it's me, Brenna."

At first there was no response. Then his eyes flew open, looking wild and unfocused. There were flecks of odd colors in the irises, and whatever he saw must have been horrible, because he screamed again and struggled against his chains. His wrists and ankles were already scraped and bleeding.

"Keep talking to him, Brenna." Laurel's voice

was calm and controlled, but fear was there in the set of her mouth and in her eyes. "Maybe you can get through to him."

"Blake, concentrate on my voice. It's me, Brenna. Remember? You've been protecting me from that evil Regent, the one who killed my father."

That set off another episode of chain rattling. He struggled to raise his head, the veins in his neck standing out in sharp relief. "My fault, my fault!" Blake cried. "I killed the judge."

Brenna put her hand on his chest. "No, Blake, you caught the man who did it. It wasn't you who planted that bomb. You've fought to keep me safe."

He turned his face toward her, those strange changes in his eyes worse than before. "Let me go. Let me go. Let me *go!*" He yanked against the restraints with all his strength.

"No, Blake. I'm sorry, but I can't let you go." She deliberately misunderstood his meaning. "I love you, Blake Trahern. I'm not about to let you walk away from me."

A movement on the other side of the table caught her attention. Dr. Young was preparing an injection. Tears streamed down her face as she held the syringe up to check the dosage.

"What's that?"

"He's suffering, Brenna. I care too much for him to let that go on." Her hands trembled as she drew back on the syringe a little farther.

Laurel's words hit her like a blow. "You can't kill him, Dr. Young, not yet! You haven't even given him a chance to make it back!"

Devlin interceded. "It's his eyes, Brenna. No one's ever come back from this point. When they change like that, nothing can be done."

"You *have* to give him a chance. Give *me* a chance to get through to him. I know it's bad—even really bad. But I'll never forgive you or myself if we don't try."

She met Laurel's gaze. "Please. He calmed down for me before. I know this time is worse, but there has to be something we can try."

Laurel slowly nodded and set the syringe down, close by in case she needed it in a hurry. "Dim the lights, will you, Jarvis? And Devlin, go get some chocolate. He has a sweet tooth; maybe the familiar scents will help."

"Make that snickerdoodles if you can find some," Brenna said. He loved them when he lived with us. Our housekeeper always made them specially for him."

"There's a bakery in town. I'll go." Looking relieved to have something to do, Jarvis disappeared out the door.

"What now?" Devlin asked.

"We wait." Laurel dragged a chair over to Brenna. "You're going to need to conserve your strength. This could be a long haul for all of us."

The light over the table cast the rest of the room in shadows, lending a feeling of intimacy, and Brenna caressed Blake's face.

"Blake, I need you to come back to me. I love you, and can't imagine the world without you in it." She kissed his cheek, then his lips. "And your friends Devlin and Jarvis, they need your help to get to the bottom of this mess. We've made progress, but rooting out one corrupt Regent may not cure the problem."

She talked until her voice was all but gone. Then she laid her head against the table and held his hand, gently stroking the back of it with her fingertips. Was it a good sign that he'd been calm for so long? Or had the madness retreated to reappear later, stronger and more violent.

She hardly noticed when Jarvis came back. He gently tapped her on the shoulder. "Here are the snickerdoodles. They were just taking a fresh batch out of the oven."

"Bless you, Jarvis."

She took the bag and opened it. The scent of fresh baked cookies filled the air as she held it near Blake's nose.

"Blake, remember that scent? Nothing is better than snickerdoodles. Maisy used to bake them just for you because she liked you so much."

"I'm going to eat one now." She bit into the rich cookie and savored the taste of sugar and cinnamon. "I wish you were awake so I could share."

His head moved restlessly, but his eyes didn't open. "There's only a dozen cookies, Blake. If you don't wake up soon, they could all be gone." That was a lie. She'd make sure there were cookies left for him no matter what.

"We're all here, Blake. All your friends—me, Devlin, Laurel, and Jarvis. Come back to us. Please."

"Brenna, you've been at it nonstop for almost two hours. Take a break. I can talk to him for a while."

"I can't leave him, he's been calm since I've been here. I think he knows I'm here."

"At least get something to eat. You need your strength, and he needs it, too. We'll stay here, I promise."

Jarvis joined in. "Come on, Brenna. The kitchen's nearby. We'll be gone twenty minutes tops."

Her stomach rumbled noisily at the thought of food. Maybe they were right. "All right, but don't leave him for a second."

Laurel had already taken Brenna's seat and was murmuring something about cookies. Devlin stood right behind her, his hands on her shoulders.

Content that Blake was in good hands, she allowed Jarvis to lead her to a small kitchen. He gently shoved her toward a table and started rummaging in the refrigerator.

"Mayo or mustard?"

"Mayo."

"American or Swiss?"

"American."

He threw together a couple of sandwiches, and then joined her at the table. "Brenna, no matter how this turns out, I appreciate what you're trying to do for Trahern. We all do."

"I haven't done anything yet." The sandwich felt like a lump stuck in her throat. "I'm so scared."

He reached across and put his big hand on hers. "We all are. Devlin and I know that we'll both end up strapped to that table someday. But if you can save Trahern, then there's hope for all of us."

"And if I can't?"

"Then at least you eased his passing. That means a lot."

"He deserves better. You all do."

"We all play the hands we're dealt, Brenna."

They quickly ate and returned to the lab, where Blake was fighting his chains again.

Brenna ran to his side. "Blake, please stop. It's okay. I'm back and you're safe."

She laid her head on his shoulder and wrapped her arms around his struggling body as best she could. "Blake, please rest easy. I'm here."

To everyone's relief, he immediately relaxed. Brenna listened as his heartbeat gradually slowed down. When he seemed once again to be at peace, she sat in her chair and took his hand in hers. "Sleep all you need to, Blake. I'll be here when you're ready to wake up."

Then she squeezed his hand and rested her head against his arm. Gradually, she slipped into a light doze. She was vaguely aware of Laurel and the others in the room, but if they spoke it was in whispers.

An hour later, or maybe a little longer, something touched her hair. She froze, waiting to see if it happened again. When it did, she thought her heart would leap from her chest. Blake's fingers were stroking her hair.

Slowly, she lifted her head and looked up. Silver gray eyes, a bit sleepy but otherwise clear, gazed down at her.

"Blake?"

"Brenna?" His voice was rough.

"Oh, thank God, Blake, you're back."

He tried to lift his hand, but the chain prevented him from moving very far.

She caught his hand and squeezed it. "Hang on, big guy. We'll get the chains off." She called out, "Laurel, bring the keys. I need to unlock the chains."

Laurel and Devlin, who had stretched out on the bed in the other room, came at a run.

"Trahern?" Devlin stood over his friend with relief and wonder on his face. "I didn't think I'd ever see your ugly face again."

Laurel checked the readings on the machines hooked to her patient. As she recorded the numbers, she started smiling.

Trahern blinked up at her. "Doc, what are you doing here?"

She beamed at her patient. "I always take care of my guys, Trahern. You should know that."

Jarvis joined the party around the table. "Leave it to you, Trahern, to have two beautiful women fussing over you."

Blake turned his head toward his old friend. "Did we get the bastard?"

"Yeah, we did. He hasn't told us much, but I'll bet he'll start chatting away when he hears that you're back." Jarvis's grin was positively wicked.

"How long was I gone this time?"

"Long enough to worry your woman, but she fought for you every inch of the way. She helped run off Dr. Crosby, and not even the guards dare poke their noses in here now."

Brenna blushed. "I didn't do much." Then she realized that no one had moved to unlock the chains. "The keys, Laurel?"

"I can't for another hour at least. We have to make sure these readings are stable before we turn him loose."

"Just one hand? Please?"

Laurel hesitated only a second before handing the key to Brenna. "Just one."

Brenna released the lock. "I hate these things."

Trahern gently squeezed Brenna's hand. "It's okay, Brenna. That's how things are done. I can wait." As long as she was close by, he could put up with it.

"Hey, Doc, before you start poking and prodding, can I have a couple of minutes alone with Brenna?"

Laurel nodded. Jarvis and Devlin stepped out of the lab, no doubt guarding the door, and Laurel disappeared around the corner to Dr. Crosby's desk.

Brenna was still holding his hand for dear life.

"Did I scare you?" he asked.

"A little." The truth was there in the dark circles under her eyes.

"I'm sorry you had to see me like that."

She gave him a weary smile. "I wouldn't have missed it for the world."

He spotted the bandage on her arm and frowned. "Ritter shot you. Are you all right?"

Her smile warmed up. "I am now."

He closed his eyes, remembering the nightmares. "I could hear you talking to me in the darkness. I was so cold—but then I'd hear your voice and feel warm again."

"It was the blankets. They were warm."

"That might have been part of it but not the best part. It was what you were saying that made me want to come back. Say it again."

"Say what again?" Her expression said she knew exactly what he wanted to hear.

"That you love me."

"I love you," she whispered with a smile.

"Damn straight you do." He reached over with his free arm and pulled her close. "That's only fair, since you made me fall in love with you, too."

Then he kissed her.

Several of the machines beeped at the change in his pulse and breathing rate, but he didn't give a damn. With Brenna in his arms, he was feeling just fine.

epilogue

"How the hell did they get to him?" Trahern stood over Ritter's dead body, burning to hit somebody, anybody. Damn it, this wasn't supposed to happen!

"I don't know, but I'm damn well going to find out." Jarvis banged his fist against the wall. "The doctors say the guard should survive, and he might remember something. Otherwise, we're back at square one."

"We'll get them eventually," Trahern said. "No use in beating yourself up over it."

"I've already got Jake working on the disk again. It keeps his mind off his leg hurting."

"Thank him for me." Trahern looked down at the dead Regent's body, resisting the urge to kick it. "I'll be heading back to Seattle with Devlin and Laurel's pet Other. We'll see what we can find there. One way or the other, we're going to get some answers."

"I suspect Brenna is going to take up a fair amount of your time," Jarvis teased.

It was strange to think of himself as half of a couple. Never in his wildest dreams had he expected her to fall in love with him. That he loved her came as no surprise, though. He'd fallen for her the minute he'd met her all those years ago.

They left the cell. "I worry about her uprooting her whole life to be with me—giving up her job at the college and all."

"Don't be a jackass, Trahern; you've found something we'd all like to have. Besides, you should have seen the look on her face when Devlin told her about the archives of Paladin history. She can hardly wait to get her hands on it, trying to figure out what makes us tick."

"She's sure something, isn't she?" Blake shook his head in wonder.

Jarvis looked more than a little jealous. "She sure is."

And she was waiting for Blake back in their room. He was better with actions than with words, and he was looking forward to showing her exactly how he felt about her.

He grinned and took off running.

Pocket Star Books
proudly presents

In Darkness Reborn
Alexis Morgan

Available in paperback
from Pocket Star Books
in 2007

Turn the page for a preview

chapter 1

Get that goddamned freak out of here!"

The wounded Paladin could barely speak, but there was no mistaking the venom in his words. Barak quietly picked up a tray of sterile instruments and put it away. After arranging the supplies and equipment exactly as Dr. Young preferred them, he walked past the man and made eye contact. He took pride in knowing he wasn't the one who blinked first.

The badly wounded patient had been conscious for just over an hour and had been cursing Barak for almost all of it. Paladins were never easy patients, and having one of their mortal enemies in the room only made them worse. Barak retained enough of his own hatred of the Paladins to take some pleasure in knowing his enemy was chained down on the steel table while he walked free. He savored the sweet taste of the man's fury in the air.

Dr. Laurel Young set aside the chart she'd been writing in and crossed the room to stand near her patient. She, too, paid little attention to the Paladin's curses and demands for his sword, concentrating instead on the array of machinery that monitored his progress. Judging from the frown line between her eyebrows, she wasn't pleased.

Barak braced himself for the request he knew was coming. Rather than wait to be shooed out of the lab like a troublesome child, he started for the door.

"Barak . . ."

If she said more than his name, he didn't hear it. They both knew there wasn't anything she could say to make his situation any more palatable. When he'd entered this world, he'd fully expected to die within minutes at the end of a Paladin's sword. But that hadn't happened, leaving him alone in this confusing place. Although it wasn't too late to end his own life, his suicide would only serve to please his enemies among the Paladins. And if he could not defeat them in combat, then he would irritate them with his continued presence in their midst.

The guards who manned the lobby desk looked up, preventing him from slamming his fist against the wall in frustration. Any such action on his part would be reported to Dr. Neal, the local head of Research. He, in turn, would pass along the information to the Regents. For now, they tolerated his continued existence, as long as he did not become too much of a problem. For Laurel's sake, he behaved—at least most of the time.

It would be some time before he could return to the lab without upsetting their current guest, which wouldn't have bothered Barak in the least. It was for Dr. Young's sake that he had walked out of the lab. He owed her that much. He swallowed his anger and considered his options. He *so* wanted to teach the insolent Paladin a lesson in manners with his fists. Instead, he would settle for a long work-out in the gym.

The elevator was closer than the stairs. He pushed the button, still marveling at all the conveniences that humans took for granted. Their casual use of power appalled him at times. They had no idea how blessed they were. Or how wasteful.

When the doors slid open, a pair of the building guards immediately shuffled to one side of the elevator, as if to make room for him. It was far more likely that they were avoiding any possible contact, as if he still carried some contagion.

He forced a small smile as he nodded his appreciation for their false kindness. As the doors shut, he considered whether he was overreacting by assuming that everyone he met had a hidden agenda. Maybe they had problems of their own and had meant no slight. But until he better understood these humans and how their minds worked, he could only rely on his own instincts. It was safer to assume they were the enemy than to be stabbed in the back by a false friend.

Several seconds later, he escaped the narrow confines of the elevator. Pausing outside the locker room, he cocked his head to the side and reached out with his senses to see if anyone was inside. The gods were with him; the whole place was empty. Inside, he stripped down and pulled on the shorts he kept in his assigned locker. After tying back his shoulder-length hair, he entered the gym.

He closed his eyes, searching for the silence deep within, to let go of the day's frustrations. Moving slowly at first, he lost himself in the ha'kai, the "death dance" of his people. Through its familiar rhythms he could almost imagine himself back home. The origin of the dance was lost in antiquity, but those who learned its graceful, lethal maneuvers had long kept the practice alive in his world. Here, in this land of too much light, it was an unknown art.

Even without an opponent, the death dance pleased Barak greatly. There was so much confusion in this new life that he drew comfort from bringing this one little part of his world with him. However, the peace was short-lived as three—no, make that four—Paladins came swaggering into the gym. They dropped their weapon cases on the tiled floor and drew their swords.

The closest one groused, "Aw, hell, nobody told me that they let that silver-haired bastard roam free. I thought Seattle had a leash law."

The words were followed by raucous laughter as the others encouraged the speaker to continue. "I think you're right, Roy. Maybe we should call Animal Control and have them haul it off to the pound with all the other flea-bitten dogs."

Barak kept his eyes firmly closed and finished a last twirl and lunge before acknowledging the intruders' presence. He picked up a towel and wiped his face clean of sweat and smiled. A fight was inevitable; he couldn't find it within him to be sorry. His opponents looked impossibly young, although with Paladins it was difficult to judge their real age. Something about these made him suspect that they'd yet to face their first combat against his people. He relished the chance to teach them some respect for his kind and their ability to fight.

He tossed the towel toward the hamper. "Better the dogs for company than two-legged cowards." Cocking an eyebrow, he sneered at the Paladins, "Or do your people consider four against one to be honorable?"

Their response was both immediate and predictable. The one who'd done all the talking so far took a long step toward Barak. "Listen here, asshole, I wouldn't go around calling other people cowards. Everyone knows the only reason you're still alive is that nitwit Dr. Young took pity on you and let you hide behind her skirts."

That did it. They could insult him all they wanted, but he wouldn't tolerate anyone treating Laurel Young with disrespect. Before, even if the squabble had come to swords, he would have settled for running them in circles without doing any real damage. But for bringing Dr. Young's name into the discussion, he would demand payment in blood. And if word of their taunts got back to Devlin Bane, the whole bunch would be lucky if they lost only one life each.

He calmly crossed the room to the rack of swords that the arms master kept on hand in the gym for practice. After rejecting several, he settled for the one that came closest to the feel of his own, which had been lost to him.

Already the Paladins were forming up to attack. The biggest one stood a few steps ahead of the others, no doubt planning on challenging Barak's arm first. Barak took a couple of practice swings with the sword before touching the blade to his forehead to signal his readiness to fight. Judging from his opponent's stance, the young fool depended on his size to win most of his fights. That might work when it came to fists, but he would soon learn the error of his ways.

Barak held his sword at the ready and used his other hand to encourage his opponent to attack.

"Shall we dance, Paladin? Have you any skill with that sword, or is it only for decoration?"

Roy's face flushed with anger. "I'm ready whenever you are."

The other Paladins arranged themselves along the wall, calling out their encouragement. "That's it, Roy. Teach him some respect for his betters!"

As Barak expected, the young Paladin lunged forward, using his weapon with graceless power. If his blow had actually connected it might have taken Barak's head, but experience counted for much in any battle. Roy stumbled past, fighting to regain his balance. It didn't take much longer for Barak to have young Roy pinned against the wall, the point of his sword at the boy's throat. The flash of fear in Roy's eyes tasted sweet.

"Now, what was that about teaching me respect for my betters?" Barak crowded closer. "I'm listening."

When Roy didn't respond, Barak indulged his own anger with a flick of his wrist, slashing a shallow but painful cut down the side of Roy's face. To give the boy credit, he stood his ground, ignoring both the pain and the blood dripping down his cheek.

Barak leaned in close, letting Roy see his full rage. His lips drew back, showing a lot of teeth. "If I ever hear another disrespectful word about Dr. Young, I will slice you into tiny little pieces. Then I'll report you to Devlin Bane and Blake Trahern and let them finish the job. Do I make myself clear?"

Roy nodded very slowly. The mention of the two scariest Seattle Paladins had definitely struck home. Devlin and his friend Trahern were the stuff of legends. Maybe Roy and his friends hadn't yet heard that Dr. Young and Bane were mates, but it wasn't Barak's job to inform them. It was enough that he defended her honor.

"Get out of here." He'd deliberately kept his back to the rest of the pack, saying without words that he considered them to be of no real threat. "And the next time you see me, I suggest you turn and walk away."

Another voice entered into the conversation. "Is there a problem?"

"Nothing I can't handle." Barak picked up a towel to wipe the small splash of blood off of the tip of his sword, then turned to face Devlin Bane. "I was just teaching young Roy here that size doesn't always decide the winner."

Bane made Roy look a bit on the small side. "Really? I've never found it to be a handicap." He sauntered over to the sword rack and picked one at random. He eyed Roy, obviously taking the younger man's measure. "Let's see, there are four of you and two of us. What do you think, Barak? Would it be unfair odds?"

Barak considered the matter. "Maybe if we promised to use our weaker hand, it would give them a better chance."

Devlin's grin was pure evil as he switched the sword to his off hand. "I like it."

Barak did the same and moved to stand next to his mortal enemy. "We shouldn't hurt them too badly, though. I don't feel like mopping blood up off the floor."

"Fair enough." Devlin turned to Roy's companions, who looked as if they were about to make a dash for the door. "Come on, gentlemen, pick up your weapons. I've got just enough time to show you how it's done in the real world."

Barak stood watching their exhausted opponents stumble out of the gym, each of them glad to have escaped with only their pride bruised. At least Bane hadn't asked what had caused the initial confrontation. He probably assumed that Barak's presence alone was enough to trigger a Paladin's inborn need to fight any Others that they encountered, and Barak didn't tell him any different.

"Were you looking for me?" He kept his voice carefully neutral. Rather than look directly at Bane, he focused his hands and eyes on cleaning the sword he'd been using.

"Laurel said you were probably up here." Bane returned his borrowed weapon to the rack with a little more force than was necessary. Clearly his temper still simmered just shy of a full boil.

"She didn't need to send you to check on me." But it was just like her to do so.

"She worries."

"And you hate that." As a physician and Handler, Laurel Young took a deep personal interest in all of her charges, even one who was her lover's lifelong enemy.

Devlin Bane shrugged. "How I feel about it doesn't matter."

Barak understood the Paladin's obvious frustration. People of his world and this one were born to hate each other. Unfortunately, Laurel Young didn't seem to accept the normal way of things. Since Barak and Devlin both cared about her, they were forced to set that hatred aside and find some common ground. Sparring in the gym fit that need. If they couldn't kill each other for real, then they could draw what satisfaction they could from pretending to.

"Are you up for another practice?" The skirmish with the younger Paladins had whetted Barak's own appetite for violence; exchanging blows with Bane would help him burn out his own temper.

Devlin stood at the weapon rack, picking up

various swords at random and testing their weight in his hand. "Knives or swords?"

Barak wasn't allowed weapons of his own, and being forced to borrow them rankled.

"Swords."

And so the dance began.

In his former life, he and Devlin Bane were mortal enemies, sworn to kill each other upon sight. In Barak's youth, he'd sworn the same vows of hatred as had all of those of his generation. Over the years that followed, their numbers had dwindled as death had claimed many and insanity still more.

When he'd gone looking for answers to the great madness, he'd found nothing but locked doors and accusations of cowardice. He didn't mind the idea of dying, he'd argued long and hard, he merely wanted to know the why of it all. Finally, he'd quit asking and quit fighting and quit everything.

Like so many from his world, he'd sought to end his own pain with an honorable death at the end of a Paladin's sword. Instead, he'd found a human woman being pursued by one of her own kind, a man who had reeked of cowardice and greed. Laurel Young had offered Barak her healer's touch, and then her friendship. To his amazement, even the strongest of the Paladins had been unwilling to refuse her the gift of Barak's life.

That didn't mean they liked the idea.

With a powerful lunge, Devlin's sword came uncomfortably close to Barak's throat, reminding him that now was not the time for reminiscing. Barak danced back out of the way and grinned at his opponent. "Is that the best you have to offer?"

"Go to hell." Bane charged again, this time whacking Barak across the back with a blow that would leave bruises.

The pain faded quickly in the triumph of using one of his favorite ha'kai movements to drop Bane to the mat with a satisfying thud, followed by a string of curses after Bane could draw enough breath to speak. Barak offered him a hand up that was rudely ignored. He backed away, giving the Paladin a chance to rejoin the battle.

"You've got to quit," Bane said.

The man was moving more slowly, but Barak knew better than to underestimate him. "Why should I when I am winning?"

This time it was Barak who hit the floor. Even a practice blade looked sharp when held at his throat.

"Not this. You've got to quit working with Laurel."

Bane backed away, giving Barak some space. Barak wiped some blood away from his mouth with the back of his hand. He was in no mood to ordered around by a Paladin, not even one who stood between him and certain death. Ignor- newest set of bruises, he slowly climbed to his feet and brought his sword back up into fighting position.

"I won't quit just because you don't want me near your woman." He backed up his vow with a flurry of thrusts that Bane met with a renewed attack of his own.

"I've never liked you being near her, you stupid bastard. That hasn't changed."

"Then what has?" A sick feeling settled deep inside him. If the newest members of the Paladins were talking about Laurel, others must be, as well. He stepped back and dropped the point of his sword in a sign of surrender. At least Bane was breathing as hard as he was. When it came to fighting the best, a draw was nothing to be ashamed of.

"Does she know that people are talking?" He hoped not.

"She probably suspects, but so far no one has had the balls to say something directly to her." They both knew that Bane would kill anyone who dared to hurt Laurel—and that Barak would help him.

"I will leave immediately." His sword suddenly felt twice as heavy as he carried it back to the rack.

"That's not going to happen. She'd only make me drag you right back here."

"Make up your mind," Barak snapped. "First you say that I have to leave; now you're telling me I must stay."

Unless he was mistaken, there was actually some sympathy in Bane's eyes. "I'm working on a plan. The only way she'll let you go is if she believes that you'll be happier with the move."

That was an unlikely scenario, since Laurel was the only real friend he had. But for her sake, he'd be willing to lie. He nodded slowly. "Tell me about this plan."